MW01123104

The Call of the YUKON

William Stanley

ARCHWAY PUBLISHING

Archway Publishing books may be ordered
through booksellers or by contacting:

Archway Publishing
1663 Liberty Drive
Bloomington, IN 47403
www.archwaypublishing.com
844-669-3957

ISBN: 978-1-6657-5330-2 (sc)
ISBN: 978-1-6657-5331-9 (e)

Library of Congress Control Number: 2023921819

Print information available on the last page.

Archway Publishing rev. date: 11/27/2023

DEDICATION

In memory of my mother and father, who were always there
when I needed them.

RUDY

CHAPTER ONE

Spring had returned to the Yukon. The early April sun melted the snow from the roof of Steward's cabin. The constant dripping of water from the eaves was a reassuring sign of warmer weather to come. After a long cold winter, life would return to this wilderness; the sunlight and warmth will start an explosion of growth in the forest. Over the course of only a few short weeks, the landscape will turn from brown to green as nature takes its course. Babies, born in the spring to mothers who live here, were in abundance at this time of the year, which is how Steward acquired Rudy.

Rudy was a wolf pup Steward had found in his den crying, abandoned by his mother. Rudy was the runt of the litter, whose mother thought would be more trouble than he was worth. When the pack moved on to a different location, the wolves abandoned Rudy in the den. Steward scooped him up sensing the young wolf pup had no fear, only wanting security as he nestled into Steward's arms. He took Rudy home and decided to nurse him back to health before introducing him to his sled dogs. He hoped an allowance would be made in heaven for Rudy, and his huskies, who viewed all wolves as their mortal enemy, would accept this pup.

Steward had many dogs, but none were pets. Rudy would be the exception, kept in Steward's cabin. He would become Steward's most trusted dog, an alpha male who would eventually dominate the smaller huskies. He would be trained to be the lead sled dog, when Steward felt his time was ready. But for now, Rudy had to regain his strength and grow.

Shortly after Steward brought his wolf pup home, Johnathan and Shining Star arrived to return Ginger and Shirley. The two huskies would be boarded with Steward for the summer, as his business was equipped to care for many dogs. Steward, pleased to see his cousin and her husband, said he was expecting Jason and Wendy and their son to arrive soon. They were also dropping off their sled dogs and he had been expecting them for the last two days.

Steward laughed aloud when he heard barking huskies approaching. He knew it was his sister and brother-in-law finally arriving. Jason and Wendy, accompanied by their young son, were coming down the trail toward his cabin. Warm embraces and greetings were exchanged between these relatives. Steward was glad to see his sister, Wendy, as he had not seen her in what seemed like a long time. Steward took the sled dogs from their harnesses. He took the working dogs to their kennels and let Chase and King, the couples' personal pets, have play time together. These dogs' friendship had a long history. Considered best friends, Chase and King were always glad to see one another.

The day was warm, and the company was welcomed by Steward. He invited them to spend the night and said he would cook dinner for everyone. As luck would have it, Steward had shot a bear cub, thinking he could smoke and eat the small animal before the meat went bad. Two of Steward's huskies had scared off the cub's mother, driving her far away. She did not return to her baby, forcing Steward to make a difficult choice.

There was enough meat from the small bear to feed all the company, including Chase and King. He would cook the bear meat over the open flames of the wood; the bear cub would be eaten by a predator, called man.

CHAPTER TWO

Steward was Wendy's older brother, a man who liked to be alone. He had trapped during the winter months, staying with his tribe where his survival through the harsh winter was easier. During the summer, Steward left his village and panned for gold. He lived in the bush, feeding himself with the small game he shot, sleeping in the forest wherever his travels took him.

On one of his gold panning expeditions, Steward discovered a promising looking creek to search for this precious metal. The fast-moving water gushed out of rock high above where Steward had stood, creating a shallow pool of water below. The water from the pool emptied into a fast-moving stream, which meandered through the forest. Steward had waded into the pool and dipped his gold pan into the sandy bottom. As soon as he pulled the pan out of the water, his eye caught the glint of gold. A large nugget, larger than any he had ever seen before, appeared in his gold pan.

Shaking with gold fever, Steward tried panning the pool again. More gold appeared, small nuggets and gold shake filled the pan. With this one discovery of gold, he was able to sell this precious metal and buy the cabin he was now living in. The owner's dogs, sled, outbuildings, and traps for the trapline were all included in the purchase. A good supply of wood lay cut and stacked beside the cabin, providing an added benefit to Steward's purchase of the building. The need to cut wood, back-breaking work difficult to do by oneself, was eliminated for the near future.

One of the huskies the trapper had owned was a young female who was pregnant. After the birth of her four puppies, Steward decided to keep the pups and sell the animals for sled dogs. This was how Steward's business was born. He kept his business small, only raising and selling one litter of huskies per year. Steward boarded dogs during the summer for his sister, Wendy, and his cousin, Shining Star. He ordered large stocks of dog food, made in Seattle, for his dogs. This non-perishable feed provided a special blend of protein and vitamins for his animals. Fresh fish, caught with Steward's nets, and a moose or deer kill, rounded out the huskies diets.

Shining Star had started the campfire, and the coals were now hot enough for Steward to cook the bear meat. Within one hour, the group, including King and Chase, were eating their fill. After dinner, while enjoying coffee which Wendy had provided, Steward announced he had a surprise to show them. Steward entered his cabin and brought out Rudy, the wolf pup he had rescued. Everyone sitting around the campfire was shocked to see the wolf, but happy Steward had brought it home to take care of. To their amazcment, King and Chase showed no aggression towards the pup, adapting well to its presence.

CHAPTER THREE

The wolf pup was passed among the two couples as they sat around the campfire. Wendy and Shining Star adored the small animal, Jason and Johnathan not so much. A wolf's reputation was he could never be fully domesticated, the wilderness traits used for survival could never be extinguished. When raised by humans, such wolf pups were often trained to be sled dogs. The males would carry the title of alpha and act as the lead dog when pulling the sled. Female wolf pups, if found alive, were usually killed, as a female wolf in a pack of huskies did not typically work well.

Steward told his visitors he planned to raise Rudy to be a sled dog. He would become the team's leader and be his best sled dog in the future. Steward gathered Rudy from the adoring arms of his nephew, Kuzih, and his mom, Wendy, and returned the wolf cub to the cabin. The bright moon, which had been shining earlier, was now obscured by cloud cover. The blackness of the night and the campfire, which had burned down to embers, made the group of relatives decide to retire to Steward's cabin to sleep. With Chase and

King added to the mix, it would be a full house in Steward's home tonight.

Outside, looking for food scraps around the campfire, was a skunk, who had been waiting for the people to go to bed. After a thorough search of the area, the skunk found nothing. Disappointed, the animal left to continue his trek looking for food in the forest.

The lake, which Steward's cabin sat on, was still covered in ice and would stay that way for a short while longer. Steward was looking forward to the return of the game birds, geese and multiple varieties of ducks, which called this lake home during the summer months. These provided an easy source of food for Steward, who exploited their presence to his advantage. What Steward missed the most when the lake was frozen was the call of the loon. He loved laying in his bed, awakened before dawn by the haunting song of this bird. The spirit of the loon's call captured his soul, filling it with joy and leaving him in awe at nature's ability to astound.

Steward's company wanted to rise early to return home. The snow was melting fast, as above normal temperatures had moved into the area. Soon the sleds would be riding in mud on the trail, rather than snow. The couples rose from their beds at daybreak. After loading their dogsleds in the melting snow, they thanked Steward for a wonderful visit. The couples then left for their respective cabins in the forest, their pet dogs pulling their sleds as they walked alongside.

Steward left the cabin to feed his dogs, the smell of spring all around him. The long, cold Yukon winter was finally over. The dogs were more excited than usual, as they sensed the change of seasons also. Like their human counterpart, the animals were also sensitive to the transition taking place. The honking of Canadian geese caught Steward's attention. Looking up, he saw geese looking for open water on the lake. Steward finished feeding his dogs and returned to his cabin to tend to his new pet wolf, Rudy, who was waiting to be fed.

Steward added water to the dog food he fed his huskies, making a mash for Rudy. This method of feeding the small pup was working out well for him. Rudy ate his fill and then slept in front of the woodstove all day, not waking until the early evening. The wolf pup then prowled all night, an instinctive behaviour, which allowed wolves to establish a common bond and maintain a family mentality, hunting together as a group. This was nature's way of assuring the survival of these animals in a savage land, bringing them together as a tight knit pack. Rudy was no longer part of a wolf family. He now belonged in Steward's family; a life Rudy would never adapt well to.

CHAPTER FOUR

The warm sun shone through the open window of the cabin. The snow had melted all night, the water dripping off the roof and loudly hitting the ground. That sound seemed magnified ten-fold by the quiet of the forest. Steward rose from his bed and got dressed. He went outside to feed his dogs, who made a lot of noise in anticipation of their meal. Arriving at their kennels, Steward noticed the dogs were pulling their ropes toward the tree line and barking loudly. He realized they must have seen or sensed something in the forest.

Steward went to investigate, walking toward the edge of the woods where his dogs' attentions were focused. He looked for animal tracks in the melting snow and found a large set of bear prints. This was Steward's second bear encounter this spring, the other one being when he shot the bear cub. These omnivores seemed plentiful in the area this year. Steward envisioned an abundance of bear meat this spring, with plenty of leftovers for his dogs to feed on.

As the bear had left the area, Steward returned to feed his dogs. The ground underneath the dogs' shelters was melting, leaving a muddy mess for the dogs to navigate.

Soon the entire yard would be a large mud hole, filled with dog waste which had frozen and been buried under the snow over the winter. Steward had completed a secondary place to shelter his dogs while he removed and disposed of all the dogs' solid waste and the main yard dried out. Steward thought now was the right time to complete this job.

The day was warm, feeling like the temperature could reach sixty degrees. Steward decided he had better move the animals today or they would be up to their knees in a potpourri of mud and sewage by this evening. After much yelping in disagreement, the dogs were moved to their new space. This spot was located on higher ground, which was drier, but was further from the cabin. This location made it more difficult for Steward to get to his dogs in case of an emergency.

The ice on the lake was disappearing, large areas of water were appearing along the shorelines. Waterfowl returning from their winter break congregated in these areas of open water. Steward went to the cabin and retrieved a sleeping Rudy. Snarling, the wolf pup showed his displeasure at being disturbed when Steward picked him up. Steward scolded Rudy for this bad behaviour. Once outside the cabin Rudy loved it, running and jumping in what snow was left on the ground, sliding in the mud and rolling in it. This was exactly what wolf pups do on warm spring days, bathe in the mud, an opportunity this pup would never turn down.

CHAPTER FIVE

The honk of Canadian geese flying over his cabin woke Steward from his peaceful slumber. Dawn's early light shone through the dirty cabin window. Ravens cawed in the forest behind the cabin, the remnants of a carnivore's kill the probable cause of the birds' excitement. The ravens in the forest were sending out a call for others of their species to join them, as there was food for all who were hungry. The remnants of a young moose, hunted down by wolves, lay on the forest floor ready to be picked clean.

Steward decided to take Rudy and find the carcass the ravens were eating from. He retrieved his rifle from the cabin and headed into the woods, accompanied by his wolf pup, Rudy. As they moved closer to the source of the activity, Steward could hear an animal snarling. He immediately knew the cause of the commotion in the typically quiet forest. As he got closer, Steward saw a small mammal in control of the remains of the moose calf, exhibiting threatening behaviour. It was an animal neither the ravens nor the waiting fox would challenge. A wolverine had taken over the carcass, and he was in no mood to share his found spoils. Steward laughed at how fast the animal had changed the equation.

Steward set Rudy down, quickly raised his rifle, and took aim at the unsuspecting animal. An explosive sound rocked the forest, followed by a brief period of silence. The hated predator lay dead, its blood soaking the once white snow. Rudy bounded over to the scene where the wolverine's body lay, his wolf instincts kicking in. Curious, he circled the wolverine, sniffing its body. Rudy's primal instinct told him this dead animal was a feared member of the forest.

The wolverine is viewed as a threat and avoided by most animals living in the wilderness, a savage killer who spares no one if encountered in the forest. The wolverine eats almost anything it happens upon, if hungry. Steward picked up the dead animal to take it back to the cabin, with Rudy following closely behind.

Returning to the cabin, Steward decided he did not want to be bothered with processing the wolverine he had shot. He hated this animal who took many unnecessary lives in the bush. He decided to give him a taste of his own medicine. Steward took the wolverine a mile from his cabin and slit his belly open to make his smell more attractive to the scavengers who would come to feast on his remains.

Before heading back to his cabin, Steward checked on his dogs, who were doing well in their new location. After tending to his huskies, Steward returned home with Rudy. He fed the wolf pup breakfast, after which the animal retired to his favorite spot beside the woodstove. Steward had added wood when he returned from outside, resulting in a roaring fire to keep Rudy warm.

Steward spent the rest of the day completing spring related jobs which needed to be done every year at this time. He would soon be travelling to pick up supplies, which were arriving by riverboat. Such boats were used to resupply Dawson with goods depleted over the winter. Steward would be using Jason and Wendy's donkey, Omar, to carry the items needed for his business back to his cabin. Steward would have to limit his purchases, not wanting to make two trips from Dawson, as the other donkey he had access to, Honey, was not available for work. Omar had had his way with her, and she was pregnant, unable to carry anything heavy on her back. Omar's spur of the moment desire had created a lot of extra work for him.

CHAPTER SIX

The howl of the wolf pack filled the night with sound. Steward awoke, listening to the chorus of music emanating from the forest. His huskies, hearing the howls of their fellow canines, returned the sound with a symphony of their own. Rudy lay awake, his ears pointing skyward. He listened to the howls coming from his wolf pack, who still lived in the area. The wolf pup wondered if his mother was looking for him. The wild characteristics of this animal would never be tamed. Rudy would always be a wolf; his instincts would have it no other way.

Steward awoke the following morning with an uncomfortable feeling. He wondered how Rudy reacted to the familiar howls from the wolf family which abandoned him. Steward gathered up his new companion and snuggled him tightly. He knew the wolf pup needed love and attention, which he would never receive from his mother.

Steward fed Rudy and then went outside to take care of his sled dogs. He noticed that during the night the rest of the ice had disappeared from the lake. Steward was glad he could canoe and fish on open water again. His trip to Dawson was coming soon. He had arranged for his sister,

Wendy, and his brother-in-law, Jason, to stay at his cabin and care for his dogs while he was gone. He would return with Omar, their donkey, with his back ladened down with goods purchased in Dawson.

During the winter months, Omar was boarded in Dawson at Steward and Wendy's aunt's house. Bev's stable was a safer place for Omar to stay, as survival in the bush during the cruel winters of the Yukon cannot be guaranteed for a donkey. Exposure to the brutal cold and hungry predators looking for an easy meal would be the probable cause of the donkey's demise, if he stayed year-round at the cabin.

Omar would work hard during the summer, packing in goods on his back for the trio of relatives who called this part of the forest home. His pregnant girlfriend, Honey, would remain in Dawson and have her baby in the fall. Omar would return to Dawson in October to Honey, and hopefully a healthy, new baby donkey.

Steward resigned himself to complete the job he was not looking forward to this afternoon, cleaning the sled dogs' yard. A top layer of waste had to be removed from the ground before the dogs were relocated back to their familiar surroundings. This task kept Steward busy all day. The sun was setting as he moved the last husky to its clean pen. He was happy to return to his cabin, planning to spend a quiet evening with Rudy, a true companion of the north.

CHAPTER SEVEN

Steward awoke the following morning to a surprise. When he had returned to his cabin last night, after moving his sled dogs back to their original yard, the outside air was mild and the sky was clear. During the night the wind had shifted, blowing from the north, dragging a strong cold front down from the arctic. With this change, came black menacing clouds and cold wind-blown snow.

The cabin was cold; Steward had let the fire go out not expecting this April snowstorm. This snow event was not uncommon for late spring; snow in June is not unusual in the Yukon. Rudy lay on his blanket in front of the warming woodstove. The crackle of the burning fire was the only sound to break the silence in the cabin.

After lunch, the warm sun peeked through the departing clouds. The fresh snow lay like a blanket over the trees, shining like sparkling diamonds before melting and disappearing forever. The skies cleared completely, and the afternoon sun shone brightly, melting the snow which dusted the ground.

Steward had been watching the activity on his lake. Geese and ducks of various species used the lake as a stopover on their migration north. A wide variety of waterfowl could be found on the lake at anytime, now that the ice had dissipated. Colonies of beavers and muskrats lived at one end of the lake, where the wetlands were located. This marshy environment harboured numerous species of birds, who ate food found only in the water. The rest of the lake was deep with a rocky bottom, having been formed by glaciers a millennium ago. This cold, clear water was habitat for lake trout and whitefish, as well as a variety of other species. All fish Steward caught were used for food, with those considered inedible by man being fed to the dogs, providing a good source of protein during the warm months of the year.

Steward launched his canoe into the calm waters of the lake. Pushing the canoe forward, he hopped aboard and positioned himself in the small boat. His gun, food, and water lay in the bottom of the canoe, as he paddled toward the beaver colonies. Steward wanted to check on the status of the beaver dams, looking for signs of recent work activity. The colony typically completed repairs from storm damage done during the winter months once the ice was off the lake.

Steward was a careful man when it came to beaver. If he harvested too many from the colony, the family might collapse. This would be a tragic situation for both the beavers and Steward, who would lose a valuable source of income from the loss of these animals' fur. As Steward paddled his canoe closer, he noticed activity on the other side of the dam. A half-eaten carcass of a large beaver was floating in the still waters of the beaver pond, which squawking ravens were pecking clean. Upon examination, Steward found no evidence of a violent death and surmised the beaver had died of old age or disease. When the warm spring days melted the ice and snow around the dam and beaver lodge, the body must have floated to the top of the water, where it was eaten by a variety of scavengers found in this ecosystem.

Steward left the area happy with what he had observed, a heathy colony of beavers. Rudy was at the cabin waiting for Steward to return, wondering where he had gone for such a long time. As he paddled toward home, Steward thought about Rudy and the pup's long journey ahead. He was now living in an unnatural world for a wolf, the world of humans, unlike the one he had been born into.

CHAPTER EIGHT

A sudden knock on his door surprised Steward. As he approached the door, he could hear a dog whining and conversation between two adults. He was pleased when he opened the door to the smiling face of his sister, Wendy, and her family, including King, the family dog. Heartfelt greetings were exchanged, and the group was invited into Steward's cabin.

Wendy explained she was happy they had made it here before darkness had settled in, or they would have had to spend the night in the bush. This was not something she and Jason would have enjoyed. They were relieved to reach the safety of Steward's cabin before dark. Jason and Wendy's dog, King, loved Rudy, letting the wolf pup crawl all over him as he laid on the floor beside him. Rudy would growl, bite King's ears, and stand on top of him as if he had conquered the large animal beneath him. Everyone was amused by Rudy's antics.

Wendy had arrived with smoked duck and goose, which Jason had shot at their lake earlier in the week. They shared this food with Steward, who was thankful to be eating something other than fish, which had been his primary diet for weeks. While eating, Jason and Wendy told Steward they were having issues with a wolverine coming to their cabin at night looking for food. Steward suggested Jason set a trap ladened with fresh fish or meat. As the wolverine was apparently hungry, he would most likely let his guard down if his senses were tantalized by this delicious offering. Jason liked the idea and told Steward he would try it when he returned home.

Now that Jason and Wendy were there to watch the dogs, Steward planned to leave for Dawson tomorrow. But tonight, they would enjoy spending the evening together. After dinner, Steward went outside and started a campfire. The Yukon evening was cool with a light breeze and the sky was clear. The family savoured the atmosphere created in this moment of time as they huddled around the outdoor fire. As the wood burned down to embers, the tired adults decided to return to the cabin and sleep. Jason and Wendy's baby and Rudy had both fallen asleep and were carried to the cabin and put to bed.

Steward planned to rise at daybreak for his trip to Dawson. He would leave Rudy in the care of Jason and Wendy until he returned. A sudden howl broke the silence. Rudy's ears perked up and he lifted his head, listening to this familiar sound. One howl from a lone wolf was all Rudy heard. He went back to sleep in his bed by the fire, enjoying the warmth radiating from the sides of the old cast iron stove. Rudy knew he was an orphan, his mother abandoning him in the den where he was given life. Resentment was starting to build in the pup's mind, making him feel angry and unwanted, emotions Rudy would take with him to his grave.

CHAPTER NINE

Steward left for Dawson at daybreak, having packed his belongings needed for the trip the night before. He bid Jason and Wendy goodbye and cuddled Rudy, telling the pup he loved him and would return home soon. Steward would walk the trail to Dawson, something he had done many times in the past.

The day was sunny and warm, and the birds filled the forest with their song. The beauty of nature was returning after the end of the frigid Yukon winter. Steward readied his rifle. He was approaching an area of evergreen trees which he knew harboured grouse. His thoughts were on dinner tonight as he approached the stand of trees quietly. His rifle was cocked and ready to fire. Steward reached the edge of the thicket, pausing to listen for the grouse's song. Coming from the trees he heard a faint murmur from a bird's throat. Steward needed to flush the grouse out into an opening where he could get a clear shot.

Steward devised a plan; he would stand to the side of the fir trees and throw a large rock into the birds' habitat. He hoped this would startle the grouse, making them leave their roosts and fly out into the sights of his gun. The execution of his plan worked perfectly. Two dead grouse lay at his feet, ambushed when they left their cover. He stored the birds in his pack and continued his journey to Dawson, stopping for lunch on a scenic overhang he knew was on this trail. This location was the highest point a traveller would encounter when walking this route to town.

At the point, Steward sat on a large rock; the view was breathtaking. The forest was starting to wear its summer coat of green and the pristine lake's waters were sparkling in the sunshine, two of nature's displays of beauty his eyes beheld. Steward ate his lunch in silence. looking out over the horizon. His mind became lost with the splendor before him. After a short nap he was on his way, traveling until dusk.

The halfway point of Steward's journey was a large lake. Arriving earlier than he expected, Steward cleaned the grouse he had shot and collected wood for a campfire. Dusk had settled over the lake; nighttime was drawing near. The fire sizzled as the grouse were cooking. The smell of the cooking meat had been noticed by a hungry animal lurking in the forest, waiting for Steward to leave. Luckily, it was just a wayward fox, who did not have the nerve to intervene in Steward's cooking.

The forest was quiet. A pair of loons which called this lake home sang, the sound of their melancholy voices reverberating across the lake and beyond. Steward ate in silence, thinking about reaching Dawson tomorrow and staying at Bev's house overnight. He finished eating his dinner and found a spot by the water to sleep. The gentle lapping of the waves against the shoreline helped lull him to sleep. He would wake up refreshed, ready for another day in the morning.

CHAPTER TEN

Steward slept poorly on the cold damp ground. He had placed fir boughs beneath him to lay on, hoping they would starve off some of the dampness. The branches helped little, as the ground was still cold from being frozen during the winter. Steward pulled himself up off his makeshift bed and stretched his stiff muscles. He started a fire to warm his aching bones before continuing his trip to Dawson City.

Steward looked at the lake. The morning sun was burning the fog off the water, as the cold lake interacted with the warmer air above. Steward could see the eerie shadows of waterfowl hunting for breakfast in the dissipating fog which covered the lake. He sat by the fire, the roaring flames throwing a warm heat over his chilled body. Steward let the fire burn down, extinguishing the last flames before he left the campsite. The second half of the trail to Dawson would be much easier to traverse and should put him at Bev's house before dark. He left the lake, his thoughts on the warm bed and good meal he would have upon reaching his ever-gracious Aunt Bev's home.

One hour outside of Dawson City, Steward was surprised by the sound of two gunshots coming from the bush. He continued walking, when he heard the crashing sound of a large animal running through the forest in a bid to escape a life-threatening situation. Steward stopped and took cover behind a group of trees. A large buck, an adult male deer, came out of the forest stopping to rest on the open trail. The animal had been wounded by a hunter, the bullet grazing the animal's side. Steward took aim and a loud shot rang out as the animal went down. Steward ran to the fallen deer, its dead body on the ground. A well-placed shot to the heart had ended the animal's life. The sound of men talking interrupted Steward's thoughts.

Two Indigenous men appeared out of the trees and walked up to Steward and the deer. The men told Steward they had shot twice at the deer, one of their gunshots hitting him. The blood trail was easy to follow, leading the hunters here. Steward told the men to keep the deer, knowing the meat was going to a good cause. The men were hunting to provide food for the most destitute in Dawson, keeping these men, women, and children from starving. Thanks to Steward, they could now say their hunt was a success. The men embraced Steward for his kindness, wishing him a safe journey to Bev's house.

Before arriving in Dawson, Steward met two Mounties riding horseback. This was the first year the North West Mounted Police had their horses stationed in Dawson and were a sight to behold. The proud constables gave Steward a gracious greeting in passing.

Steward was soon being greeted by his Aunt Bev. With outstretched arms, she welcomed him into her warm household. Bev knew Steward was hungry, so the first thing she did was feed him. Bev asked about the welfare of the rest of her family living in the bush and was glad to hear they were all well. Bev told Steward she was glad the winter was over, as she was looking forward to working in her garden again. Bev was an avid gardener, who grew numerous varieties of vegetables successfully. People joked she had a special gift from the spirits when it came to growing food.

Steward was bone tired. Bev wished him a peaceful night's sleep as he retired to a warm bed in his own room upstairs, a privilege Steward rarely enjoyed.

CHAPTER ELEVEN

Steward woke from an undisturbed sleep. Ten minutes after wishing Bev a good night, he was sound asleep under the covers, his head buried deep in a comfortable pillow. He slept soundly through the night, waking only to the smell of Bev cooking breakfast. The odor of frying pork this morning set Steward's sense of smell on fire. The aroma reminded him of cooking deer meat over an open campfire at the cabin.

After the delicious breakfast was finished, Bev asked Steward for a favor. The stalls in the barn where Omar and Honey lived needed a spring cleaning. The manure piled up in a corner of the barn over the winter needed to be removed and placed by Bev's garden. Mixing this donkey manure with dirt from her garden was one reason Bev was able to grow beautiful vegetables. Steward told Bev he would be more than happy to do this chore for her.

When Steward entered the barn, Omar's heart sank. The donkey knew he would be going with Steward and be used as a pack animal this summer in the bush. He would miss Honey, the mother of his new baby which was expected to be born in the fall. His life would be in danger daily from hungry predators he shared the forest with, all who would like to eat him for dinner. Omar hated staying in the wilderness, where he never felt safe.

Steward greeted the two donkeys, rubbing their heads and talking to them in a nice way. He then got to work. He moved the pile of manure from the barn to Bev's garden with a wheelbarrow. Steward then moved animals around while cleaning their stalls. This fresh manure was also taken outside to the garden. After four hours of hard work, Steward was finished moving manure from the barn to the outside. He went from the barn to Bev's house, where lunch was on the table waiting for him.

Bev was like a mother to Steward, anxious to take care of all his needs. After eating lunch, Steward headed into Dawson to buy ammunition for his rifles and handgun. Over the winter, guns are discharged regularly for hunting and personal protection. One of the greatest fears of wilderness trappers and gold prospectors is running out of ammunition. Steward would also stop by the saloon and drink two beers. Visiting the saloon was a ritual he enjoyed whenever in town.

Steward completed other errands as well, visiting the mercantile store and picking up a new axe and saw for cutting firewood. He purchased foodstuffs, such as flour, sugar, and salt, along with a large bag of dogfood for his dogs. This fifty-pound bag of dried food was needed for emergencies during the summer in case fresh food became scarce. Steward gathered all his supplies at Bev's place, except for the dog food, which he planned to pick up with Omar on the way out of Dawson tomorrow.

Omar knew his first day back to work was not going to be pleasant, he was not looking forward to it. He would cooperate with Steward, knowing life could be worse for him somewhere else. Honey, his pregnant girlfriend, did not want Omar to leave for fear she would never see him again. Omar felt the same way. He would miss Honey and worry about her and the baby.

Even donkeys' have personal issues living in the bush, some of which are greater than those of their owners. The animals' caretakers do not see them or care. The donkeys believe their feelings are important and should be considered in the decisions made by their owners. Such as, not keeping them in the forest all summer, an idea neither Steward, Jason, nor Wendy ever considered.

CHAPTER TWELVE

The morning sun was peeking over the horizon when Bev yelled at Steward to get out of bed. Steward dressed and joined Bev downstairs for breakfast. Steward thought about Omar and Honey, the donkeys in love whom he had to split up until the late fall. Omar and Honey would see each other when Jason and Wendy visited with Bev this summer. Omar would return in mid-October and winter over at Bev's with Honey and the couple's new baby donkey. Omar hoped Honey's baby would be born before he returned to Bev's for the winter.

Steward thanked Bev graciously for her hospitality, hugging her tightly not wanting to let go. He walked to the barn to prepare Omar for his journey to his cabin. Steward had bought Omar and Honey a special treat from the livery stable, the finest hay the proprietor of the business sold. The hay was made of sweet clover, donkeys' favorite food to graze on. Steward had also purchased some of the man's grain mash which he made at his stable, also one of the donkeys' favorite. He offered these items to the pair before heading out.

Steward led Omar from the barn. He loaded the goods he had already purchased and placed them on the donkey's back. He led Omar back into the barn to say goodbye to Honey. Tears welled in Steward's eyes when he witnessed the love these donkeys showed toward one another. From Steward's place, Jason and Wendy, who owned Omar, would take the donkey to their cabin for the summer. It was clear to Steward how much they would miss each other.

Omar and Steward finally left the barn to pick up the dog food Steward had purchased. This was the last stop in Dawson before hitting the trail back to Steward's cabin. Steward was missing his wolf pup, Rudy, and would be thrilled to see him. The man at the store had divided the bag of dog food into two twenty-five-pound packages to balance the weight on Omar's back. With the proprietor's help, the donkey was securely loaded and ready to make the trip into the bush. Steward thanked the man and left his store, leading Omar out of town and into the wilds of the Yukon forest.

Omar did love the aroma of the fresh outdoors. His sense of smell was invaded by a hundred different scents all at once. In the barn all winter, the only thing he smelled was hay, dry brown hay. Omar had walked this trail before with Jason and Wendy, ferrying supplies from Dawson City to the couple's cabin in the forest. With Steward prodding Omar to keep moving, the pair made it to the familiar lake where they camped, which was the halfway point of their journey to his cabin. Steward started a fire to produce light as the sky was dark, ladened with storm clouds. Steward ate beef jerky in silence and thought about returning to his cabin tomorrow. He was exhausted and would sleep on that thought tonight. Tomorrow he would be home, cuddling a grateful companion. It was a moment Steward was waiting for.

CHAPTER THIRTEEN

Steward opened his eyes. The honking of geese woke him as a large group of the birds flew over where he was sleeping and landed on the lake. The geese would forage for food until tiring and then move on to a more productive spot. The sun was slowly making its way over the horizon when Steward pulled himself up from the hard ground. He approached Omar, wishing him a good morning and rubbing the donkey's neck. Omar basked in the attention Steward lavished on him.

Steward's plan was to take Omar to a nearby meadow, where he could graze until his stomach was full. Steward would join him and eat the food Bev had prepared for his overnight trip home. The duo left the lake, embarking on the last half of their journey back to the cabin.

Thirty minutes later they reached the meadow. Fresh shoots of tender green grass were in abundant supply. Omar delved into this smorgasbord of fresh greens, hoping it would not upset his stomach later. Steward felt the same way, hoping the food he left Dawson with was still good after this amount of time in the open air. Luckily for the pair, neither suffered any ill effects from their breakfast.

The day was sunny and warm. The hours of daylight were getting longer, and the sun rays were getting warmer. Winter was finally giving up its tight embrace, letting life thrive once again. Steward led Omar down the trail. Coming toward them from the other end of the trail was a man leading a donkey. When their paths crossed, the men stopped to talk, viewing each other as harmless. The man told Steward his name was Leonard and he lived outside of Dawson. He had delivered supplies to a friend who lived in the bush and was on his way back home. After a brief conversation, the men wished each other good luck and parted ways.

The remainder of Steward and Omar's trip was uneventful. Dusk was falling as Steward's cabin came into view. Steward yelled out to Jason and Wendy. The couple responded by meeting Steward and Omar at the cabin door. Omar garnered all the attention, stealing the spotlight from Steward, who had just seen Jason and Wendy before he left for Dawson. The couple had not seen their beloved donkey since Christmas. Even King, the family dog, had missed Omar. Omar liked King because he watched out for Omar's safety while he was at Jason and Wendy's cabin. King had saved Omar's life more than once from hungry predators.

Upon entering the cabin, Wendy told Steward that Rudy would not allow Jason or her to pick him up. Trying to do so elicited an unfriendly greeting of snarling and biting from the wolf cub. Rudy did not want to be handled by human hands. Steward knew he had to take charge and become Rudy's master. Keeping Rudy would become intolerable if, as an adult, the domesticated wolf thought he was in control, an unsuitable ending Steward knew would not work for Rudy or himself.

CHAPTER FOURTEEN

Steward walked over and picked up Rudy. The pup was glad to see him, burying his head into Steward's chest. The men unloaded the goods from Omar's back and settled him into his enclosure for the evening. He would leave with Jason and Wendy in the morning, returning to their cabin for the summer months.

While Steward was gone, the couple had used his canoe to fish for subsistence and to provide protein for his dogs, who had been living on dry dog food and were hungry. Their efforts had proven fruitful, using Steward's nets to catch numerous fish. Rabbits were plentiful in the woods surrounding the cabin, resulting in Jason successfully shooting three rabbits, which Wendy was cooking for dinner. The timing of Steward's return home could not have been better.

Rudy did not like Jason and Wendy's child. Whenever Kuzih approached Rudy wanting to play, the pup would show its displeasure by growling menacingly at the baby. Kuzih grew weary of Rudy and learned to keep a safe distance from him. After dinner, the warm evening beckoned the siblings and friends outside. Steward built a fire and retrieved his pup from inside the cabin. King checked on his friend Omar secured in his enclosure. He knew the donkey depended on him to provide extra security when it was necessary. King tried to do the best job he could for his buddy, Omar.

The warm evening was accompanied by a cloudless sky. What seemed like a million stars illuminated the blackness of the night. The full moon was but a backdrop in this celestial show put on by the Creator. A set of curious eyes watched from the forest; the animal's musky odor caught by the wolf pup. A growl came from the back of Rudy's throat, warning Steward of the danger lurking nearby. Steward, ready for unexpected danger, always had his rifle by his side.

The howl of a nearby wolf caught the group by surprise. Rudy, hearing the call, lifted his head high returning his mother's call. Who should Rudy stay loyal to, Steward who had saved his life by rescuing him or a mother who had abandoned him? She left her pup to die, cold and alone in a deserted wolf den. Rudy lay his head back down in Steward's lap, quickly falling back asleep.

For now, Steward was making the choice easier for Rudy. Being the pet of one of wolves' biggest predator made him feel like a traitor to his species, but Rudy felt he had no choice but to take this pathway in life for his own survival. It was a direction which would lead to many hardships in the future, as Rudy grew into a companion for Steward and his fiancée, Blossom. Steward and Blossom would soon be getting married, and she would join him at his cabin. Rudy would not be agreeable to sharing his space and attention with a new human companion, something Rudy would have to learn to live with.

CHAPTER FIFTEEN

Rudy slept fitfully; the howls of his mother's wolf pack filled the night air with sound. Two members of the pack had surprised and killed a deer, now they were calling the rest of the family to feast on the prize. Steward was awake listening to the wolves, which appeared to be nearby. Tomorrow, Steward was planning an overnight camping trip. He would take Rudy to the kill site on their way to the creek they were going to visit. Noisy ravens feeding on the carcass would direct him to the remains.

The morning sun crawled up over the horizon, another beautiful day full of life was beginning in this vast territory of wilderness called the Yukon. Jason and Wendy rose at daybreak. Jason went out to Omar's enclosure to prepare the donkey for his trip home. Wendy collected the couple's personal gear, some of which was loaded on Omar's back. With the baby strapped to Wendy and King leading the way, the family said goodbye to Steward and left his cabin. Silence prevailed when Steward was left alone. The only sound in the cabin was Rudy snoring, sleeping by the woodstove, which Steward kept burning on cooler nights so the cabin would not get cold.

Steward had plans for today. He would take Rudy and show him the carcass of the wolves' kill from the previous night. Some of the remains were surely left by the wolves for scavengers to feed on. Steward and Rudy would then go on an overnight adventure. Steward wanted to try panning for gold in a fast-moving stream bolstered by recent rains. On their way home from there, they would visit Johnathan and Shining Star's cabin. Steward needed a favor from them, as the time for his wedding was coming soon and he needed someone to stay at his cabin to take care of his huskies. He wanted Shining Star, with her calming spirit, to care for Rudy while he was away. Steward fed his dog team, packed supplies for an overnight stay in the bush, along with his gold pan, and headed out.

Rudy followed Steward to the deer carcass, where remains of the animal lay scattered about the area. Rudy sniffed with abandon, finding every piece of carrion left to rot in the forest. The primitive instincts of the wolf cub returned as he gobbled down this meat from the forest floor. The pair continued their walk to the waterfall and cold, spring-fed stream. Two hours later they arrived and set up camp. The rushing current through the rocks was a prime location to find gold nuggets flushed out of the ground by the underground river. The stream was also full of rainbow trout, who lived in the cold, fast-moving water. This habitat was perfect for this trout species and Steward never went hungry when he visited this site.

Before fishing, Steward gathered enough firewood for the evening. He needed a fire for light and to cook the fish, if he was lucky enough to catch any. He had packed some fishing line and found some grubs to bait the hooks. With coaching from Rudy, Steward had four large trout in his possession within a one-hour period. Steward happily cleaned the trout, throwing the remains to Rudy to eat what he wanted. Rudy loved the outdoor camping trip. He was starting to listen and obey Steward's commands, becoming the dog Steward expected him to be.

CHAPTER SIXTEEN

Steward spent the rest of his day panning for gold, with poor results. He found not a single nugget or even a trace of gold flake while working the pan all afternoon. Rudy played in the cold spring water of the creek while Steward unsuccessfully tried his luck at finding the precious metal.

The afternoon was turning to dusk, as Steward lit the campfire to cook the trout he had caught earlier in the day. He had left the fish in the cold water of the creek to keep it fresh until dinner. The wood crackled and snapped, the flames leaping upward and the smoke rising skyward in a grey column. Steward waited for the coals from the wood to glow red. He then cooked the trout over the hot coals. Steward and Rudy enjoyed a delicious meal together for dinner.

The forest was quiet, not a creature was stirring or moving about. A brisk wind blowing through the leaves on the trees was the only movement Steward heard coming from the darkness of the night. He added more wood to the fire, enjoying the quiet and serenity nature had to offer on this beautiful star-lit evening. Tomorrow they would continue their journey to Johnathan and Shining Star's location, which Steward planned on taking three-hours.

Steward lay down beside the waterfall with Rudy by his side. He stared up at the night sky, knowing soon he would have a wife to share these moments with. Steward and his wolf fell asleep. Only the curious owl watching from a tall tree knew of their presence in the forest. The rising sun and the sound of the waterfall woke Steward. Rudy was awake and playing in the water. He had been digging in the sand on the bottom of the creek, where the swift current, acting like a wash, picked up the loose sediment and sent it downstream.

Steward watched Rudy dig furiously, as if he was looking for something. He dove face first into the hole he had dug and came out with a leather pouch in his mouth. Steward jumped up, surprised at what Rudy had found. Rudy was not willing to give up this prize he had found buried in the sand easily. A large piece of fish changed his mind on the matter, taking food over his found treasure. Steward's hands shook as he took his knife and cut open the leather sachet. In the bag were silver and gold coins, probably the cache of some lone prospector who lost his small savings and his life in this unforgiving land called the Yukon.

CHAPTER SEVENTEEN

Steward placed his newfound wealth in a safe place. There was a total of ten coins in the bag, the largest being a twenty-dollar American gold piece. The rest of the coins had limited value, with half of the cache being American silver dollars. The combined face value of the gold and silver was thirty dollars. The mystery of how these coins ended up buried in the sand in the bottom of the creek would never be known.

Steward packed up his camp, called out to Rudy, and the duo left the site, walking toward Johnathan and Shining Star's cabin. The day was sunny and warm, with a brilliant blue sky. Rudy was growing fast. He could now keep up with Steward when walking on the forest trails. He was an alert and highly intelligent canine, and Steward knew as an adult Rudy would make an excellent work dog. He would become a true leader and be known as the best sled dog in the Dawson area.

It was an easy walk to Johnathan and Shining Star's cabin. Steward and Rudy's visit would be a welcome surprise to the couple. Having visitors while living in the remote bush of the Yukon was not a common occurrence. Upon arriving at their cabin, only the family dog, Chase, was home. Steward checked the lake, noticing one of the couple's canoes was gone. Steward surmised they had gone fishing and would return to their cabin shortly. He sat with Rudy by the lake waiting for them to come home.

The sun shone brightly on the placid turquoise water of the lake. Steward caught sight of a canoe, looking like an anomaly on the large expanse of water. As Steward waited, the canoe moved closer to the cabin. Johnathan and his wife were on their way home. As the couple approached the shoreline, Steward yelled out and waved a greeting. Rudy yelped loudly, looking for attention. The couple returned Steward's greeting, glad to see him and his new dog, which had grown considerably since they first met him.

Steward helped the couple beach their canoe. Five large lake trout lay in the bottom of the boat. It had been a lucky day for fishing. After welcoming gestures, the trio retrieved the fish and walked to the cabin. Chase welcomed the trio into his home, except for Rudy, whom he was not sure of. Chase wondered if he should treat the wolf pup as a friend or a foe, although there was something a bit familiar about him. Rudy soon won over Chase's heart with his playful puppy antics, and Chase enjoyed the entertainment Rudy brought to the cabin during his stay there.

Over dinner, Steward asked the couple about them taking care of his dogs for a few days, including Rudy, his wolf pup. His new wife would soon be waiting for him in Dawson, where a private wedding ceremony would be performed by an elder of the tribe at Bev's house. The newlyweds would leave to return to Steward's cabin the following day to start their new life together as man and wife, a marriage built from companionship and love, which Steward hoped would last forever.

CHAPTER EIGHTEEN

The following morning, Steward said his goodbyes to Johnathan and Shining Star. He thanked them for the hospitality he was shown while staying here. He was also grateful the couple agreed to take care of Rudy and his sled dogs while he travelled to Dawson for his wedding. On the way down the trail, Steward thought about the news Shining Star told him before he left. She was pregnant, expecting her baby in the late fall. It was news Steward had not expected to hear, but he was very happy for his cousin and her husband.

As the trail moved deeper into the forest, the sky darkened. Thunder sounded in the distance and a cool steady breeze rustled the canopies of the trees. A storm was moving closer, the thunder getting louder. Lightning lit up the forest and the sound of driving rain could be heard coming through the trees toward Steward and Rudy. The pair took cover in a clump of evergreen trees, but the torrential rain soaked them. There was no escaping the deluge of water from Mother Nature.

The quick moving thunderstorm left the area, and the returning sun began to dry Steward's wet clothes. Rudy had received a needed bath, courtesy of the rain, and Steward had his clothes laundered. These gifts from nature were not requested but were appreciated. Cleanliness was not a common condition to enjoy when living in a wilderness environment.

Steward and Rudy continued their journey. Grouse were plentiful on this walk, allowing Steward to take full advantage of this gift. He shot three of the gamebirds for dinner. After a lengthy walk, Rudy and Steward reached the cabin. A pair of ravens sitting on the roof squawked at them loudly. This pair of birds were the newest residents in the forest surrounding Steward's home, nesting in a tall tree nearby. They often visited, looking for food.

Steward entered his cabin and was surprised to see a note on the table, alongside a package of coffee and sugar. The Mounties had stopped by, patrolling with their horses for the first time this year. Like sled dogs in the winter, the horses provided an easier and faster way for the Mounties to get to their destination. The horses also could be utilized to carry needed supplies between Mountie outposts during the warm weather months.

The note from the Mounties indicated they were sorry to have missed Steward and they would stop by later this summer. Steward liked the fact there was now a contingent of law enforcement stationed in Dawson, bringing order to the gold rush town. It was a presence which was sorely needed in this new frontier and untamed land called the Yukon.

CHAPTER NINETEEN

Steward had been busy preparing to leave for Dawson in a week. Since his return from Johnathan and Shining Star's house, he had been performing maintenance around his cabin and been cleaning the interior. His wife-to-be, Blossom, was the adopted daughter of his Aunt Bev's close friend. Bev had played matchmaker, introducing Blossom to Steward a little over a year ago. Blossom had been an invited guest at Bev's annual Christmas party and Bev thought it would be a match made in heaven if they were to marry.

Steward had discretely asked for Blossom's hand in marriage about six months after their meeting. His relationship with her was a well-kept secret, with Bev being his only family member aware of the impending nuptials. Steward's shy demeanor kept him from wanting to draw attention to himself and his fiancée. Bev insisted he tell his family and friends. When Steward continued to refuse to do what Bev asked of him, she did the job for him. She announced his upcoming marriage to everyone in attendance at her house the previous Christmas. Steward was looking forward to being a married man, having a reliable helper and companion to share his life with. His sister, Wendy, was glad her brother had found Blossom, whom she met at the same Christmas party. She felt Blossom was a woman Steward would love and trust.

Time was here for Steward's trip to Dawson. Johnathan and Shining Star had arrived at his cabin the previous evening. Chase and Rudy, the two-family pets, kept each other occupied. To Steward it appeared Chase was the babysitter for his rambunctious wolf dog, who was hard to keep entertained in the cabin. Steward bid farewell to Shining Star and Johnathan, promising to come back within the week. Johnathan and Shining Star assured Steward everything would be fine until he and his new wife returned.

The day after his arrival in Dawson, a wedding ceremony was performed at Bev's home by an Indigenous shaman. The ceremony was attended by Bev and Blossom's adoptive parents. After the ceremony, the new bride and groom left, happy to be retiring to the best hotel in town to have dinner and spend a romantic evening together. Steward was looking forward to their wedding night, as all grooms do. He hoped Blossom felt the same way about spending the evening alone together, consummating their marriage. Steward expected they would discover love and their life together would blossom into a loving marriage, a union in the Yukon meant to last forever.

CHAPTER TWENTY

A ringing bell woke Steward and Blossom from their peaceful slumber. It was the proprietor of this family-run hotel notifying his guests breakfast would be served shortly in the dining room downstairs. The man's wife was the chief cook and bottle washer of this establishment. Her reputation as the finest cook in Dawson drew people like a magnet to her hotel dining room to eat. The excellent cooking and baking skills she offered to her guests were second to none.

The young couple ate a hearty, delicious breakfast at the hotel before leaving on the long walk to Steward's cabin. They had purchased jerky, a nonperishable food item, to satisfy their hunger on their trek to Blossom's new home. Fish caught or fowl shot would add to their meager diet as they travelled through the forests and wetlands of the Yukon.

The late April day was warm with the sun shining brightly in a cloudless blue sky. However, recent rains made the trail muddy, slowing the newlyweds' progress. The couple passed many travellers during their first morning on the popular trail. Gold seekers from the lower forty-eight states made up the bulk of these men, who were travelling to the Klondike to seek their fortune. For many of these men, their future would bring death, as they succumbed to the harsh realities of a winter they were not prepared for. Many families would be left at home, never again seeing their fathers or husbands.

After an uneventful day, the couple reached the lake which was the halfway point of their journey. It was the only lake they would encounter on their way to Steward's cabin. The sun was setting as Steward built a fire for ambience. Twilight settled over the lake and the soulful call of a loon pierced the quiet of the evening. The male loon's call for his mate echoed across the open water. The couple quietly sat and talked.

Blossom was the adopted daughter of a family friend, who Bev had known for many years. Blossom's birth father had been mauled and killed by a grizzly bear when she was four years old. He had surprised a sow and her baby eating berries in the forest. The mother bear attacked him, protecting her baby. Blossom's father was no match for an angry grizzly bear, losing his life in the struggle. Unfortunately for Blossom, her mother died two years later of an illness which ended her life quickly. Blossom was sent to live with an aunt and uncle, who raised her as their own child. This aunt, a member of another Indigenous tribe in the Dawson area, had been friends with Bev since they were teenagers.

Blossom became a great asset to her aunt and uncle, who lived alone in a cabin in the wilderness. She provided an extra set of hands, which was always welcomed when living in the bush. Bev had picked a good woman for Steward. She had been raised in the environment like that he chose to live in, secluded with his dogs in the forest. This was the only life Blossom knew, living alone with Steward in the bush was fine with her. Blossom was falling in love with Steward and wanted to be with him all the time. She did not want to feel the loneliness she experienced living with her aunt and uncle.

The couple fell asleep in each other's arms. The sound of the waves lapping against the shoreline was drowned out by the calls of the lovesick loon looking for attention from his ignoring mate. Blossom loved life in this brutal land where nature rules and men must pay attention, as second chances are rarely given.

CHAPTER TWENTY-ONE

Steward awoke as the morning sun was rising over the horizon. Fog hung over the water obscuring the waterfowl present on the lake, only the sounds of the birds' song could be heard through the mist which covered the water. Steward reached down and pulled the blanket up over himself and his wife. The morning was cool and damp. He snuggled with Blossom, the warmth from her body making Steward feel comfortable. After a brief time of play under the blanket, tickling and caressing each other, the couple pulled themselves up from the hard ground. Steward was hoping they would reach his cabin by late afternoon if there were no distractions on the trail today.

As the morning wore on, the day grew warmer. The sun beat down on Steward and Blossom, who were not expecting to be overwhelmed by this sudden, unseasonal heat wave. The land was quiet as the birds and mammals living in the forest sought shelter from the hot sun. The couple's supply of water was low, but luckily Steward knew of a bubbling spring just yards from the main trail up ahead where they could refill their bottles. This provided Steward and Blossom with enough of this life sustaining liquid for the remainder of their trip home.

Dusk was descending on the forest when Steward's cabin came into view. A haze was forming over the lake, as the warm moist air interacted with the cooler water below. As the couple moved closer to the cabin, Steward yelled out a greeting. His huskies, excited at hearing Steward's voice, barked out a loud greeting in return. Johnathan and Shining Star appeared in the open doorway of the cabin. Rudy ran to meet Steward when he called out for him. Rudy's friend, Chase, followed behind the wolf pup, who was quietly growing into a wolf dog.

Steward introduced his new bride to Johnathan and Shining Star. Shining Star thought Blossom and Steward made a beautiful couple. Steward gave Blossom a walking tour of her new home. She was happy with what Steward had created and felt comfortable joining him to live her life here with the man she loved.

Shining Star had prepared smoked lake trout for dinner, a meal appreciated by Steward and Blossom who had been eating only jerky since they left Dawson. Calm swept through the cabin as the cooler air of the night blew in through the open window. A peaceful sleep was had by all, the quiet night interrupted only occasionally by the long soulful call of the loon on the lake, a bird representing a symbol of peace and hope in this rugged land.

CHAPTER TWENTY-TWO

The early morning found Johnathan and Shining Star getting ready to leave Steward's cabin to go home. After best wishes from Steward and Blossom, the couple called Chase and started their journey back to their cabin. They expected to reach home before lunch. The newlywed couple watched as their company disappeared out of sight into the forest.

Unfortunately for Rudy, Steward realized some changes had to be made. Rudy had displayed some aggressive, jealous behaviour toward Blossom, and he knew things would not end well if this were left to continue. It had become obvious a wolf of his character could not be confined to a cabin. Rudy needed to be outside. His wild instincts were suited for the wilderness, not life as a family pet.

Steward decided to keep Rudy outside, in a shelter away from his huskies. When the snows came, he would train Rudy as a sled dog and try to incorporate him into the dog team as the alpha male. Steward hoped this winter Rudy would lead his dog team to victory in the gruelling Dawson City dog sled race, where first prize was a hundred dollars paid in gold.

Rudy hated being confined to the cabin and was always at the door wanting to be let outside. However, Steward knew if he did not restrain Rudy he would leave and rejoin the wolf pack. The wolf's instincts were telling him he was in the wrong place; he was a wolf, not a human. He felt he needed to be living in the forest, not inside a building where food was provided daily. Steward believed having a shelter outside the cabin would be a good start in making his wolf dog happy.

Steward took Rudy to his new home, an emergency shelter he had previously set up for keeping sick or injured dogs away from the rest of the pack. The space was also used as a maternity hospital, where a pregnant husky could have her babies. This would be Rudy's new home. Steward would build another shelter for sick dogs and pregnant huskies. Rudy loved his new home, except for the strong fence enclosing it, which confined him to a relatively small space. Rudy would stay loyal to Steward, as he remembered who saved his life and who deserted him. It was a conflict he had within himself, which was difficult to resolve; should he be loyal to Steward or his pack? For now, Rudy's choice was Steward.

Blossom asked Steward if they could go out on the lake today. She loved the water and the wildlife which lived there. Fish and an assortment of mammals and waterfowl harvested from such lakes supplied nourishment for her people, helping them survive the difficult life they faced in the wilderness. These Indigenous people were the true spirits of the north. Their presence will always be felt here, as their spirits roam the forests of this untamed land, called the Yukon.

CHAPTER TWENTY-THREE

Blossom watched as the young beaver, with a fresh cut branch of aspen in its mouth, headed back to its lodge. Through proper management, Steward had nourished the beaver colonies. By not trapping many of these mammals, their numbers remained strong. With the birth of new babies in the spring, the number of beavers in the colony were replenished every year. Proper management of beaver colonies was important to the fur trade industry. Beaver pelts were the most desired and valuable fur harvested in the Yukon. Experienced trappers knew the benefits of proper management when it involved this busy animal.

Steward turned the canoe around and paddled toward the cabin. The bright sun shone its warm rays down upon the couple. They returned to their cabin to barking huskies and a sullen Rudy, who lay motionless in his shelter. Steward wished he had just left Rudy where he had found him. Now the animal was caught between two worlds, not knowing which one he belonged in. Rudy could no longer be returned to the wild by Steward, as the wild wolves would kill him. He was contaminated with the scent of man.

Blossom walked to the cabin, while Steward went to see Rudy. He entered his compound and was greeted by the dog. Rudy jumped on Steward, knocking him to the ground and licking his face in a show of affection. His wolf was his companion. Steward cared for Rudy and understood the issues he was facing, adapting to this way of life. He talked to Rudy softly, telling him he cared about and loved him. Steward knew no one could replace this wolf cub's mother.

Steward returned to the cabin and discussed Rudy with Blossom. She told Steward she felt over time Rudy would adapt to the situation he found himself in. When he became the alpha male dog, pulling the sled through snow this winter, he would be a happier animal.

The summers in the Yukon are short, and preparations for winter must be started early. One job was cutting enough wood to keep the cabin warm all season, including procuring extra wood in case of an especially cold winter. Running out of firewood usually meant death from exposure to the brutal cold for early fur trappers. The stove pipes needed to be cleaned, as a house fire was something to be avoided at all costs. The logs of the cabin needed to be chinked to keep out the cold draughts of winter air and the roof needed to be cleaned of all debris. These were some of the tasks which kept these early settlers busy. It was a lifestyle embraced by Steward and Blossom, who knew no other way of life.

CHAPTER TWENTY-FOUR

The hungry bear roamed around Steward's cabin looking for food. Steward and Blossom were awakened by the barking huskies. Steward jumped out of bed and dressed himself. He retrieved his rifle from the corner of the room and walked toward the front door of the cabin. As he neared the entry, the sound of wood being torn from the structure could be heard. Steward knew it was a bear invading his property. He could hear the growls of this predator as it tried to break into the cabin.

Steward thought this was unusual behaviour on the bear's part. Barking dogs were usually a deterrent which kept bears away. Showing no fear of the dogs and trying to enter an occupied dwelling was not what these predators usually do. Afraid the animal might be sick, Steward felt he needed to kill the bear so it would not return to the cabin again.

Blossom watched out the window, telling Steward when the bear moved away from the door of the structure. Steward readied his rifle in one hand and threw open the door of the cabin with the other. The startled bear had little time to react as he took a bullet in the head. The animal staggered backwards, collapsing dead on the ground in front of the cabin. A look of triumph spread across Steward's face, as he realized he had defeated this feared enemy which lived in the forest.

After examining the bear, Steward recognized it as a young bear, born last year. The animal was hungry and an inexperienced hunter, which explained his unusual behaviour earlier, when the hunter had become the hunted. The bear would be butchered tomorrow by Steward and Blossom. For now, Steward dragged the young bear to the shed and secured it in the building for the night. When finished, Steward returned to bed with his wife, who was waiting for him. The couple, feeling exhausted after this midnight encounter with the bear, immediately fell back asleep.

The morning sun filtered through the dirty window of the cabin. The ravens who lived nearby were on the roof of the home. Their annoying calls for food echoed through the quiet forest. Steward went out to feed and water his dogs. He took care of his huskies first, who always appreciated their breakfast. Steward took special care of Rudy, spending more time with him, making the wolf dog feel more important than the huskies. Steward paid little attention to his huskies, treating them like his work dogs.

As the summer wore on, Rudy would continue growing. Steward was the only human Rudy trusted, with Blossom being the only other individual Rudy would listen to or be civil toward. He would bite anyone else who tried to touch him. Rudy was going to be a large strong dog, evident in the way he handled himself. Rudy looked and walked like a dominant alpha male. Unlike the huskies, he was the true leader in this land, where only the strong survive and the weak perish. Succumbing to weakness would never be an outcome for this wolf dog, he was the king of the north.

CHAPTER TWENTY-FIVE

After breakfast, Steward and Blossom went to the shed, which was used during the trapping season to process and store furs caught on Steward's trapline. This was where he had dragged the dead bear he had shot and killed, for safe keeping. The night had been cool, which helped preserve the meat until morning.

The couple got to work butchering the bear. Blossom took some meat for stew and Steward would take some of the better cuts and smoke them, a method of preserving meat which works well when faced with no refrigeration. The couple would eat the stew cooked on the woodstove in the cabin for dinner. The rest of the meat harvested from this predator would be used to feed the dogs and the scavengers living in the forest.

Steward had built a primitive cart for moving things around during the summer. He would hook up one dog to the cart and pull anything which needed to be taken to or from the cabin. The scent of butchered animals tended to draw hungry wolves and bears to the scene. Taking the remains of these animals far from the cabin usually solved this problem.

The bear was butchered before lunch. Blossom took her bear meat inside the cabin to start working on preparing the stew. Steward started a fire in the smoker before he took the remains of the bear from the fur shed to the forest, figuring the smoker would be ready for use upon his return. Steward hatched a plan, to use Rudy to pull the cart to the forest. He would reward Rudy's positive actions with bear meat, something the wolf dog loved. Rudy's instincts told him food was not easy to come across. This was the reason for wolves' selfish behaviour at large kill sites, like deer. The wolves' overindulgence in eating, sometimes to the point of throwing up, and display of a lack of civility toward each other, were a result of their instinctual fight for survival.

Steward retrieved the cart and pulled it over to Rudy's shelter. He fed Rudy some bear meat, which he enjoyed immensely. He fastened a harness to his growing wolf dog and connected it to the cart. Rudy seemed to enjoy playing this game. It got him out of his shelter and Steward kept feeding him large pieces of raw meat, which he was rarely fed. With Steward leading the cart, he guided Rudy over to the fur shed to pick up the carcass of the bear. After loading the remains, Steward led Rudy and the cart down the bumpy trail through the forest.

A half hour later, Steward deposited the remains of the bear in a clearing where the raptors and ravens could see it plainly from above. Along with wolves, wolverines, and other scavengers, the chances of there being any remains left uneaten by tomorrow morning would be few.

Steward and Rudy returned to the cabin. Steward was happy with the way Rudy took to pulling the cart. He knew by winter, Rudy would be big and strong enough to be the lead dog pulling the sled. He put Rudy back in his enclosure and walked to the cabin to join his wife. Steward wanted to share his positive story about Rudy with Blossom. Now, he was even more sure Rudy was the dog he envisioned he would be, a true warrior with a strong back. No sled dog in Dawson would have the power to pull such large loads on their sleds; Rudy would be hard to beat in any competition. He was not just another sled dog.

CHAPTER TWENTY-SIX

The days of summer passed quickly. The latter part of August brought with it cooler nights and shorter days. The vegetation was already turning from green to brown and the leaves on the deciduous trees were starting to change to their fall colours. Rudy was growing into a young adult wolf, with an attitude to go along with it. The huskies were afraid of him. Rudy would be their leader and the other dogs would follow him.

A trip to Dawson was being planned before winter. The couple needed supplies before the snows came. They would use Omar, the donkey, if Jason and Wendy were not using his services. Blossom would stay home and look after the dogs. Steward would make sure there was a large quantity of fish on hand to feed the dogs before he left. Fresh fish and meat were lasting longer as the weather cooled. Blossom needed to have enough food to last until Steward returned from his trip to Dawson City.

September weather saw below freezing temperatures at night more times than not, during this transitional time of year. Steward suggested to Blossom he might be at Bev's house when Honey's baby is born, as the donkey was expecting her new foal sometime in the latter part of September. Steward hoped he was present at the time of the baby's delivery.

Steward had been using the cart to train Rudy for his duties this winter. He would pull loads of firewood with ease to the cabin from long distances away. His focus on duty was remarkable, his instincts for the bush were fine tuned. Steward could not wait for the arrival of winter so Rudy's strengths could be tested in the snow.

The morning came for Steward's departure for Dawson. He kissed Blossom goodbye, wished his dogs farewell, and was on his way. Steward expected to hunt for his food on this trip. Gamebirds were plentiful and easy to shoot on this journey. Steward loved the succulent breast of a partridge when the meat was cooked over a wood fire. Steward never stopped for lunch, planning to make it to the lake, the halfway point to Dawson, in the early afternoon.

Steward set up his camp on the shores of the lake. He had shot two game birds on his trek and cooked them both for dinner. The northern sky cast an unnatural glow, as nighttime descended over the waters and forests of this desolate land. The soulful call of the loon coming from the lake was the only sound which broke the stillness of the moment.

Steward gazed skyward, mesmerized by the power of the universe. The sky, now black, was filled with a million twinkling lights shining down on him, making Steward question the reason for his own existence in this world he did not understand. He hoped one day, when he left this earth, he would be one of those shining stars everyone loved to look at.

CHAPTER TWENTY-SEVEN

The call of the Yukon has led many men to a premature death. Drawn by an untamed land and dreams of gold, these men flocked north to find their fame and fortune. Most of these hapless folk found disappointment when they arrived and a life that they were not prepared for.

Steward woke to a light misty rain, with the sun already well above the horizon. Steward jumped up and prepared to leave, as he wanted to reach Dawson before dark. Picking up his pace on the trail, Steward knew he could gain back the hour he lost sleeping past sunrise. He was hungry and would be glad to arrive at Bev's house for her home cooking and fresh baked bread.

The day's walk was uneventful, and the buildings of Dawson City came into view just as twilight was approaching. Steward knocked at Bev's door and was greeted by a surprised aunt. She was expecting him to visit in the fall but did not know when. Steward entered Bev's house. Bev told him to sit, knowing he was hungry. Bev prepared Steward some moose meat, potatoes, and carrots for dinner, followed by apple cobbler for dessert.

Steward asked Bev how Honey was doing with her pregnancy. Bev reported the donkey should be giving birth soon. She also shared Omar was back in her barn. Jason and Wendy had told Bev Steward was coming to borrow Omar and had asked Bev to tell Steward to return the donkey to them when he was finished using him. Jason and Wendy had more work to do with Omar before he was brought back to Bev's for the winter.

Bev also told Steward Shining Star was arriving shortly. She planned to give birth at Bev's house and spend the winter with her, instead of returning to her own people. Johnathan and Shining Star's cabin was isolated in the bush. The weather was too extreme for a new baby to be born there unless it was necessary. The birth should be in a safe place, where the child's chances of survival were better. Johnathan would stay at their cabin for the winter, running his trapline and coming to town to visit whenever possible.

After dinner, Bev took Steward to the barn where Omar and Honey were staying. Entering the structure, the couple heard a lot of activity coming from the animals which boarded there. She knew what all the commotion meant, Honey had given birth. Bev grabbed Steward's arm, leading him to Honey's pen. Honey was laying on her side in the corner of her birthing pen, nestling and feeding a healthy baby donkey. Bev entered Honey's pen for a closer look at the newborn. It was a male donkey, born healthy to a happy mother. The new addition to Omar and Honey's family would be called Baby Jack, a name which would be with him his entire life, even as an adult.

Johnathan and Shining Star would be happy to hear Honey's delivery was problem free and all participants in this venture were healthy. Bev and Steward returned to the house, surprised and happy at the outcome of their visit to Honey and Omar, two happy donkeys with a newborn named Baby Jack.

CHAPTER TWENTY-EIGHT

A cold north wind was blowing in Dawson this morning. Steward pulled on a jacket he carried with him for such an occasion. Steward knew Omar was going to be upset about having to leave Honey and his new son, Baby Jack, behind. He would be going with Steward on a dangerous expedition through the forest. Omar never knew if he would survive the jobs these fur trappers used him for. His tales of survival were many, having had numerous near-death experiences with hungry predators.

Omar went with Steward willingly but begrudgingly. Their first stop was the feed store where Steward bought Omar a treat, the proprietor's well known pack animal mash. This food had never been turned down by any donkey or mule the man had ever owned. Steward bought Omar enough of this concoction to feed it to the donkey sparingly, planning to use this mash as a treat for good behaviour.

Steward's next stop was the mercantile, to pick up a large quantity of dry dog food he had ordered, the second of his twice-a-year special purchase. He also bought a quantity of flour, sugar, salt, and coffee, as well as a large purchase of jerky. This nonperishable food was a great emergency item to have on hand when no other nourishment was available. With all the purchases Steward had made on Omar's back, there was no room to spare.

Steward and Omar returned to Bev's house, where Omar's back was unloaded, and he was returned to the barn with Honey to spend one more night. His back would be reloaded in the morning for the trip back to Steward's cabin, where Omar would have a new enemy, Rudy, the wolf dog, who would view Omar as dinner rather than part of the family. This would be another potential foe, who would like nothing better than to eat poor Omar.

Steward was up at daybreak, loading Omar with the supplies he had purchased yesterday. He said his goodbyes to Bev and wished her luck with Honey and her new offspring. Steward left Dawson with the sky full of dark storm clouds, which hinted of an early snowfall. Winter came quickly and with a vengeance this far north. It was important for Steward to get to his cabin quickly and then return the donkey to Jason and Wendy. They would be responsible for returning Omar to the safety of Bev's barn before winter. If Omar stayed in the forest too long, he would die of exposure to the cold, an ending not fit for a poor helpless donkey.

CHAPTER TWENTY-NINE

After a long day on the trail, Steward and Omar reached the lake. The duo would camp here for the night. On their way home from Dawson City, this body of water was the halfway point back to their cabin. Omar was familiar with the lake and liked this camp site. The donkey felt safe here, having stayed in this location many times in the past without any harrowing experiences happening to him.

The skies had cleared but the air was cold; the threat of snow had passed. Steward built a large campfire trying to fend off the dampness and cold of the nighttime air. He had carried only a lightweight blanket with him on this trip, now wishing he had packed a heavier one. The campfire was soon roaring, the flames from the burning wood sending spirals of smoke skyward. Steward tethered Omar close to where he would be sleeping, knowing Omar was petrified about spending the night in the bush. Steward hoped this would make Omar feel safer than being tethered to a tree yards away from where he was. Steward's rifle was always by his side, if needed for an emergency.

A long, eerie call from the lake broke the silence of the black night. The loon's haunting song echoed across the water. After a moment of silence, the call was returned by its mate who was swimming on a distant part of the water. When the loons call, time stops, as one's mind is captivated by the sound of these birds. This encounter with nature is indicative of the birds' power over the human psyche, interrupting one's ability to think as their cries echo across the lake.

Steward fell asleep, but not Omar. The scared animal heard every noise coming from the dark forest. Omar surveyed the woods as beady, red eyes watched his movements from among the trees which surrounded their location. Steward woke after constant displays of Omar's uneasiness. He listened to the quiet forest and heard animals moving about, seemingly trying to encircle them. Steward and Omar's backs were against the lake.

Steward was sure it was hungry wolves who had picked up Omar's scent and were ready to make a meal out of him. The easiest way to get meandering wolves to leave in a hurry is to spray the forest with gunfire. Realizing the danger, the wolf pack will run for their lives once bullets start flying. This is what Steward did, saving Omar's life again from a hungry pack of wolves.

Once back asleep, the night passed quickly. Steward woke with the first rays of sunlight peeping over the horizon. The fire had burned down during the night and the flimsy blanket he had placed over himself provided no warmth. He decided the best way to warm up was to start moving his stiff limbs by walking. He fed Omar some mash while he ate jerky and within a brief time the duo was on their way, walking the forest trail to Steward's cabin. With luck, he expected to be home by 4 p.m., anxious to see his wife and his dog Rudy, both whom he missed while away.

The day had warmed; the cold front had passed leaving only a sample of what was to come later in the season. After an event free afternoon of walking, Steward's cabin came into view. Blossom was feeding and providing water to the dogs when the pair arrived home. After a loving greeting, Steward went to see Rudy, who was excited to see him. Rudy had wondered where Steward had gone. Steward gave Rudy a large beef bone he had purchased for him in Dawson.

Leaving Rudy to enjoy his treat, Steward and Blossom unloaded Omar, placed him in a secure pen, and fed him dinner. Steward decided against introducing Rudy to Omar, fearing what the wolf's reaction would be. Steward had to return Omar to Jason and Wendy's cabin before the donkey became a heart attack victim, a mishap the couple would never be forgiven for.

CHAPTER THIRTY

S teward and Blossom were happy with the supplies Steward had purchased in Dawson. These purchases had been delivered on the back of the couple's favorite donkey, Omar, who was owned by Steward's sister, Wendy, and his brother-in-law, Jason. Steward and Blossom would return the donkey to Jason and Wendy's cabin tomorrow, Steward deciding to spend one day at home before leaving again.

Steward suggested to Blossom they should take the canoe out on the lake. The last of the migrating waterfowl would soon be a distant memory, as the lake froze and became covered in snow. It would soon be the beginning of October, a time of great change in the Yukon. The bird song, which makes this land so inviting in the summer, would soon be forgotten. The enchanting hardwoods would lose their canopy of green leaves, leaving the forest bare and void of most life.

Steward and Blossom paddled the canoe across the lake in silence. The couple were admiring the beauty of nature which surrounded them. Steward paddled towards the beaver dam, as migrating birds were attracted to areas flooded by beavers. The habitat created by these aquatic mammals provided a good source of food for migrating waterfowl. Ducks and geese tended to congregate at this popular spot to eat and rest.

Steward was right. Approaching this area on the lake, many geese could be seen swimming about. With Blossom maneuvering the canoe, the couple caught the Canadian geese by surprise and within minutes four of the large birds were lying in the bottom of the canoe. Satisfied with the amount of food they harvested, the couple returned to their cabin. They took the geese to the fur shed and butchered the large birds. Some of the meat would be smoked, while the rest would be cooked and eaten at the cabin. The goose parts deemed inedible would be fed to a hungry Rudy and Steward's huskies.

The storing of meat in Steward's outdoor freezer was now feasible, as nighttime temperatures regularly dropped below freezing. The changing weather made it too early to store large quantities of meat, such as moose or deer, but it was fine to use the freezer for storing small game animals, such as birds and rabbits. Steward smoked three of the goose breasts for future consumption and took the breast of the fourth goose to cook for dinner. The succulent breast of any large gamebird was delicious to the pallet of hungry couples living in the wilderness.

The sun was setting as Steward and Blossom sat down to eat. The goose breast was delicious, the meat was tender and succulent. The forest was silent as darkness took over. The mood of the land changed, as predators roamed the forests looking for food. Omar would become the hunted if left in the forest to live. He would become food for hungry wolves if he was not protected. This fact was one reason he would be returned to his rightful owners tomorrow. Jason and Wendy would soon take Omar back to Dawson, to the comfort of his waiting wife and child, for the winter. This arrangement would make the displaced donkey very happy.

CHAPTER THIRTY-ONE

Steward and Blossom rose from their bed early, as today they were going to return Omar to Jason and Wendy's cabin. Their destination was a three hour walk from here; they planned to return home this evening.

The early morning was sunny and cool. Steward walked to Omar's enclosure and retrieved the donkey. Blossom had packed a smoked goose breast to share with Jason and Wendy for lunch. The entourage left with great fanfare, the barking huskies saying goodbye and a not so nice Rudy who snapped, growled, and lunged at Omar as they walked by. Omar was glad he was leaving this hostile place, where the constant barking from the huskies bothered him. He would be glad to be back in the comfort of Bev's barn in Dawson. This donkey hated being stuck in the forest.

The trail the group walked on passed through a hardwood forest. The ground was covered with fallen leaves of many different colours. As Blossom looked skyward, a gust of wind sent a flurry of leaves from the trees above drifting down toward the forest floor. The trio walked along the trail, the fresh leaves crunching under the weight of the donkey's hooves. As the group moved closer to their destination, Steward noticed an abundance of deer sign and would be sure to tell Jason and his sister, Wendy, about this location.

With colder weather arriving soon, deer and moose meat could be stored outside in the trapper's underground freezer. Any meat kept there would stay frozen from mid-October to the following April, nature providing six months of natural refrigeration.

Blossom noticed smoke rising above the trees in the forest, which was coming from the chimney of Jason and Wendy's cabin. In a brief time, Steward sighted the building, a cabin sitting by itself on a beautiful lake which provided subsistence for this couple, who had built a life for themselves in this unforgiving land.

King, the family dog, ran out of the cabin with his tail wagging and barking to greet the visitors. Wendy invited the group into the cabin. Jason had a fire going in the woodstove, making the interior of the cabin comfortable and warm. Steward and Blossom shared the smoked breast of meat they had carried with them for lunch.

As they sat together, Wendy told Steward and Blossom Shining Star was at Bev's house and was expected to have her baby soon. When they travelled to Dawson to return Omar to Bev's barn, the couple would learn if Shining Star's baby had arrived yet. She was anxious to hear if it was a boy or a girl.

After a pleasant lunch, Steward and his wife left to return home. Without Omar they would cut an hour off their return trip. They said their goodbyes and left happy. Friendships were rare when living in the bush, as survival, not friendship, was the true mantra of the north.

CHAPTER THIRTY-TWO

Steward and Blossom walked in silence, their thoughts on the upcoming winter and the hardships which soon would be thrust upon them. A cold north wind blew through the forest, as Steward and Blossom traversed the trail home to their cabin. The forest was quiet, as all the migratory birds had left and would not return until spring.

The snow would return to the Yukon soon, covering the landscape in a sea of white. The couple noted dark storm clouds now filled the afternoon sky. Steward told Blossom they needed to pick up their pace, as he feared an early season snowstorm was approaching. The snows started when the couple were a short distance from home. In the beginning, the snow was light, but that changed to almost white out conditions shortly after they reached their cabin.

Upon arriving home, Steward went to check on Rudy and his huskies. Blossom entered the cabin to start a fire in the stove; the heat would provide warmth for the couple. After being caught in the snowstorm coming home, the couple felt lucky to be at their cabin where it was warm.

Steward checked on Rudy first, marvelling at the wolf's size and strength. Steward knew Rudy's training would need to start soon. He would teach Rudy how to pull a snow sled and work with his huskies as team leader. Rudy would be the alpha male and lead dog for his dogsled this winter. Saying goodbye to Rudy, Steward's next stop was to check on his huskies. The snow was something the sled dogs welcomed. The huskies knew soon they would be off their leashes, running in the wilderness, pulling the dogsled, and working the trapline. His dogs were glad to see Steward and appeared to be happy about receiving the first measurable snowfall of the year. Steward hugged each of his dogs accordingly, before feeding them dinner. He walked to his cabin to join his wife.

Blossom had a hot fire burning in the stove and was heating water for coffee. The strong wind from the storm had died down, but heavy snow continued to fall. From this point until mid-November, snow would accumulate on the ground and then briefly melt before accruing again. This would allow Steward to run his huskies for conditioning, as well as begin Rudy's training. He figured it would take at least two weeks to get the dogs and Rudy ready for working together. The trapping season for Steward and Blossom would start in the first week of December.

Blossom cooked some venison, which Wendy had shared with her and Steward. Jason had already been hunting in the spot Steward had planned to tell him about. He also had seen the deer sign and shot a doe two days before Steward and his wife arrived with Omar.

After the couple ate dinner, the snow stopped. The bright moon, in the now clear sky, caused the forest to shine, the snow-covered trees making it look like a winter scene. This was Canada's Yukon, where winter dominates the seasons and hardships are many for the men and women who chose this way of life. For most of these hardy souls, they would have it no other way.

CHAPTER THIRTY-THREE

Today was the day Steward would hook Rudy up to a sled for the first time. Fresh snow had fallen during the night, covering the landscape in a new coat of white. Time had slipped by quickly and it was now mid-November. The snowpack had increased from the frequent storms which had developed over the last two weeks.

Steward pulled the dogsled over to Rudy's enclosure, attached a harness to Rudy, and led him outside of the place he called home. Steward talked softly to Rudy as he hooked the canine's harness up to the sled. There was no opposition from Rudy, making Steward believe Rudy was glad to get out of captivity. If this was the way he could get out of lockup, Rudy would cooperate with Steward, at least for now.

When Steward was ready, he yelled for Rudy to go. With his powerful shoulders thrust outward, the sled moved forward on the new layer of snow. Rudy ran with abandon; he had not used the muscles in his legs for running before at top speed. Steward had locked him up as a young dog, thinking Rudy could not be trusted to remain with Steward and not return to his wolf pack. Rudy had enjoyed pulling the cart, but he loved pulling the sled through the snow. Steward knew his wolf would be the lead dog on the sled this winter.

The next step was to see how Rudy fared sharing a harness with the huskies. Wasting no time and with Rudy being in a good mood, Steward thought this would be the opportune moment to harness his other dogs to the sled with Rudy. He steered Rudy back to the cabin and yelled at Blossom to come outside to help him with the dogs. She was surprised at how well Rudy had taken to pulling the sled.

Blossom was good at taking care of the sled dogs, as she had been raised with huskies and had been around these dogs all her life. The huskies became quiet when they realized they were being hooked up to the sled with the wolf. He was the alpha male and lead dog for the sled. Rudy turned and looked at the huskies hooked to the harness behind him. The smaller dogs cowered when Rudy growled and gave the huskies a hateful look, exposing his true feelings toward them. Rudy loved being a leader and would dominate over his underlings, making the huskies work hard. He accepted no complaints, his wrath a given for any husky who exhibited disruptive behaviour.

Steward and Blossom worked with the dogs over the next two weeks. The huskies fell in line, following Rudy's demands after they realized he was a threat to be reckoned with. Crossing Rudy and making him angry could lead to bodily harm, or even death, for any husky involved. This was a problem neither Steward nor Blossom could come up with an answer for; it was an issue Rudy would have to solve himself.

CHAPTER THIRTY-FOUR

The training of Steward's dog team, with Rudy as the lead, went well. The huskies knew their boundaries with the wolf. They listened to Steward's commands and worked hard trying to avoid conflict with Rudy, who could turn on them instantaneously for making trivial mistakes. Steward and Blossom felt the dogs were ready for the trapping season.

The first of December brought visitors to Steward and Blossom's cabin, Jason and Wendy came to pick up the two huskies they leased from Steward for the winter. These huskies would help King, who presently was the only dog they owned, pull their sled. King was the family dog who did not enjoy being used as a sled dog. He was a spoiled family member, who preferred the warmth of the inside of the cabin over the cold outside Yukon air.

Wendy was glad to see her brother Steward. The couple and their young son were invited inside Steward's cabin, where a robust fire made the room comfortable and warm. Blossom heated some water on the stove for coffee. Jason had brought a large package of venison for Steward and Blossom. He told them his hunting trips were a huge success this winter, with many deer living in the area around his cabin. No wolf pack had claimed this territory as their own, leaving all the deer for Wendy and himself. Steward said he has also had good luck hunting this season and his outdoor freezer was full of meat.

Jason and Wendy were invited to spend the night. The two couples would share the venison Jason and Wendy had supplied, along with some rabbits Steward had snared. He had been successful in capturing several rabbits, which were also in his freezer. Blossom was happy to cook two of these rabbits, along with the venison. Any leftovers would be given to Jason and Wendy to eat on their journey home tomorrow.

After dinner, the couples talked about current events. Upon returning Omar to Bev's home in Dawson, Wendy and Jason learned Shining Star had given birth to a baby boy. Both mother and baby were in fine health and doing well. Steward asked how Honey was doing, to which Wendy said both she and Baby Jack were fine. Baby Jack was growing fast and was already as tall as his mother's mid section. She knew Honey and Omar were happy to be back together and both doted on their son.

Wendy also shared with Steward news from Johnathan regarding the trapping season. He would not need dogs from Steward, as he had acquired another husky over the summer. With Shining Star in Dawson at Bev's home all winter, the two dogs he had were all he needed to run his trapline. Steward was glad Johnathan had reached this decision, because two of his own dogs had mysteriously died in the fall, leaving him short of dogs.

Bev had asked Wendy to extend an invitation to Steward and Blossom to attend Christmas at Bev's house again this year. Steward and Blossom could now go to Dawson, as they would have no animals to care for at home. Rudy and all the huskies would be pulling the sled to town.

It was near midnight when everyone in the cabin retired to bed. The forest was dark and silent. The snow blew around the cabin, which sat cozily snuggled in the bush. The inhabitants inside slept, relaxed in the peace nature provided them.

CHAPTER THIRTY-FIVE

The morning sun shone through the cabin windows. The ravens on the roof were calling out loudly looking for food. This loud activity annoyed the waking couples, prompting Steward to get out of bed to shoo the obnoxious culprits away. Steward thought he could scare the birds by shooting off his rifle toward them. He hoped the ravens would get the message, they were not welcome here and to never return to his cabin.

After telling his comrades inside of his intentions, he went outside with King. Seconds later, a loud gunshot was heard, followed by silence. The cold north wind blowing through the barren treetops was the only sound coming from the forest. A stillness in the air followed, which belonged in this wilderness setting. Steward returned to the cabin telling his wife and company he hoped he had taken care of the problem with the ravens permanently. This issue had been ongoing since he had fed the ravens, a decision he had made without reason.

After breakfast, Steward took Jason out to see Rudy, his wolf, who had become the formidable king of the domesticated dog world. Upon seeing Rudy in his enclosure,

Jason was apprehensive about Steward's trust in Rudy. The wolf was a wild animal, who could display unpredictable behaviour when least expected. When Jason moved closer to Rudy's enclosure, the dog lunged at him, snarling aggressively. Jason told Steward he needed to be careful dealing with this aggressive animal. Rudy knew he had to be loyal to Steward only, and no one else mattered to this wolf, who hated the scent of humans.

After feeding the huskies, Steward and Jason returned to the cabin. Wendy refused to go with Steward to see Rudy. She hated wolves, believing they were demons in fur coats. Years earlier, one of Wendy's cousins had been attacked and eaten by a starving pack of wolves. That year, a disease had decimated the deer population, leading to starvation among the Indigenous population living in the area. Wolf packs, who also were dependent on the deer for food during the winter, were devastated. Finding and eating wayward humans in the forest was how the wolves helped stave off their persistent hunger and survive.

Jason, Wendy, and their son, Kuzih, were leaving to go home. Wendy thanked Steward and Blossom for showing their family love and kindness on their visit. Their paths would cross again at Christmas, when family and friends were to gather at Bev's home in Dawson. The couples hugged and wished each other well. With King leading the way, the dogs pulled the sled away from the cabin in the direction of home. Steward and Blossom, standing in the doorway of their cabin, turned and went back inside.

As they sat down for a final cup of coffee, they discussed getting ready for the trapping season. The couple had three dozen traps and a good dog team. Steward decided to work twenty traps until Christmas, when they would have to pull the traps while away. Once the couple retuned from Dawson after the holiday, they would add the other sixteen traps to their route.

After catching and skinning the animals caught, the remains of these mammals were used to bait traps and feed the dogs. Early fur trappers sometimes even fed themselves with this bounty of meat they procured from the forest. A good trapper, in this land of plenty, never went hungry. If the man died, it was either from exposure or an attack by a hungry predator. Men living in this unforgiving wilderness were part of the food chain, as many of these early settlers perished at the hands of surprise wolf and bear attacks. Their bones would be picked clean by hungry scavengers, making a tasty meal for starving animals.

Tomorrow, Steward and Blossom would go out on the frozen lake and place their fishing net under the ice. The scraps of any fish caught would be used to bait the traps they would set out the following day. The couple needed a good night's sleep, as it would be a hard day on the frozen lake with no shelter from wind and blowing snow. The beginning of the winter season was upon them; Steward and Blossom hoped they were ready.

CHAPTER THIRTY-SIX

The day dawned sunny and clear; the northern sky shone with a brilliance not seen often during the winter months in the Yukon. The couple marvelled at the scenery, as they looked out upon the lake. The interaction of blue sky and white snow, with the forest in the background, was a spectacle created by nature, not man.

Steward and Blossom decided to use Rudy today to pull the sled on the lake for their fishing trip, leaving the huskies at home. Tomorrow, the couple were planning on setting out traps to begin their fur season, when they would use the entire dog team. Steward hooked Rudy, his wolf, up to the sled. This strong animal would have no problem pulling the two passengers and fish across the flat surface of the frozen lake.

Rudy pulled the sled past the shackled huskies, who responded by barking loudly and pulling on their chains. The huskies wanted to be part of this mission, which Rudy was leading. The dogs did not like to be left at home. Rudy pulled the sled and its passengers a half mile out onto the lake.

Steward had kept several holes open in a lucrative spot to fish for lake trout and whitefish during the winter. He reopened the holes in the ice with an axe he had carried with him from the cabin. Blossom lowered the fishing nets skilfully through the holes in the ice into the water below. The first catch was good; pulling the net from the water, four large whitefish appeared on top of the ice. Steward threw Rudy the largest fish. His primeval response was to viciously take possession of the food, consuming the entire fish leaving nothing for the scavengers which were now flying around the area looking for a handout.

After two hours of fishing, Blossom and Steward had accumulated more fish than they expected. They gathered up the nets and fish, loading them onto the sled. On Steward's command Rudy started for home. The sled skimmed smoothly over the snow-covered lake. Blossom motioned to Steward, pointing to six wolves coming out of the forest ahead of Rudy. It appeared the wolves would try to cut the sled off at an opportune moment. The overwhelming smell of the fish had made these hungry wolves throw caution to the wind, as they launched this misguided attack. Unfortunately for the wolf pack, they got bogged down in deep snow, hindering their progress in catching the sled.

Rudy left his brethren behind, safely taking Steward and Blossom back to the cabin, following the same route on which he came. After unloading the dog sled, Steward rewarded his wolf with another fish. Rudy had ignored the pursuing wolves and delivered the couple home safely to their cabin. He had shown Steward where his loyalties lie, to the hand that feeds him.

CHAPTER THIRTY-SEVEN

After arriving back at the cabin from their fishing trip, Steward unloaded the fish from the sled. He returned Rudy to his enclosure, providing him with fresh water to drink. Blossom entered the cabin to stoke the dying embers of the fire and add fuel to the woodstove. Steward and Blossom had spent two hours on the frozen lake, with a bitter cold wind blowing. The couple were cold and wanted to feel the warmth of the cabin to comfort them.

After securing the fish in the fur shed, Steward returned to the cabin to join his wife. A sudden chorus of barking from the huskies signalled unexpected company was on its way. Blossom looked out the window and noticed a dog team pulling a sled with two occupants in it. Steward told Blossom he was sure it was the North West Mounted Police, as he knew part of their law enforcement duties was to patrol the surrounding wilderness. The Mounties had recently acquired horses for summer patrols but used dogsleds in the winter to visit cabins in the bush.

These cabins were registered with the North West Mounted Police headquarters in Dawson to be checked routinely. Some of the old-time trappers would not agree to this policy, not wanting this unwanted intrusion on their property. These were men left alone to their own doing, their demise sometimes was never known. A chance discovery of a hunter out looking for food, finding a decrepit cabin with human bones inside, was the likely ending for these men who refused human contact. Alone in their cabins, injured or sick, was the way these loners preferred to die.

Steward and Blossom gladly welcomed the Mounties into their cabin. The men brought gifts from Dawson of coffee and sugar. Blossom boiled some water on the woodstove, a cup of hot coffee sweetened with sugar was a favored drink of these men and women who lived in the bush. After an amicable conversation, the Mounties got ready to say goodbye. Steward went outside with the men, to show the curious Mounties his wolf.

Rudy was walking his enclosure, like a pent-up animal who needed to be released. The Mounties asked Steward if Rudy was trained to run a dog sled. The inquiring men told Steward Dawson ran their annual dog sled race the week between Christmas and New Year's Day. Mushers entered their dog teams, hoping to win first prize, one hundred dollars paid to the winner in gold. This was a substantial amount of money for a trapper living in the bush. The Mounties thought Rudy was a special dog who could win. Steward agreed, telling the men this was his plan.

Steward waved at the departing Mounties, as they headed out for their next destination. He headed to the fur shed to clean some of the fish they had caught for dinner, saving the innards to use as bait. The rest would be used to feed the dogs. Blossom came to the shed to check on

Steward's progress, saying she was glad they would start setting their trapline at daybreak. Steward agreed, and when his work was completed, the couple spent most of the rest of the day in bed. They enjoyed the only free thing the wilderness provided them, solitude and passion on a grand scale.

CHAPTER THIRTY-EIGHT

It was late afternoon when the couple awoke and roused themselves from bed. Steward went out to feed and water his dogs. He threw the huskies a whole frozen whitefish each to eat. He knocked the ice from the dogs' water dishes and replenished it with water from the lake. Steward kept an open hole in the ice during the winter season, ensuring water for his dogs and for the cabin was always available. Steward, after taking care of his huskies, focused his attention on his wolf. Rudy was waiting for Steward, having watched him take care of the huskies. Rudy seethed with jealousy and anger, his hatred for the huskies was intense and unforgiving, while his love for Steward was self-rewarding and selfish.

Steward brought his wolf more fish than he fed his huskies. Rudy was becoming a large animal, mean and rotten to the core. His body was strong and muscular, which solidified Steward's decision to enter Rudy into the Dawson City dog sled race. He would mush Rudy to the finish line and win the hundred dollars in gold, the first prize for winning Dawson's most prestigious event of the year.

Steward knew the other mushers he would compete against hated wolves. However, the rules said wolves could participate. The other mushers claimed the wolf owner had an unfair advantage during the race, their rage often taken out on the owner of the wolf before it was taken out on the wolf itself. None of this talk bothered Steward; he owned the wolf, an animal these mushers feared and loathed. Challenging Steward meant challenging his wolf. This was an action most of these men would avoid, but Steward knew there would always be one man who would challenge him for supremacy.

Steward finished socializing with Rudy. The north wind was blowing stronger, causing snow to swirl around the structures and across the flat landscape of the lake. Steward sensed an abrupt change in the weather was taking place, the first blizzard of the year would soon be upon them. Steward returned to the cabin knowing his canines could take care of themselves during the storm. He told Blossom he feared they were going to experience the worst from the blizzard.

The couple prepared for the coming storm. Blossom carried in extra firewood from outside the cabin while Steward retrieved food from their outdoor freezer. They secured the windows and used the extra bolt Steward had fastened on the cabin door for such an occasion. The oil lamps cast a ghostly light in the cabin, while the snow swirled and danced outside the little building. The cabin was a warm recluse for a pioneer couple, snuggled in the woods of Canada's north, a mysterious land they called the Yukon.

CHAPTER THIRTY-NINE

The fury of the blizzard raged all night. Cuddled under the blankets on their bed, Steward and Blossom felt safe and warm. Like being wrapped in a cocoon, the cabin was their saviour. Without shelter from the storm, death would be quick and unforgiving as this brutal land would take another victim.

The dim light of the early morning sunrise shone through the cabin window. An eerie calm greeted the waking couple. The snowstorm had ended, and blue sky was appearing within the dark storm clouds. Steward pulled himself out of bed and dressed. He added fuel to the dying fire in the woodstove, pulled back his security bolt on the cabin's front door, and pushed the door open. A foot of newly fallen snow greeted him. Steward pulled on additional clothing, wanting to check on his dogs.

The huskies were glad to see him and greeted Steward with much banter. Rudy was not so happy; the wolf paced in his pen, a sullen expression never leaving his face. Steward thought it best to leave Rudy alone for now. He would return later to Rudy's enclosure. Steward would take his wolf for a run today to break the trail for tomorrow's hopeful start to the trapping season. This venture had been delayed twice from their planned starting date.

Steward returned to the cabin. Blossom was awake, boiling water on a now hot woodstove. The coffee the Mounties left for them was a treat not to be denied to the Indigenous people and the early settlers who invaded the Yukon seeking their fortunes. Steward told Blossom he was going to hook up Rudy and break the trail for their trapline. As they were only setting a portion of their traps, he would take Rudy to the mid-point, near the beavers' dam. During the winter months, this frozen marshland allowed the dogsleds to travel on the solid surface. Steward would use this to his advantage, setting beaver traps across the area which was now accessible by sled.

After eating breakfast with his wife, Steward bid her farewell, promising to return to the cabin in a few hours. He walked to Rudy's enclosure, the wolf waiting for Steward's return. Steward had pushed the snow sled to a waiting Rudy, letting the wolf know what was coming, the freedom to run in his environment without the huskies in tow. This was something Rudy would enjoy immensely. Being alone with Steward was what the wolf loved the best.

An enthusiastic Rudy let Steward hook his harness up to the dogsled. With a mush from Steward, Rudy pulled the dogsled forward. He ran past the barking huskies, who wished they were going on this adventure. Rudy pulled the sled through the snow, a trail of flying white powder following behind them, obscuring the sled as it moved down the trail.

After a major snowstorm, many different animal tracks are visible. Curious animals living in the forest come out to investigate their territory after a blizzard. Like humans, they need to get out after a storm. Rudy pulled the sled to the beaver dam and Steward steered Rudy onto the frozen waters, locating the beaver lodge. This was the home of the beaver and where the traps would be set. Steward marked three areas where the couple would set traps tomorrow.

Steward, happy with his mission today, returned home with Rudy. He placed the wolf in his enclosure, fed his animals, and returned to the cabin to join his wife. The smell of moose meat frying on the woodstove caught his attention. Steward would enjoy this meal after not eating while on the trail today. Savouring his favorite meal was an excellent end to a great day in the Yukon, a land Steward would never leave.

CHAPTER FORTY

The sun slowly rose above the horizon in the early morning sky. Steward and Blossom were awake and moving around the cabin. Today the couple were setting out traps, their fur season was beginning. Steward had loaded the traps on the dogsled the previous evening under the light of the full moon. He left the cabin to retrieve Rudy and the huskies to put his team together. The canines were all cooperative, knowing they would have all day to enjoy life outside of their lockups.

Within thirty minutes, the team was ready to go. The animals tugged on their harnesses in anticipation of pulling the sled through the snow. The dogsled flew down the open trail, the animals pulling their hardest. Exercising their cramped legs, having not run for a long time, was a goal the huskies wished to achieve today.

After reaching the bush, the couple started setting out their traps. The route the couple had chosen would end at the beaver dam, where they would set beaver traps before heading back toward home. This followed the route established by the previous trapper, who had also built a couple of safety shelters along the way. After a long day, twenty traps were set out. The couple had decided this was enough to deploy until after Christmas. They headed home, happy with their day's work.

Darkness settled in once the couple reached the cabin. Steward unharnessed the huskies and Rudy and placed the animals where they belonged. He threw a frozen fish to each of the canines and refreshed their water bowls. Steward was pleased with his dog team. The dogs worked well with Rudy when they worked the trapline together. The relationship between his wolf and the huskies had worked out better then Steward expected.

The month of December was passing quickly and Steward and Blossom's days were busy with the trapline. Collecting and resetting traps, skinning animals for their hides, and hunting for food for themselves and the dogs took up most of the couple's time. It would soon be time to go to Bev's house for Christmas. All the traps would be collected from the trapline and stored in the fur shed until the couple returned from Dawson. Upon their arrival in town, Steward would register his dog team for the dogsled race. This would be Rudy's opportunity to prove his worth as a leader, a job the wolf would not be denied.

CHAPTER FORTY-ONE

The morning sun was rising in this land called the Yukon. The snow sparkled in the early dawn, casting a feeling of serenity over the land. Steward and Blossom had been preparing for their trip to Dawson to spend Christmas at Bev's house. The couple's preparations for the trip were completed and their itinerary had them leaving today.

Steward and Blossom had climbed out of bed before the light of dawn. The couple ate a quick breakfast and would not eat a meal again until their arrival at Bev's house in Dawson. Steward went to feed his dogsled team. The animals needed to eat well to maintain their strength pulling the snow sled to town. Steward paid special attention to Rudy; the animal was his usual sullen self. He fed Rudy some moose meat, hoping this would lift the spirits of this displaced wolf. Steward let Rudy eat while he hooked up the huskies to the sled.

The huskies were excited, sensing they were working somewhere other than the trapline today. The dogs grew silent as Steward reached Rudy's enclosure. The huskies sense of joy turned sour upon encountering the foul mood of Rudy. He was the alpha male of this group and the unspoken leader of the dogsled team. Steward hooked Rudy's harness to the sled, after which the couple loaded their last few personal belongings and prepared to leave.

Steward mushed his dog team. The movement of the team running together as one impressed Steward. He knew with Rudy as lead dog the huskies would be pushed to their maximum output in the upcoming race. It meant so much for Steward to win the Dawson City dogsled race with its first prize of one hundred dollars in gold.

Rudy's strides were long. With the huskies behind him pulling hard on their harnesses, the sled was fast. The dogsled raced toward Dawson. The animals were enjoying their day in the snow away from the cabin and their enclosures. The sky was sunny with no wind, making for good travel conditions. As Steward and Blossom drew closer to Dawson, seeing dogsleds on the trail became more common. Most of the mushers and their dogs they came across were local. The rest of the dogs and sleds they encountered were heading to Dawson for the dogsled race. It was one of these latter mushers Steward would have his first threatening encounter with.

The man had passed Steward on the trail and noticed the wolf pulling Steward's sled. The man was inflamed, his future victory might fall to this wolf. He turned his sled around, catching up with Steward's team. This man motioned Steward to stop his sled, as he wanted to talk about his wolf. Steward obliged the man, not wanting any trouble for refusing his request. Steward's first impressions were not positive regarding this stranger's character.

The man had one eye, having lost the other at the end of a whip during a dispute over a dog race he stole years ago. He was a mean, brutal man who loved to threaten and intimidate men smaller than himself. He told Steward he was not allowed to run Rudy in the race. He told Steward there was a bounty out on his wolf and he planned on collecting it. Rudy hated this man. Anger welled within him as he heard the man talking. The wolf hated the black patch which covered One-Eyed Jack's scarred eyeball. This was a man who never accepted defeat.

Upon leaving, One-Eyed Jack cursed Steward and used his whip on Rudy's back as he passed by. A sneer with a mouth full of rotten teeth left a parting memory of this man on both the wolf and Steward. Steward realized this was just the beginning of what could develop into a serious affair regarding this outcast who threatened and intimidated people. Steward hoped the Mounties would oversee the race, putting an end to such behaviour by the hoodlums who infiltrated what was an honest group of mushers testing their dogs and skills in a local race, a race Steward and Rudy hoped to win.

CHAPTER FORTY-TWO

The sun was sinking below the horizon when Steward, his wife, and their sled dogs reached Dawson. After living in the bush in a small cabin, it was always a change to see houses, stores, places of business, and other structures built together in one place. Dawson was booming as prospectors from the lower forty-eight used the town as a jumping off point to the gold fields of the Klondike and beyond.

Fur trappers, who lived in cabins in the bush surrounding Dawson, resupplied with goods purchased here. Fur brokerage houses in this growing town bought fur from the trappers and the Indigenous people. The fur would be sold for a profit to brokers in Seattle and Vancouver. From these port cities, the furs were sent overseas to be sold for high prices in the European market. Wearing fur from America in Europe was considered a status symbol of the wealthy. The demand for fur outstripped the supply that was available, which kept the prices high. Beaver pelts were especially sought after and were soaring in value. The fur trappers living in the Dawson area did well selling their fur to the growing overseas market.

Steward steered his dogsled down the roadway to Bev's house. Bev, hearing Steward coming from all the barking dogs at her house, stepped outside to greet the couple. Bev would host many dogsled teams over Christmas. Jason and Wendy, with their son, also greeted Steward and Blossom, happy to see them again so soon.

Bev was thrilled to see her nephew and Blossom but not Rudy. She associated wolves with evil and felt the only good use for this animal was its coat. Wolf fur would be used as decoration during ceremonies by Indigenous tribes as a reminder of this evil spirit which lived in the forest among them. Bev had a special place to keep Rudy, away from the other dogs and their mushers. She did not trust any wolf, including Rudy.

Bev invited everyone inside to meet Shining Star's new baby. The boy, born in late September, had been given the name Grey Eagle. Indigenous children were traditionally named after animals which shared the forest. Grey Eagle, now three months old, was healthy and content, being raised in Bev's happy household.

Jason had arrived with fresh beaver for Bev, which she had prepared in a stew for dinner. It was accompanied by root vegetables from Bev's cellar and fresh baked bread from her oven. It was mentioned at dinner that Johnathan would be arriving in two days, as on his last visit to see his wife and child he told Shining Star he was coming on Christmas Eve day.

Steward went outside to feed and water his dogs. He felt sorry for Rudy, who he knew felt out of place and angry for having to be here amongst all his enemies. Steward gave extra attention to his wolf, who he knew most people hated. Steward viewed Rudy as his pet and would protect him like he protected his huskies. Steward's second brush with One-Eyed Jack and his hench men was coming shortly to Bev's house, an incident Steward had hoped to avoid.

CHAPTER FORTY-THREE

The night was black as the two men from Dawson entered Bev's property. The men's goal was to steal Rudy. A man in Dawson had offered these two drifters twenty-five dollars each to take Rudy from Steward and bring the dog to him. This man was One-Eyed Jack, who neglected to tell the men Rudy was a wolf and a dangerous animal. Jack told these men Rudy was not a mean dog, just an excellent sled dog he could use for his own team.

The theft of a dog was a crime which was prevalent in Dawson during the time of the goldrush. Dogs were a commodity needed by the early prospectors and fur traders. Selling stolen dogs in Dawson was a serious problem the Mounties wished to solve. One-Eyed Jack had taken these men to where Rudy's enclosure was. Jack's spies had learned the location of the wolf by following Steward to Bev's property as he arrived in Dawson. One-Eyed Jack was a sadistic man, caring for only himself. He knew these thieves would not bring Steward's wolf to him, as they would be attacked and gravely injured by Rudy. His goal was to create chaos for Steward and additional controversy over his wolf. Jack hoped this plan would alienate Steward from the other mushers, who were already leery about Rudy's participation in the dog sled race.

Rudy's pen was a short distance from the huskies location. The men quietly made their way to the wolf's enclosure. Rudy heard the men coming and kept quiet, knowing these men were up to no good. If they entered his space, he would ambush them, attacking with a vengeance. The thieves laughed between themselves, thinking how easy this job would be. They planned on spending the money Jack had promised them to buy tickets in the spring on a sternwheeler. An eventual return to Seattle, where these men originated from, was their goal.

Rudy quietly waited in the shadows, sensing these men wanted to do him harm. He heard the entrance gate to his pen open. The men entering Rudy's space thought someone had taken Rudy from the enclosure. They quietly called Rudy, hoping he would come out of the shadows and willingly go with them. Disappointed at getting no response, the men turned their backs to leave. This was when Rudy attacked these hapless men from behind and total chaos broke out. The screams from the victims of the wolf attack, and every huskie at Bev's house barking, woke Bev and her company out of their sleep.

Hearing the screams of the men, Steward reckoned this 3 a.m. encounter had something to do with Rudy. He grabbed his rifle, and with Jason at his side, rushed to Rudy's pen. Steward entered Rudy's enclosure. In the shadows of the darkness, he saw a man's body lying on the cold ground. The man's friend had managed to escape the attack, but this man had not been so lucky. Rudy had savagely killed him, relishing in the fact he finally got to fight his enemy and defeat him. Rudy watched from the shadows as Steward dragged the dead man's body out of his pen.

Steward would go to the North West Mounted Police office with the corpse in the morning to report this crime and the death of one of the participants involved. Steward and Jason returned to Bev's house. They explained to the curious audience waiting for them what had happened. Bev knew this wolf would be a bad omen and a constant source of trouble. She loved Steward, but wished he had not introduced Rudy into her life or brought him here.

In the morning, the Mounties took the body from Steward and wrote a report, classifying the event as a dog napping gone wrong, resulting in death at the hands of a wolf. The Mounties tried to convince Steward to drop out of the race to avoid any further conflict, but Steward's answer to that request was a firm, "No!".

CHAPTER FORTY-FOUR

The mood around Bev's breakfast table the following morning was sullen. Rudy had brought despair to Bev's spirit; a man dying at the hands of Steward's wolf disheartened her. Bev tried to put this incident in the back of her mind. It was Christmas Eve day, a time for happiness, not despair. Johnathan was arriving today to join his wife, Shining Star, and their baby for Christmas. As in previous years, Bev had invited two close friends for Christmas Eve dinner.

Steward left Bev's house shortly after breakfast. He put his dog team together to travel to Dawson to register for the race. He left Rudy at Bev's house, for his own protection. Word was spreading around town that Steward's wolf had the taste of human blood in its mouth and had turned into a savage animal, who Steward had little control over. A short time after leaving Bev's house, Steward found himself at the registration office. He signed up his dog team and received a number, which was to be displayed on his sled during the race.

After finishing his registration, he walked out of the building right into the path of One-Eyed Jack. The man sneered at Steward, the smell of alcohol permeating from him, his rotten teeth a testament to this man's dignity. One-Eyed Jack insisted Steward meet his sled team's leader, his alpha male, Satan. Satan was a wolf dog, the result of a domesticated dog, a husky, who mated with a wolf. The offspring of this matchup was neither dog nor wolf, but known as a hybrid dog and was much meaner and stronger than his husky mother.

One-Eyed Jack laughed, calling his dog Satan. The dog was cruel and hateful. Under the sadistic nature of One-Eyed Jack, the wolf dog had been whipped into submission by this evil man. The dog's sense of glory was gone, replaced by a vengeful, hateful spirit which would follow Satan forever into his future. One-Eyed Jack challenged Steward to a dog fight between Satan, his wolf dog, and Rudy, Steward's wolf. The fight would take place the day before the dog sled race. The losing dog would have to drop out of the race. Steward kept walking, ignoring the man and leaving on his sled.

Steward steered his sled back toward Bev's house. He returned the huskies to their chains, fed and watered the animals, and then went to check on Rudy. Steward questioned whether he made the right choice by taking this wolf out of his environment and forcing man's way of life upon him. Rudy was a loner and a killer. Steward was sure Rudy could win a fight against Satan, a smaller opponent, but Steward would not accept One-Eyed Jack's challenge. He wanted Rudy to win the battle against Satan on the trail, not in a dog fighting arena in Dawson.

CHAPTER FORTY-FIVE

After Steward finished taking care of Rudy and his huskies, he walked to the barn to see Omar and Honey, the two donkeys the family used as pack animals. Baby Jack was the newest addition to Honey and Omar's family, born in late September. Omar gave Steward a welcome greeting. The donkey loved Steward because he treated him with love and respect. Steward never overloaded Omar's back with heavy goods, leaving him sore for days afterwards, as some members of the family did. Baby Jack was a beautiful young donkey, who loved to be hugged, caressed, and talked to. He nestled his head into Steward's chest while his hands caressed the baby animal's head.

After a brief visit with the donkeys, Steward wished them goodbye and a Merry Christmas. He turned, leaving the barn and returning to Bev's house. The smell of food cooking greeted Steward's senses when he entered the house. A Canada goose, shot just before the freeze up, had been stored in Bev's outside freezer. This goose was on Bev's menu for dinner tonight.

Bev's invited guests arrived and all the attendees for her Christmas Eve dinner squeezed into her large living room.

The Christmas tree sat elegantly decorated in a corner of the room. Some guests added ornaments they had crafted the previous year for just this occasion. This was a traditional gift brought by Bev's family members to place on the beautiful tree at Christmas.

Bev was troubled this Christmas. She wished Steward had not brought Rudy here. The wolf had caused a serious problem, resulting in the death of a man and she feared the worst was yet to come. Bev tried to hide her true feelings for Rudy from her guests, not wanting to ruin their happiness on this important holiday. Stories were exchanged among the group until the familiar call that dinner was ready was announced by Wendy, Bev's helper in the kitchen. The guests sat around the large table and prayers were said. Generous helpings of goose and vegetables were passed around. Hot home-made bread with butter was on the table. The Christmas season was when Bev used the last of her root vegetables which she had stored in her cellar since the fall. The dinner went well, with traditional apple pie served for dessert.

After dinner, Steward prepared his dog sled to give Bev's two invited guests a ride home before it got late. These women were elderly and tired easily. Their homes were only a short distance into town, making the trip easy for Steward. The remaining people left in the house retired to the living room with tea or coffee in hand. After a brief time, Steward returned from his errand and joined them.

As the evening wore on, the couples gradually went to bed. Tomorrow was Christmas, a much quieter time at Bev's house. Bev had decided this Christmas, with the help of her family members, she would cook a large amount of surplus moose meat and fish. This food had been donated to Bev by members of Dawson's Indigenous community. The moose meat would be cooked on a large fire outside and served to the needy from Dawson. The family agreed it was the right thing to do, helping the hungry people who surrounded them on this important holiday.

The men would be responsible for the fire and cooking the meat. Bev and Wendy would hand out a portion of meat to each family, until it was gone. There would not be leftovers, only hungry people looking for more food. Christmas would soon be in the past, but normality would not return to Dawson until the chaos surrounding the town's preparations for the dog sled race were over.

Satan and Rudy were the focus for most of the bettors on the dog race. The odds were in One-Eyed Jack's favour, two to one, because of Satan's years of experience. One-Eyed Jack and Satan had not lost a dogsled race in five years; they were a hard team to beat, never accepting a loss. They won by bullying fellow participants and threatening grievous harm if they didn't let One-Eyed Jack win. Steward and Rudy had a chance to change this outcome with a clear, honest victory, ending One-Eyed Jack's dominance of this race. It was a feat the town never dreamed would be accomplished.

CHAPTER FORTY-SIX

The morning after Christmas Day in Dawson was bright and sunny. Jason and Wendy left early for home, wanting some time to prepare for resetting their trapline the following day. Johnathan was planning to visit with Shining Star for three more days before returning to his cabin. He hoped Steward would be declared the winner of this year's Dawson City dog sled race and wanted to be in Dawson when Steward crossed the finish line with his dog team.

Steward was nervous. His dog sled team, with Rudy as lead dog, was ready to go to town to compete in the race. Steward took Johnathan with him in case he ran into problems with the other mushers he could not handle alone. The gathering area for the start of the race was busy. A hush fell over the crowd when Steward steered his dog team toward the starting line. Rudy, the wolf who was already a legend in Dawson, stood alone but proud. The other dog teams cowered in his presence, except for one; Satan and One-Eyed Jack, who moved his dog sled closer to Rudy's position.

The race would begin with groups of three sleds departing the starting line in five-minute intervals. The course was twenty-five miles long and the winner would be who had the best time traversing the route to the finish line in Dawson. With the first three mushers in a line, the crowd roared their approval as a gunshot officially started the race. A silence fell over the crowd as the last two mushers pulled their sleds to the starting line. One-Eyed Jack sneered at Steward and his wolf, exposing his rotten teeth which were stained yellow from chewing tobacco.

The gunshot went off and the dog teams lunged forward. Steward's team was in the lead as the sleds rounded the first corner and disappeared out of sight. Rudy ran fast, his pace hard for Satan to keep up with. After an hour of hard running, Steward's huskies were getting tired. This is where Satan and One-Eyed Jack had the advantage, as their team was better trained and conditioned for long distance running. Rudy's stamina could not be worn down. He pushed forward motivating the rest of the team to do likewise.

Steward and One-Eyed Jack both began to pass dog teams which had started the race before them. Satan was in hot pursuit, with Jack formulating some devious schemes to overcome Steward's sled and win the race. As Satan edged Jack's sled closer to Steward's, One-Eyed Jack whipped Satan viciously causing him to overtake Steward's sled. One-Eyed Jack started to use his whip on Steward and Rudy. Caught up in the moment, and not paying attention, Jack let the runners on his sled get entangled with Steward's. This caused One-Eyed Jack to lose control of his speeding sled and crash into the brush and trees on the side of the route. His harnesses got tangled and he ended up crossing the finish line unharmed, but dead last, a defeat for this conniving character who was outsmarted by an honest man and his wolf.

Steward finished the race to the roar of the pleased crowd, crossing the finish line ten minutes faster than the second-place finisher. Steward and Rudy won the title and the first-place prize of one hundred dollars in gold. One-Eyed Jack was furious. He had lost the race and one of his sled dogs had suffered a broken leg during the accident with Steward's sled, ending his mushing career. One-Eyed Jack was the laughingstock of Dawson after his humiliating defeat at the hands of Steward and his wolf, Rudy. Revenge would be Jack's, as he planned to ambush Steward on the trail and kill Rudy.

CHAPTER FORTY-SEVEN

S teward decided to go straight home to Bev's house, rather than attend any of the end-of-race parties at the saloons around town. Unlike the other mushers attending these events, he could not leave Rudy alone while he was in a saloon drinking. Steward collected his winnings and headed back to Bev's, where he stayed while in town. Johnathan was with Steward, having promised his friend he would be there when he crossed the finish line.

With Johnathan on the sled, they headed home. The two men were excited about telling the women the good news, Steward had won the dog race and the one hundred-dollar first prize. When the men arrived at Bev's house, they returned the animals to their living quarters. They joined their wives and Bev in the house and told them the story of One-Eyed Jack and his humiliating defeat at the hands of Steward and Rudy and his team of huskies. Bev offered that such an evil man got the punishment he deserved. She also warned Steward to be aware of receiving retribution from this man. In Jack's mind, it was Steward who created the predicament he now found himself in. He lost the race, a dog, and his reputation as a tough guy was shattered.

Revenge was on Jack's mind now, revenge against Steward and Rudy.

Steward and Blossom planned to leave Bev's house in the morning, to return to their cabin and life of trapping in the bush. A man hired by One-Eyed Jack was watching for any sign of when Steward might be leaving town. The spy reported to Jack in the early evening he had seen Steward preparing his sled and believed he would be on the trail travelling home early tomorrow morning. Jack would set his trap and exact his revenge on Steward and Rudy, his wolf.

With hugs and good wishes, Steward and Blossom left Bev's house the following morning for their journey back home. Only a half-mile outside of town, a surprise was awaiting the young couple; an ambush was waiting for them. Approaching a wooded area, a gunshot rang out. One-Eyed Jack stepped out from his cover, pointing a rifle at Steward and Blossom, ordering them to stop the sled. The young couple obliged, knowing this man was not mentally stable.

Jack told Steward he would give him a fair chance to survive this encounter, but first they had to throw their two rifles in the snow. Jack told Steward he wanted Satan and Rudy to fight to their death. If Rudy won, they could continue on their way but without the gold they had won. If Rudy lost, he was going to take the gold anyway. Jack told Steward if he did not agree to these terms, he would shoot them, along with Rudy, and leave their bodies in the bush for scavengers to eat.

One-Eyed Jack called his dog team to come. Satan led them out of the trees where they had been hiding. Jack's dog team approached him cautiously. Jack whipped Satan savagely, thinking it would infuriate him and make him fight harder against Rudy. Steward had his hands on Rudy's harness, ready to unhook it if Jack did likewise with Satan. Before Steward had a chance to react, Jack set Satan free. The wolf dog lunged for Jack's throat, tearing a large hole in his jugular vein. One-Eyed Jack fell to the ground, holding his neck and gasping for air, as the once white snow turned crimson. Satan ran into the forest, never to be seen again. Jack bled to death on the trail, a fitting end for an evil man who would not be missed. His legacy would always be in the minds of the Yukoners, who knew him as One-Eyed Jack.

CHAPTER FORTY-EIGHT

Steward and Blossom were dumbfounded; One-Eyed Jack lay dead in the snow. His hybrid wolf dog, who was responsible for the man's death, had disappeared into the forest after committing this act of murder. Steward knew he and Blossom needed to return to Dawson and file a police report with the Mounties over the unfortunate incident which had just taken place.

Steward put One-Eyed Jack's dog team back together, selecting another dog to lead, as Satan was missing. Blossom would mush their sled back to Dawson, while Steward, with the body of One-Eyed Jack tied on the sled, would drive the other. Blossom followed Steward to the Mountie headquarters in town. They would leave One-Eyed Jack's body and his possessions with the Mounties after they filed their report. Steward hoped to be back on the trail with Blossom before lunch.

The constable listened to Steward's story. He was not surprised the man had died at the hands of his own dog. He had witnessed Jack give Satan a horrific beating in the past. He had personally put an end to it, fearing for the dog's life. It was not a crime to beat a dog in the Yukon. Frustrated and disillusioned gold seekers often beat their dogs in rages of anger. These simple men had no one else to turn on, their failure to find gold and the hard life they endured took a toll on the mental health of these greenhorns from the south. Many of these men died in the bush alone, eating the very dog they beat daily to fend off their starvation.

Steward was conversing with one of the Mounties, who had checked on Blossom and him earlier in the month while on patrol. He offered a small cabin the Mounties used on the trail, knowing the couple were too far away to make it home before nightfall. The shelter was located at the halfway point to Steward and Blossom's home. The couple graciously accepted the offer from this kind man.

With Rudy anxious to leave, they soon found themselves travelling at breakneck speed down the open trail. After burning off their excess energy, the dogs slowed to a more normal pace. Three hours later, Steward pulled the dogsled up to a cabin. A large sign on the door identified the building as a Mountie Outpost, typically used by the force when needed while on patrol, or if they were looking for someone lost, or who had broken the law. The interior of the shelter was warm and friendly.

Steward started a fire in the fireplace which graced the corner of the cabin. A blazing fire soon warmed the interior space to a comfortable temperature. The darkness of the forest surrounded the couple, the only sound being from an owl searching for his mate. The couple lay in bed, the twinkling stars shining in through the window. A peaceful sleep tonight was assured in this special piece of paradise called the Canadian north.

CHAPTER FORTY-NINE

Steward and Blossom awoke to what promised to be a bright, sunny day. Before leaving, they tidied up the cabin, happy for the night's stay here. Steward fed Rudy and the huskies whitefish from a bag he had carried with him from Dawson. He had purchased the fish from native friends of Bev's to feed his wolf and hungry dogs on the way home. The dogsled was readied to leave the Mountie's shelter, with Steward and Blossom expecting to be back at their cabin around lunchtime.

The trail ahead of the sled was a brilliant white. The sunshine reflecting off the snow covering the land and trees created a wonderland of spectacular, frozen beauty. Even the sled dogs noticed the stunning scenery surrounding them. The animals moved forward as a well-synchronized team, something Steward never expected, a wolf and a team of huskies happily working together.

Dark storm clouds were filling the sky when the couple arrived home. Steward placed Rudy and the huskies in their right spaces and walked to the outside freezer to retrieve whitefish for Rudy and the huskies to eat. It was easier for

Steward to feed the animals now, rather than during the blizzard he anticipated would arrive later.

Steward returned to the cabin, where Blossom had a roaring fire in the woodstove warming the interior to a comfortable temperature. She sent Steward back to the freezer for meat for themselves to eat for dinner and beyond. He retrieved some venison and two rabbits, ready to thaw and cook. Steward had shot the rabbits near the cabin shortly before the couple left for Dawson to enjoy Bev's Christmas celebration. He had butchered and placed them in the outdoor freezer, expecting to eat this game upon their return home.

When darkness fell over the wilderness cabin, the storm raged outside. A strong wind blew around the structure, making the cabin look like it was in a snow globe, glowing in the dark night as snow swirled around it. The storm subsided before sunrise, allowing the blue sky to return to the Yukon for another day.

CHAPTER FIFTY

Steward rose from his bed, anticipating a busy day. The couple were planning to rework their trapline today, setting out as many as twenty traps. Steward went outside to feed Rudy and his huskies. With this chore finished, he rejoined Blossom in the cabin for coffee and to plan their day. The blizzard had dumped a foot of new snow over the land. Steward consulted with Blossom about the snow being too deep to make significant progress today. The couple decided to set out the traps over the course of two days, staying at one of the two shelters which had been strategically placed along the trail for just such a purpose.

Steward went out to prepare the sled, while Blossom gathered up the personal gear they would need for an overnight stay at the shelter. Steward loaded the traps and bait on the dogsled. With room for no more baggage, the sled left the cabin ploughing through the deep snow toward the first shelter. Here the couple offloaded some of their traps, before continuing to the second shelter where they would stay for the night. They planned to begin laying their fur-bearing traps from this shelter the next morning, as they worked their way back home.

Arriving at this location, they found the door to the structure wide open. Upon closer inspection, Steward noticed an animal had entered through the front door. The interior of the shelter had been ransacked by an intruder looking for food, leaving a mess for Steward and Blossom to clean up. Steward suspected a wolverine was responsible for this disarray. The couple would watch for wolverine tracks when setting out their traps tomorrow.

Steward settled his dogs, keeping Rudy a distance from the huskies. Even though Rudy was cooperating with the huskies while pulling the sled, he refused to sleep near them. The overpowering scent of so many dogs laying too close to him, made Rudy uncomfortable.

The shelter was warm inside. Each of the two structures on their fur trapping route had fireplaces but no cooking facilities. The couple carried beef jerky and smoked fish to eat while on this trip. A sky full of storm clouds surrounded the forest around them in darkness. Sleeping soundly, the couple were awakened by loud barking and the snarls of dogs fighting. Steward jumped out of bed, pulled on his boots, and grabbed his gun. He bolted for the door of the shelter, throwing it open to a chaotic scene. Two wolves were attacking Rudy. The huskies had broken loose from their restraints and jumped into the fray, helping Rudy fend off his attackers. Two wolves, finding themselves outnumbered, were retreating to the security of the forest.

Steward resettled his huskies and rejoined Blossom in the cabin. The couple's sleep was fitful for the rest of the night, after this encounter with the wolves. These predators looked upon Rudy as a traitor, who had colluded with the enemy, and sought to harm him. To Steward, it was just another encounter in a savage land.

CHAPTER FIFTY-ONE

Steward awoke to the sound of his huskies barking. As the sun was rising over the horizon, daylight was illuminating the cabin. Steward dressed and pulled on his boots. His dogs were still barking. He opened the door and exited the shelter. The huskies were looking skyward, still raising a ruckus. Steward followed their gaze upwards and saw a porcupine high up in the tree looking down on them. Steward decided to shoot this animal, which was high in fat and protein, and butcher it for food. He would keep the best cuts of meat from the porcupine for himself and Blossom and feed the rest of the animal to Rudy.

Steward aimed his rifle and fired, the loud shot from Steward's weapon reverberated throughout the forest. With a loud thud, the porcupine hit the ground, dead from Steward's first shot. He retrieved the animal and took it to the shelter. He would carry the animal back to his cabin where he would butcher it in the fur shed.

The day passed quickly, as the couple completed their goal of setting all twenty traps. Blossom and Steward arrived back at their cabin, finishing the job of resetting their trapline, including two beaver traps set through the ice on the pond. Steward settled the dogs in their spaces and fed them dinner and then joined Blossom in the cabin. She had started a fire in the woodstove and was waiting for Steward to retrieve some deer meat from the outdoor freezer.

While his wife was cooking dinner, Steward took the porcupine from the sled and placed it in the shed to butcher later. He walked over to see Rudy, his wolf, bringing the animal a large moose bone he had found in the freezer while getting venison for Blossom. Steward wrapped his arms around Rudy, hugging him tightly. The wolf responded by licking Steward's face. Steward released the animal from his grip and rubbed Rudy's back, which the wolf liked. Steward said goodbye to Rudy, telling him he would see him tomorrow.

Entering his home, Steward noted the aroma of frying meat; the venison was cooked and ready to eat. The oil lamps in the cabin cast a warm glow over the couple's dinner table. The one course dinner was appreciated by these hungry fur trappers living in the bush. After dinner, the couple sat around the table and played cards. Steward had received a new deck of cards from Bev for Christmas. She had taught the couple new card games before they left for their cabin in the forest, which Steward and Blossom were playing now. The couple's eyes soon tired and after finishing their entertainment, they retired to bed.

Steward blew out the lamp light, pulling the warm covers over Blossom and himself. Sleep came easily for the couple, who were wrapped in each other's arms under the cozy blankets of their bed. Survival in this wilderness was a challenge they both liked to confront; living in the Yukon is exactly where the couple wanted to be.

CHAPTER FIFTY-TWO

The raven's piercing call broke the stillness of the early morning air. Steward opened his sleepy eyes and looked toward the cabin window. He rubbed his eyes, not believing what he was seeing. A set of antlers was visible in the window. Steward figured a deer must be standing directly under the window. He woke Blossom to share this strange occurrence with her. Whispering to one another, the couple decided the deer, once butchered, would fit nicely in their freezer. Steward would shoot the animal; the meat from the buck would be a welcome addition to the couple's food supply.

Steward quietly pulled himself out of bed and dressed quickly. The element of surprise would be on their side, making it easy for Steward to kill the animal. Blossom quietly opened the door. The deer continued standing by the side of the cabin. Steward stepped outside, catching the animal by surprise. Before the deer had time to react, a thunderous noise came from Steward's rifle. The buck lay dead in front of him, a bullet in his head. The couple thanked their creator for the food delivery to their cabin door, an event which was unheard of in this land which shows no favors.

Steward and Blossom pulled the deer into the forest and gutted it. They returned the carcass to the cabin and hung it from a tree. After returning from checking the trapline today, they would move the deer into the fur shed to be butchered later. Steward prepared the dogsled for today's duties, checking the trapline for fur bearing mammals. He decided to leave Blossom at home, hoping to make up the time he lost shooting and gutting the deer. The less weight the dogs had to pull, the faster they could finish the trapper's route.

By noon, Steward had checked ten of his traps and only caught two pine martens, a meager catch. He decided to go back to the cabin and butcher the deer he had shot this morning. Tomorrow, the couple would check the remaining ten traps set in the bush and the two traps they had set for beaver in the pond. Blossom had started a fire in the woodstove of the fur shed while Steward was gone. The heat would allow the frozen animals to thaw over time, allowing them to be butchered, like the deer, for food. Mammals caught in the traps needed to defrost before their hides could be removed and their meat saved for the dogs.

Blossom was surprised to see Steward return early. He told her of his plans for tomorrow and she readily agreed to go with him to finish checking the traps. The couple retired to their cabin, planning to take a nap while waiting for the animals to thaw. In the early evening, working under the light of oil lamps, Steward butchered the deer while Blossom worked on removing the hides from the pine martens and processing the porcupine. The couple hoped to finish their work early, as tomorrow would be another busy day. The work for Steward and Blossom was never ending, as they tried to survive in this unchartered land called the Yukon.

CHAPTER FIFTY-THREE

Steward and Blossom finished their work in the fur shed at 10 p.m.. The deer was butchered, and the venison was packed in the outdoor freezer, along with the porcupine. The hides from the pine martens were stretched and would be added to the fur which had been harvested before Christmas. The couple returned to a cold cabin. After adding more wood to the fire, warm air flooded the structure, radiating off the hot cast iron of the stove.

The couple retired to bed, exhausted from the long day which had started at sunrise. After a brief period of conversation, Steward and Blossom, wrapped in each other's arms, fell into a peaceful sleep. The forest surrounding the cabin was dark and foreboding. A cold north wind blew across the frozen lake which stood behind Steward's property. Steward and Blossom snuggled against each other warmly. They were under the blankets on their bed, not caring how cold it was outside. Staying warm inside the cabin was what was important to the couple.

Blossom and Steward were awakened at dawn to the annoying call of a raven on the roof of the cabin. The scavenger could smell the remains of the animals in the fur shed which were going to be discarded in the forest today. Steward prepared his dog team. They would check the beaver traps first and then circle back to check the rest of his trapline. In a short period of time Steward and Blossom were ready to leave the cabin. The sled dogs were well rested and ran with enthusiasm along the trail. Within a brief time, they were at the first beaver trap they had set. The trap yielded a large, adult male beaver with a fine pelt; however, the second trap was empty. Steward was happy with their catch, as a pelt from an adult beaver was valuable. It would be the prize of the day.

Steward turned his dogsled around, heading back in the direction of the cabin. The ten traps held some valuable fur, including a red fox with a beautiful winter coat. A lynx was found, with it's leg caught in the trap, fighting for its life. Blossom shot the animal, being careful the bullet did not ruin the fur. An ermine and two more pine martens completed the bounty from the traps. One of the martens was half eaten, apparently by a raptor who had spotted easy pickings from above.

The couple gathered their catch for the day and returned to the cabin. The mammals caught from the trapline were stored in the shed, where their hides would be processed tomorrow. Steward put the huskies away but kept Rudy aside. He was going to use the wolf to move the unsalvageable remains from the deer deep in the forest, away from the cabin. He pulled Rudy and the sled close to the fur shed.

Steward loaded the deer remains on the sled and mushed Rudy down the trail a half mile. Steward then turned the sled into a more wooded area, stopped, and unloaded the remains in an open area among the aspen trees. Steward wanted to test Rudy's loyalty to him. For the first time since Rudy was a pup, Steward did not restrain him. He unleashed his wolf from its harness, who rushed to the pile of deer remains. Rudy ate his fill and then returned to Steward, who reattached his harness to the sled. Rudy then pulled the sled back to the cabin. Rudy had passed Steward's test of loyalty, being a trusted ally, but still a dangerous foe.

CHAPTER FIFTY-FOUR

Arriving home, Steward returned Rudy to his enclosure. The odor of venison frying on the woodstove caught Steward's attention as he entered the cabin. Blossom was cooking deer meat, the only food the couple would be eating tonight. The cold winter months, along with the couple's isolation, made for few food choices. A meat diet was what these early fur trappers and gold seekers subsisted on during the winter in the Yukon. During the fall, Indigenous people foraged for edibles hidden amongst the forest. Blossom would sometimes supplement dinner with these products. Roots, mosses, fungi, and bulbs taken from plants were stored for the winter to be used as a substitute for vegetables in stews.

The couple ate dinner, the darkness folding like a blanket around them. Steward and Blossom decided to lay in bed and look at the books Bev had given Steward while in Dawson. Steward read to Blossom, who was unfamiliar with reading English. The evening was quiet and peaceful, with the couple falling asleep shortly after midnight.

Rudy was not sleeping. He was listening to a wolf pack chasing down a deer in the deep snow on the lake. Rudy paced his enclosure, his instincts telling him he would like to participate in this wilderness adventure with his brothers. The wolf's emotions were torn. Rudy's devotion to Steward was waning as the thought of freedom was gripping his wild, primitive side.

Steward and Blossom were roused from their bed by the raven squawking from the cabin roof. Annoyed, Steward went outside and shot his rifle at the bird. The bullet zoomed by the raven's head, taking the welcome mat out from under his feet. The bird's exit was swift and silent. Steward hoped the raven would never be back.

Steward returned to the cabin, motioning Blossom to get out of bed. Last night before dinner, he had lit a hot fire in the fur shed and added enough hardwood to keep it burning until sunrise. The mammals they had trapped yesterday should be thawed enough to process this morning. Steward would wait to feed Rudy and his huskies until after he harvested the fur from the animals. Blossom elected to work on the beaver, as she was skilled at skinning this animal. The beaver hide was the most prized and useful fur in the Indigenous people's culture. Therefore, Blossom had been taught how to take the hide off the beaver and butcher the carcass. The beaver meat would be used for stews, a favorite dish in the Canadian north.

The couple finished their work in the fur shed by noon. Steward planned on taking Rudy on another trip to the forest to dispose of the animal's remains, letting him eat what he wanted. To a wolf like Rudy, this food was a delicacy, which the huskies did not enjoy. Over the month of January, Steward repeated this job with Rudy many times, each time allowing the wolf freedom from restraints. And each time, Rudy explored a little bit farther away before returning to Steward's call. Was Rudy reacting to the call of the wild or was he just exploring his newfound freedom? Steward would accept Rudy's choice, whatever it might be.

CHAPTER FIFTY-FIVE

The long Yukon winter was finally getting a reprieve; January's bitter cold turned a bit warmer when the month changed to February. The warm front lasted for three days. The bright sun shone down upon the roof of the cabin, melting the snow. A constant drip of water falling from the eaves could be heard hitting the frozen ground. Then, winter returned with little warning. Steward observed the water had stopped dripping off the roof of the cabin. After feeding Rudy and the huskies, he noticed the wind had changed direction, now blowing from the north. Steward knew Mother Nature was getting ready to cast her wrath and bring winter back across the land.

Returning to the cabin, Steward told Blossom to prepare for a blizzard. After dinner, the wind grew stronger, making the trees sway, their trunks rubbing against each other. This action created an unpleasant groaning sound to travel throughout the forest. Steward looked out the window of the cabin. New snow was accumulating rapidly on the ground. The trees were covered in white, as the snow stuck to their branches, still wet from the melt caused by the warm front.

The blizzard raged until the following morning. Then as suddenly as it began, it stopped. The sun came out and the landscape shone a brilliant white, an accumulation of fresh snow covered the ground. Steward readied the dogsled to take the animals for a run in the new snow. He mushed Rudy and the huskies along the trail, noticing many animal tracks in the undisturbed snow. He suddenly stopped the sled; moose tracks crossed the trail, disappearing into the bush on the other side. Steward was ecstatic! A moose had moved into this territory. An animal this size would supply meat for three families for the rest of the winter. Steward decided he would organize another moose hunt with Jason and Johnathan.

Steward mushed the dogs to the first shelter, then turned them around and returned home. Upon his arrival, Steward was surprised to see a dog sled in front of his cabin. It was Jason and Steward's sister, Wendy, their son. and their dog, King, who had come for a visit. Steward put Rudy and the huskies in their rightful places and returned to his cabin. A warm greeting prevailed from their company. Jason had shot four game birds during their journey here today. Steward and Jason butchered the birds in the fur shed and their wives would prepare them for dinner. Comradeship would prevail among the couples, a rare commodity when living in the wilds of the Yukon.

CHAPTER FIFTY-SIX

The grouse frying on the woodstove filled the cabin with an aroma which stimulated the hungry stomachs of the couples waiting to eat dinner. Under Wendy's guidance, the birds were soon cooked and served to the hungry people sitting around the table. The couples discussed their success at trapping this winter.

Jason told Steward a wolverine had discovered their trapline and caused considerable damage. The animal had been eating the mammals caught in their traps, destroying the fur and making the hides worthless. The animal was finally caught due to his own greed. Wendy had set a trap using venison from the outdoor freezer. She thawed the deer first and then molded a large piece of the meat over the trap, obscuring most of the metal. The trap was set, and the wolverine took the bait. The couple were relieved of this small animal's destructive habits. The wolverine's hide would be going to Dawson in the spring to be sold with Jason's other furs.

Steward told Jason about seeing the moose tracks in the snow. Shooting a moose would help Jason and Wendy replenish their supply of meat for the remainder of the winter. Jason told Steward he would talk to Johnathan about the moose and the two men would return together in a week to Steward's cabin for their hunting endeavour.

After dinner, the men went out to feed their huskies. Steward took Jason to Rudy's enclosure. Rudy paced nervously around his small yard. Jason marvelled at the size and strength of Steward's wolf. The men returned to the cabin and joined their wives in a game of cards. The conversation flowed freely around the card table. Laughter was contagious, as each person took a turn at winning and losing.

Outside the cabin, the wind was calm, the forest dark and silent. The only activity was the presence of a rabbit, being pursued by a hungry fox; the fox being the eventual winner of this contest of survival. Midnight's arrival meant bed for the tired couples. Jason and Wendy were leaving in the early morning. Steward and Blossom were planning on working on their trapline after the couple left. Sleep was peaceful, as the silence which enveloped them promoted an undisturbed slumber. Everyone sleeping in the cabin awakened with the sun the following morning.

Jason and Wendy gathered their dogs and young son and left early. Jason told Steward and Blossom, they would see him soon when he returned for the moose hunt. The couples hugged and said their goodbyes. Wendy and Jason's dogsled was soon out of sight, as the couple travelled on the trail back to their cabin. Steward enjoyed visiting with his sister, Wendy. Her presence brought back memories of days gone past. The spirit of the north would always be with these siblings in this wilderness enclave they called the Yukon.

CHAPTER FIFTY-SEVEN

Steward and Blossom spent the day digging out the traps, which had been buried under the snow during the storm. Two of the buried traps contained animals, an ermine and a pine marten. These were common furs found on a Yukon trapline. After digging the buried traps out of the snow, they reset them, ensuring they had enough bait on the trigger. Afternoon was waning when they finished the job on the trapline.

Steward steered Rudy in the direction of the cabin. The sled was racing for home when a distraction made Steward stop his team. Ahead on the trail was the moose who had left the tracks in the snow. The animal was a cow, an adult female. She stood about one hundred feet down the trail looking at the couple and their dog sled. After a brief time, the moose turned and sauntered off into the forest. Steward and Blossom continued on their way, reaching their cabin with no more distractions.

The couple spent the next week tending to their trapline. Several valuable hides were harvested during this time, including a silver fox and two beaver pelts. One day, after returning home from checking the trapline, a familiar noise broke the silence, the sound of men mushing their dog teams. Steward could see two dog sleds racing across the frozen lake toward his cabin. It was Jason and Johnathan, arriving for the moose hunt.

The men anchored their sleds and let the dogs be. They would return later and make the dog's sleeping arrangements more permanent. They joined Steward in the cabin. Blossom brewed some coffee Jason had carried with him from home. Steward told his friends about seeing the cow moose on the trail. He believed the animal should be easy to find and harvest for food. The men would leave at daybreak tomorrow with two dog teams. Steward's huskies and Rudy would be left at Steward's cabin for now. If needed, the dogs would be used later to haul meat to the cabin.

After eating dinner and plotting their hunting strategies, the men talked about their lives in the bush. They agreed it was a hard life, fraught with danger; a life they chose, not one given to them. The men slept peacefully as the full moon shone down on the landscape. Its reflection off the white snow lit up the cabin and the lake, like an early morning dawn. The morning sky would soon be illuminated in brightness, signalling another day in this land called the Yukon in Canada's far north.

CHAPTER FIFTY-EIGHT

Under the early light of dawn, Johnathan and Jason prepared their dog sleds. The men loaded the supplies needed for the moose hunt and were soon ready to leave Steward's cabin. With a yell from the mushers to go, the dogs bolted forward. Jason and Johnathan's sleds followed Steward's trapline route to his last shelter. The shelter bordered a large beaver dam. Steward had noticed while checking his trapline, the moose had moved from her previous location. The cow moose was now foraging for food in this wetland, a large area which encompassed three established beaver colonies.

The men secured their sleds at the last shelter and walked into the frozen swamp looking for the moose. Steward reasoned the young cow moose was in her second year of life. Johnathan pointed out the large number of moose tracks, which were spread out across this area. The men separated, each going off in their own direction. The call of a blue jay and a woodpecker hitting the dead wood of a tree with his beak were the only sounds to be heard echoing through this quiet swamp. The silence was broken by a loud gunshot, then stillness returned to the swamp.

Jason had sighted the moose, but was unable to get a clear shot. The moose had seen Jason and started to run off. Jason's reaction was to shoot at the animal, which resulted in it being wounded, but not critically. The injured moose crashed through the swamp, trying to get away from Jason's rifle. The animal, in its haste to escape, became careless, running into a waiting Johnathan's gun sights. Two successive shots from his moose rifle brought the animal to its knees. The wounded moose gave a final try at getting back up on all four feet. A final shot from Johnathan's rifle took the moose to the ground, blood pouring from its wounds.

The men gathered around the dead moose. The meat from a cow moose was desirable, as it was tender and the flavour better than meat from an adult bull. The men congratulated each other on their successful hunt. Johnathan and Jason went to retrieve their dogs, as the tools to butcher the animal were on the sleds. When the men returned, they decided a third sled would not be necessary to haul meat. The moose was young and had not reached it's full maturity, resulting in less weight for the dogs to pull.

Butchering the moose would take the three men most of the day. While working on the moose, a sudden storm brought wind and blowing snow to the swamp, making this open-air job more difficult. Johnathan packed the last of the meat from the butchered moose at 2 p.m.. The sleds, led by Jason, returned to Steward's cabin, where the meat was unloaded into the fur shed. After dinner they would prepare and clean the meat better, as the moose had only been field dressed and quartered. The trappers called this a bad butcher job.

After the men ate their fill of moose meat for dinner, they went to the fur shed to finish processing the animal. The meat would be divided equally among the three men. Steward fed Rudy his dinner, a large piece of meat, still wet with the moose's blood. He fed his dogs the most undesirable cuts from the animal, which the huskies relished. The dogs were happy eating almost any part of the moose.

The evening slid by and soon everyone in Steward's cabin were sleeping. Their sleep was restful, their minds at peace. Nature had provided them with a bounty of food, not a given in this brutal land where survival is not guaranteed, unless there is luck involved.

CHAPTER FIFTY-NINE

Jason and Johnathan were up at dawn. The sun rising above the horizon promised a sunny day for travel. The men loaded their sleds with the moose meat and left Steward and Blossom's cabin for home. Wendy would be happy to see her husband bringing home fresh meat, as they had limited stock in their freezer. This protein was necessary for survival during the winter when game was hard to find.

Steward and Blossom were planning on spending the rest of the day fishing with nets under the ice. The couple's stock of fish to feed the sled dogs was low and needed to be replenished. Steward hooked Rudy up to the sled and retrieved an axe from the wood pile to reopen the holes in the ice. Blossom gathered her fish nets from inside the cabin. The nets were a valuable commodity, which needed to be taken care of. Without the nets, an excellent method of harvesting food would be lost, putting a strain on the trappers' ability to feed their dogs.

The Indigenous tribes crafted many of these nets, allowing for loss from inexperienced handlers. Blossom constructed her own fish nets; she had many and would never find herself without one. It was an important tool for catching fish and providing food, especially during the winter.

Rudy pulled the sled out onto the frozen lake. The couple's destination was a half hour away. at the other end of the lake. Rudy, with his strong back and large strides, delivered them to the fishing area ten minutes earlier than the couple expected. Within another half an hour, Steward had reopened the holes in the ice and Blossom was fishing. Four hours of fishing produced splendid results. Twenty whitefish and four lake trout lay on the ice. The couple gathered up their belongings and the fish they caught and mushed Rudy back to their cabin. They unloaded the whitefish into the outdoor freezer, keeping the lake trout for their dinner tonight.

Steward took the frozen fish into the warm cabin. Once thawed, he would clean the fish and prepare the fillets for dinner. Blossom added wood to the dying embers in the bottom of the woodstove. A short time later, the fire was roaring in the belly of the stove warming the inside of the cabin to a comfortable temperature. Steward and Blossom decided to lay down for a well-earned nap after spending the day on the open lake fishing. The couple's reward for their hard work was fresh lake trout for dinner, a special treat any time of the year in the Yukon.

CHAPTER SIXTY

The remaining month of February brought brutal cold to the Yukon. For two weeks the temperature never rose above zero degrees Fahrenheit during the day. The sun shone down daily from a bright blue sky, but the cold arctic air trapped over the Northern hemisphere made the sun's warmth irrelevant. The couple's trapline become less productive, as the animals living in the forest sought shelter from the brutal cold. Steward and Blossom were happy they had cut extra firewood for the winter to cover such an event.

The bitter cold receded in early March, ushering in warmer days. Steward knew it was time to take their furs to Dawson. He would need to make two trips, if Blossom accompanied him. The season had been productive, and the couple had been rewarded for their hard work. He told Blossom they would both travel to Dawson to sell their furs. Blossom would stay with Bev while he travelled back to the cabin to pick up the second load of hides from the fur shed. In agreement, the couple decided they would leave for Dawson tomorrow morning.

Blossom and Steward enjoyed a quiet evening together. The night was serene; only the occasional breeze could be heard blowing through the bare treetops. The couple lay in bed thinking about their trip tomorrow, looking forward to seeing Bev and being in town. Steward was up with the sun. He fed Rudy and the huskies and prepared them for their trip. With Rudy as lead canine, the dogs pulled the sled in front of the cabin. They waited here until Blossom was ready to leave.

Blossom gathered up the couple's personal belongings and packed them on the dogsled. It was a tight fit, with the hides that had already been loaded. Steward secured the cabin before leaving. He gave the command to Rudy to mush. Rudy's shoulders strained under his harness, pulling the heavy load on the sled. The wolf led the dog team down the trail to Dawson. Rudy pressed the huskies hard, pushing them to their limits of endurance. After only one short rest for the canines, the buildings of the frontier town came into view.

Steward decided to go to the fur broker in Dawson he had used for years. He was an honest man who offered fair prices to the trappers. Before going to Bev's house, Steward would take care of this important business, the reason he had travelled to Dawson. The broker took Steward's fur and inspected the hides carefully. After two hours of writing down the different prices he was willing to pay, the broker came up with an offer for Steward. After consulting with Blossom, he accepted the broker's offer thinking the deal was more than fair. The couple thanked the man and continued their journey to Bev's house.

Bev was a woman who was always happy to see the couple, but not Steward's wolf. Rudy was creating a rift between Steward and Bev; she would prefer Steward not bring Rudy to her house. Bev believed the wolf's soul belonged to the devil and would cast bad luck upon her. Because of her father's strict beliefs, she had been taught to view wolves this way. Bev had a mindset which could not easily be changed.

CHAPTER SIXTY-ONE

*B*ev had a special area set aside where unruly sled dogs were kept when staying overnight at her house. These were dogs which exhibited an ill temperament and picked fights with other canines. These abusive huskies were kept by their owners because there was a shortage of dogs available in the Dawson area. To most trappers, a bad dog was better than no dog, in most circumstances. This pen is where Steward housed Rudy while staying at Bev's house.

With the wolf and dogs settled into their accommodations, the group sat down to dinner. Shining Star talked about returning to her cabin and joining Johnathan with the couple's son. Spring would soon return to the Yukon, ushering in a renewal of life for another short season before winter's snows once again covered the land. Steward told Bev and Shining Star of his plans to return to his cabin tomorrow to pick up the rest of his furs. He would return to Dawson the following day to sell them to the broker.

When dinner was over, Steward and Blossom walked to the barn to visit Omar and his family. The donkeys were always glad to see company walk through the barn door. Baby Jack was a big attraction and visitors usually showered him with treats when visiting. Omar, always vocal and wanting to be the centre of attention, brayed loudly and consistently until someone would rub his head and pat his back.

After a pleasant visit with the donkeys, the couple returned to the house. They drank coffee in the living room and ate fresh baked cookies from Bev's oven. The mood of the group was relaxed, until Steward proclaimed he had a major announcement to make. Steward, holding Blossom's hand, told his waiting audience that his wife was pregnant, and they were expecting their first child. Shock and excitement were the reaction Steward received from his listeners, followed by hugs and congratulatory affections; a joyous moment not often captured in the Yukon.

Steward woke at daybreak and readied his dog team for travel. He left his wife in bed and said goodbye to Bev. The morning was cloudy, but not cold. Steward reached his cabin with no major incidents along the trail, making good time getting home. He put the animals in their rightful places and entered his cabin. Lighting a fire in the woodstove, the cabin was soon warm and comfortable. Steward was lonely. It was his first time alone at his cabin since he married his wonderful wife, Blossom.

Steward's sleep was restless that night. He was impatient for daybreak, wanting to load his sled with furs and return to Dawson. The annoying raven on the roof demanding food woke him at daybreak. He dressed, not annoyed at this bird for the first time. The call from the raven acted like an alarm clock, awakening him at just the right time.

Collecting frozen whitefish from the outdoor freezer, Steward fed his animals. Any meat left in the freezer would need to be eaten soon before the warm spring weather spoiled the meat. Steward took extra moose meat from the freezer to give to Bev, wanting to avoid any meat going to waste. Bev knew many hungry people in Dawson, ensuring the moose given to her would be put to good use.

Steward's trip back to Dawson was uneventful, except for a wolf pack crossing the trail shortly after leaving the cabin. The wolves did not stop or threaten Steward in any way. Arriving in Dawson after lunch, Steward's first stop was at the fur brokers to sell his remaining furs. Steward was happy this would be the last time he would be dealing with anything trapping related until next winter. Blossom and Steward had removed all the traps from their trapline and stored them in the fur shed before leaving for Dawson. The traps would not be used again until next season.

Completing his transaction with the fur broker, Steward returned to Bev's house. He secured Rudy and his huskies in their approved locations and returned to the house, kissing his waiting wife and hugging her tightly. The couple would spend one more night at Bev's, leaving for home after eating breakfast with her in the morning.

The first warning came at dawn, with Steward's huskies barking. Steward dressed quickly, grabbed his rifle, and bolted out the door of the house. Steward's heart sank into the ground at what he found. Someone had opened Rudy's pen and the wolf had left his enclosure, his tracks leading into the forest. Steward knew this is what Rudy had yearned for, the freedom to let his wild instincts return, allowing him to live in a place he longed to be. Steward was not sure if he would ever see Rudy again. He returned to the house to tell his wife the news. The news was sad to some, but not the majority, who were glad to see the wolf disappear.

CHAPTER SIXTY-TWO

Steward's heart was in disrepair. He had lost Rudy, whom he had found abandoned as a young pup in a wolf den. Rudy was an animal Steward would sorely miss. He gathered up his huskies, who knew Rudy was missing. Without the wolf as lead dog, the huskies would have to pull much harder. Rudy had made the huskies lives as sled dogs easier; these animals would miss Rudy's strength, stamina, and leadership abilities greatly.

The trip back home would take longer than usual. The huskies tired more readily without the help of Rudy pulling the sled. Dark storm clouds filled the early spring sky, as the wind shifted direction and blew from the north. Steward mushed his huskies, pushing them hard. They needed to get back to the cabin ahead of the late season snowstorm which was following them. Light snow started falling as the dogs pulled the sled to the front of the cabin.

Blossom unloaded the couple's belongings and placed them inside. Steward took his huskies to their yard to be fed. Steward walked by Rudy's empty enclosure, a feeling of loss overwhelming him as he realized Rudy was no longer his wolf. He turned and returned to the cabin, where Blossom had started a fire in the woodstove and was boiling water for coffee. Blossom knew it would take time for Steward to get over his grief from losing Rudy.

The storm struck with a vengeance, reminding the couple to never let their guard down. Some of the worse weather offered by nature in the north strikes at the most inopportune time. The couple were glad to be home from Dawson and sleeping in their own bed. Waking in the morning, the couple looked out at the fresh snow, which covered the landscape. The storm was over, but dark clouds still filled the sky. Persistent snow flurries would fall for the rest of the day before the Yukon warmed again.

Steward and Blossom stayed in the cabin. Their trapping season was finished, so staying in bed late was an option the couple chose to practice. After the snow melted and the lake became ice free, the ducks, geese, and other waterfowl would return from their migration south. Steward's cabin sat on their summer home. The couple loved to hunt and fish from their canoe during the summer months. The lake was their main source of food when no refrigeration was available. The couple would have to wait another month to see these changes take place, always a welcome reprieve after the cold months of winter.

CHAPTER SIXTY-THREE

The month of May arrived in the Yukon. Steward needed to travel to Dawson to pick up supplies needed for the summer. He would use either Omar or Honey, one of the two pack animals who lived in Bev's barn, to carry goods from Dawson to his cabin. While he was gone, Blossom would stay home and care for the huskies.

The snow had melted at the cabin and the lake was free of ice. The ducks, geese, and other migratory waterfowl had returned from their migration south to the ice-free lakes of the north. Steward left for Dawson shortly after daybreak on a warm sunny day. He would walk halfway, before camping for the evening. Blossom packed smoked fish, which she had caught fresh from the lake this year, in his pack.

After a long walk, Steward reached his destination, a lake he was familiar with and his favorite place to camp when travelling to Dawson during the warmer months. The spring air was cold. Steward built a fire and gathered enough wood to last the night. Sleeping outdoors this early in the spring in the Yukon was cold and uncomfortable.

Steward lit the campfire as twilight fell. The crackling of wood burning in the firepit was a welcome sound; the promise of heat from the fire would warm Steward from the cold. Looking up to the heavens, a million twinkling stars shone back at him. Steward remembered camping here with Blossom and wishing on the falling stars while they lay together watching the night sky. The call of the loon on the dark lake had heightened that special moment together.

Steward slept well, the burning campfire and his blanket keeping him warm. The morning sun shone brightly, as Steward picked himself up from the cold ground and added wood to the dying embers of the fire. He would warm his aching bones before continuing his journey to Dawson. Thirty minutes later, Steward was back on the trail.

The foliage on the trees and vegetation in the forest was sparse, offering a good view of the immediate surroundings. Steward felt he was being followed. He stopped, scanning the forest for movement. Seeing nothing, he continued walking. As a thicket of aspen trees appeared in front of him, Steward decided to take cover and wait. Ten minutes went by before Steward saw movement in the forest. As he watched, the animal moved closer to where he had concealed himself.

Catching a glimpse of his stalker, Steward realized who it was. It was his wolf, Rudy. He had been shadowing Steward through the forest, never giving up his presence until he was tricked into showing himself. Steward, without hesitation, yelled out Rudy's name. With his element of surprise gone, Rudy bolted back into the forest, ignoring Steward's call. A wave of gratitude washed through Steward's soul, knowing Rudy was safe. He believed Rudy was curious but would never return to him. When Rudy found a soulmate, Steward knew he would no longer be important to the wolf, just part of Rudy's past.

CHAPTER SIXTY-FOUR

Steward was stunned by his encounter with Rudy. When his wolf disappeared from Bev's house, he never expected to see him again. Steward continued his journey, arriving in Dawson in the late afternoon. He walked to Bev's house on the outskirts of town, just as darkness was falling. Bev was happier having Steward stay with her since Rudy was gone. Steward and Bev's relationship was mending, after it had become strained over disagreements regarding Rudy and Bev's hatred of wolves. Bev greeted Steward at her front door, inviting him into her house.

Bev was glad to have Steward's company. She had been expecting him to come and pick up one of the pack animals in the barn. When Steward and Blossom had been in town to sell their furs, he had told Bev he would be coming back later in the spring. Over dinner, Steward shared some sad news with Bev. Shortly after returning home from their last visit, Blossom had lost her baby. She was fine, but they were both still grieving the loss. Bev was saddened by the news but told Steward this happened often with first pregnancies. Hopefully they would have better luck next time. She also told Steward Jason and

Wendy had picked up Omar earlier in the week. Honey, the other donkey in the barn, was available to use as a pack animal again. Baby Jack, her offspring, was old enough at this point to take care of himself. He did not need his mother anymore.

Steward told Bev he planned to stay two nights with her. Tomorrow he would take Honey into Dawson and purchase his needed supplies for the summer. He planned to leave Bev's house the following day to return to his cabin and waiting wife. Later in the evening, while sitting with Bev in the living room, Bev shared a story circulating around Dawson about Steward and his wolf. Apparently, One-Eyed Jack's best friend and partner in crime had never forgiven Steward and Rudy, blaming the pair for One-Eyed Jack's death. He wanted to enact revenge on Steward for committing this unforgivable deed.

Initially, the man had planned to shoot the wolf, but was afraid the death would lead back to him. Letting Rudy out of his enclosure was the next best thing, with little likelihood the man would be charged with any crime. Steward suspected something of this nature from one of One-Eyed Jack's comrades, scoundrels who should be chased out of Dawson and barred from ever returning. Unfortunately, the days of the goldrush in the Klondike drew thousands of people to Dawson. Most men, and some women, merely passed through town on their quest for gold. However, some of these recent arrivals to Dawson stayed. These bad men preyed on the weak and destitute, making more money staying in town than they could earn working the goldfields of the Klondike.

Steward went to bed, wishing Bev a good night. He slept soundly, waking with the sun shining in through his bedroom window. He dressed, went downstairs, and enjoyed coffee with Bev. Steward thanked her for being so thoughtful towards him, giving her a hug as he left the house and walked to the barn.

Unsure of how Baby Jack would react to having his mother taken away from him for the first time, Steward entered the stall and harnessed Honey. Honey came willingly with Steward, the donkey happy to get a break from her offspring, who had been with her since birth. Not so for Baby Jack, who put up a fuss when he realized his mother was leaving him alone.

Steward led Honey to the livery stable, where he picked up a bag of the owner's special mash which the pack animals loved. Steward then went to the mercantile, where he purchased a large bag of dry dog food to supplement his huskies' diet when fish were hard to catch. He bought sugar, salt, and coffee, along with a large supply of jerky, a nonperishable meat smoked and dried to perfection. Rich in protein, it was a popular food during the summer. Steward also picked up a new kettle and cooking pot for Blossom.

With Honey's back loaded with supplies, Steward took the donkey back to Bev's house. He unburdened her back for today, only to reload the items tomorrow, better securing them for the long trip home. Leaving in the early morning for home was Steward's plan, knowing Blossom was waiting for him at the cabin. Steward was anxious to be reunited with his wife.

CHAPTER SIXTY-FIVE

Steward was up with the sunrise. He headed to the barn and repacked the goods he had purchased earlier on Honey's back. Steward said goodbye to Baby Jack and walked Honey out of the barn. He returned to the house to pick up food Bev had prepared for his travels. Giving his aunt a hug goodbye, Bev wished Steward a safe trip home.

Honey and Steward left Dawson, but just before entering the forest, the donkey was given time to graze in a meadow of green grass growing outside of town. The short growing season of the Yukon is reflected in the rapid growth of the vegetation. Within a brief time at the start of spring, the landscape changes from a cottony white to a vibrant green. Life returns to a land where only the hardiest fools choose to live.

Steward entered the forest, walking the trail home. After a two hour walk, the duo came upon a babbling brook. Steward had stumbled onto this creek when looking for water one hot day last summer while travelling home from Dawson. He was the only person to use this trail to return to his cabin. During the winter months, he followed a more visible dogsled trail when traveling to and from town.

Deciding to take a break and eat some jerky, Steward led Honey to the creek for a drink of cold water. Honey loved the taste of the spring water, relishing its freshness. Watching Honey, he noticed flashes of gold at the bottom of the creek. Looking closer, Steward's heart skipped a beat. He waded into the water, picking up two gold nuggets he had seen sparkling in the sun. Steward was aware gold nuggets were numerous in fast flowing streams in the Yukon. He secured the two nuggets in his personal belongings, thinking of how surprised Blossom would be at his find.

Honey was enjoying this excursion, as she had been couped up in the barn with Baby Jack and Omar all winter. This was her first back-packing trip of the summer. Honey loved being with Steward because he was a good man who never pushed her hard. His kind treatment made being a pack animal a tolerable job.

Late afternoon brought Steward and Honey to the lake, where he stayed on a regular basis when travelling to and from Dawson from his cabin. Steward secured Honey to a tree beside where he planned to sleep. Many bears, still thin from hibernation, roamed the forests looking for delicacies like Honey to fill their hungry bellies. This was when Steward wished he had a domesticated dog, a pet who would warn him of impending danger while in the forest.

Steward built a fire, ate dinner, and sat close to his campfire. The nights in the Yukon can be cold, even during the summer months; sleeping outside in the open air always required a blanket. Just as the sun was coming up over the horizon, a flock of noisy Canadian geese flew over Steward, landing on the lake in front of him. He watched the geese as they foraged for food in the shallow waters near shore. Steward fed Honey the mash he had purchased from the livery stable, while he ate smoked venison Bev had packed for him for breakfast. Soon the pair were back on the trail, heading toward home.

When Steward was two hours from his cabin, Honey began to display nervous behaviours. She had picked up the scent of a predator which was following them. Steward stopped to listen. A hush fell over the forest, which was interrupted by a distant snapping of small branches and a large animal trampling down vegetation. Honey shook with fear, as the scent of the predator grew stronger. Steward tried to catch sight of this animal, who was cleverly concealing itself in the thick greenery of the trees.

Watching the treeline, the animal soon revealed itself; a large, hungry black bear. The animal stared at Steward briefly, then showing no fear, walked toward Steward and Honey, intent on eating his prey. Two successive gunshots rang out, as Steward fired his rifle, killing the bear. Steward felt he had no choice but to kill this majestic animal, believing if he had tried to merely scare the bear away it might have been briefly discouraged, but eating Honey for dinner would have continued to be on this hungry bear's mind.

Steward cut the best parts of the bear meat from the carcass and continued his journey home. Blossom was excited to see Steward, and had a story to tell, which would both surprise and delight him. Blossom decided to wait until eating dinner to share her news, wanting to see Steward's reaction when she told him about Rudy's return to the cabin.

CHAPTER SIXTY-SIX

Steward unloaded the supplies on Honey's back, which she had carried to the couple's cabin from Dawson. He had a secure location to house Honey while she stayed with them, as a wilderness setting was not a safe place for a pack animal to be. Steward and Johnathan, when he was at the cabin for the moose hunt, had made arrangements for Johnathan to retrieve Honey, as he needed her to complete some work around his cabin. When he was finished using Honey, he would return her to Dawson, where life in Bev's barn was where Honey preferred to be.

Steward finished what he was doing and returned to the cabin. Blossom had ventured out in the canoe earlier in the day and caught three lake trout. She had cleaned and filleted the fish and was cooking them for dinner. She couldn't wait to tell Steward about his wolf Rudy, who had made an appearance at the cabin while he was in Dawson. Steward had told Blossom about Rudy stalking him outside of Dawson and how he had run off into the forest when Steward yelled out his wolf's name.

Sitting down to dinner, Blossom told Steward that at daybreak this morning the huskies were barking loudly, like they were excited. After the barking continued for an inordinate amount of time, she got out of bed. She told Steward she dressed, grabbed the rife, and went outside to investigate the cause of the noise. When Blossom approached the dogs' yard, she could not believe what she saw. Rudy was among the huskies, tail wagging, socializing with his old friends.

Blossom watched, admiring the affection the wolf was showing toward the huskies. She eventually turned and walked back to the cabin, letting the encounter between Rudy and the huskies end on its own. Returning thirty minutes later to feed the dogs, Rudy was gone. Steward wondered if Rudy wanted to return to his old life at the cabin. He would leave his enclosure open to see if the wolf would return.

The couple retired to bed early. It was their reward, after being away from each other when Steward travelled to Dawson. The couple were deeply in love and even a short time away from each other seemed like an eternity. Their sleep was peaceful, as the quiet night allowed for undisturbed slumber until dawn. The tranquility of the land is what had drawn Steward here, to a land which time forgot.

CHAPTER SIXTY-SEVEN

The bright sunshine filtered in through the open window of the cabin. Steward and Blossom, typically up at dawn, had slept later than usual. A steady breeze blew through the tops of the trees in the forest, their new coat of leaves rustling in the wind. Steward pulled himself out of bed and dressed. He left the cabin to feed his huskies, walking past Rudy's enclosure. There was no wolf inside. Steward fed his hungry dogs, then returned to the cabin. When Steward returned, Blossom asked about Honey. With his thoughts preoccupied with Rudy, he had forgotten all about Honey, the donkey on loan from Bev. The couple laughed together at Steward's forgetfulness.

Steward ventured back outside to feed the donkey. As he drew near her enclosure, he saw large animal tracks in the soft ground which encircled the makeshift barn. Upon closer inspection, he noticed they were wolf tracks from a single wolf. Steward speculated it was Rudy. He wondered if Rudy had been around the barn because he was curious or because he was hungry. He thought of a hungry, domesticated wolf living alone in the forest. Would Honey be at risk, seen as an easy meal to fill Rudy's hungry stomach? Steward pondered what choice he would make if he was forced to shoot Rudy to save Honey's life. He would be aware of this ongoing situation, hoping it would not reach this conclusion.

Steward knew the ways of the wolf, believing Rudy's instinctive will to survive would return when the animal got hungry. Rudy's return to the wild could not be reversed. In a life-or-death situation involving Rudy, Steward would choose death for his wolf. Blossom also felt this choice would offer the best solution to this problem. Would Rudy become the hunted? Under the watchful eye of Steward, that decision may have to be made.

The early afternoon brought the sound of voices from outside the cabin through the open window. It was Johnathan and Shining Star, who Steward was expecting to arrive to pick up Honey. Shining Star embraced her cousin, Steward, always happy to see him. Blossom couldn't believe how much their son, Grey Eagle, had grown in just a few months.

Johnathan and his wife would spend the night, leaving in the morning to return to their cabin. Steward started a campfire. The two couples sat around the fire, enjoying the ambience and socializing. Steward explained to Johnathan, with serious overtones, about his wolf no longer being a captive animal. He told Johnathan Rudy's primeval instincts had returned, and he now needed to be viewed as a predator. Steward told Johnathan to not hesitate to shoot Rudy if he was posing a threat to Honey or his dogs.

The evening passed quickly. Shining Star carried her baby inside the cabin to put him to bed. The others sitting by the fire soon followed them inside, to get out of the chilly night air. A peace flowed throughout the land; a serenity enjoyed by few in this wilderness. Only the majestic eagle flying high above knew the true meaning of nature's mysterious ways in this land they call the Yukon.

CHAPTER SIXTY-EIGHT

An early summer heatwave settled over Dawson and the surrounding area. A heat dome was trapped over the Yukon, keeping temperatures near ninety degrees during the day for a week. Steward worried about fires igniting the dry forest. The vegetation was already dry from a lack of rainfall during the spring. Steward's father had told him about large, out-of-control wildfires which, in the past, had swept across the land. These fires had been started by dry lightning, which ignited the underbrush like kindling, catching the forest on fire. These fires had swept through Indigenous villages, killing many natives who were unable to escape the flames.

Blossom was the first to notice a change in the weather. A cool, north breeze lightly caressed her face. The cool air was a relief from the humid air which had haunted the couple for a week. Steward and Blossom had been sleeping outside, as the air inside the cabin was hot and stagnant. The distant sound of thunder caught Steward's attention. Flashes of lightning lit up the sky. Within a brief time, a thunderstorm was unleashing its fury upon them. Seeking shelter from the storm, the couple watched from the cabin as the rain pounded the dry ground with much needed water. This intense rainfall from the storm lessened the danger of the forest catching fire.

The couple had been living on fish they had caught from the lake during the hot weather. Steward knew meat other than fish should be on the couple's diet. The day following the storm, Blossom suggested they take the canoe to the beaver dam and harvest one of these mammals. An adult beaver would provide enough meat for a stew, with any remaining meat being smoked to eat another day.

The lake was calm; the waters were a turquoise blue. Steward and Blossom paddled to the beaver dam in silence. An overwhelming sense of loneliness struck the couple as they realized their insignificance in the enormity of the world around them. Reaching the beaver dam, Blossom took over control of the canoe while Steward readied his rifle. They waited patiently for a beaver to surface and reveal their location. One hour went by before the beavers felt safe enough to come out of hiding. They had heard Steward and Blossom approaching in the canoe. One loud splash of a beaver's tail on the water had sent the mammals swimming to safer waters, away from these intruders who had invaded their space.

Steward held his firearm ready, knowing he would soon have his shot. A young beaver suddenly surfaced, his head above the water. Steward took aim and fired, killing the animal instantly. The couple retrieved the dead beaver from the pond and paddled to their cabin. Steward would butcher the animal and Blossom would use the meat for a stew.

Being young, this animal would only provide enough meat for a pot of stew, any remnants would be fed to the huskies.

Neither Steward nor Blossom had seen any sign of Rudy. Steward hoped the wolf had moved on and started a new life on his own, leaving Steward and Blossom out of his life forever. This was an outcome of Steward's wishful thinking for Rudy, a faithful friend he had lost forever.

CHAPTER SIXTY-NINE

The bird song coming from the forest woke Steward and Blossom shortly before sunrise. The birds singing happily in the morning meant a beautiful day was in store for the Yukon. Steward noticed many noisy ravens a short distance from the cabin, the birds were scavenging on a kill left by a larger predator. Steward was curious what animal that might be, so he decided to dress and look. He was curious if Rudy was involved in this caper.

Steward left Blossom in bed, informing her as to what he was doing and telling her he would be back shortly. He left the cabin and retrieved his canoe. He launched the vessel into the calm waters of the lake, paddling his craft as close to the kill area as possible. After a brief time on the water, Steward beached the canoe on the shoreline of the lake. Many noisy scavengers were in the forest feasting on the remains of some unfortunate animal, a mammal who gave up his life to feed his fellow creatures who shared the forest with him.

Steward walked to the location of the body. The ravens squawked loudly, thinking this man was going to steal their dinner. He examined the kill site, finding the remains of a deer killed by a pack of wolves. Steward thought this eliminated Rudy as a suspect, as he would not be accepted into this established pack of animals. Rudy had the stink of human on him, not something which bode well in his favor. He would spend his life alone, never being able to live with a pack of wolves again. Having left few remains for the scavengers to feed on, Steward left the scene and headed toward home.

Crawling back into bed with his wife, Steward told Blossom about the deer and how the wolves ate the entire animal, leaving only bits and pieces of flesh for the ravens. The couple fell asleep in each other's arms, not waking till later in the morning when a knock on the cabin door disturbed their peaceful sleep. Steward and Blossom vacated their bed and quickly got dressed. Steward asked the person knocking to identify themselves. A dog started barking, which Steward instantly recognised as King, his sister Wendy's dog. Blossom opened the door to a smiling couple, as Wendy, Jason, and their son had come to visit Steward and Blossom. The couple had also brought their donkey with them.

Jason told Steward a lone wolf had been coming at night and terrifying his donkey, leaving its tracks around Omar's enclosure. Steward knew the wolf was Rudy, informing Jason his assumption about the wolf's identity was correct. The wolf had acted the same way around Honey's enclosure. Jason and Wendy spent a couple hours visiting before saying goodbye, wanting to get back to their cabin.

Blossom and Steward would spend the rest of the day replenishing their fish supply from the lake. The huskies were always hungry, never seeming to eat their fill. Steward and Blossom leisurely paddled the canoe close to the beaver dams. Steward, fishing with a line, caught his biggest lake trout to date near the rocky drop off close by the beaver dam. It was proven to be a good place to catch this prized species, the best tasting fish in the lake. The fish's estimated weight was ten pounds or more. Blossom caught three lake trout and numerous whitefish with her net.

Happy with their catch, the couple retuned to their cabin. The fish needed to be cleaned and Steward's prize lake trout needed to be smoked to preserve the fish as long as possible. Everyone, including the huskies, would be eating fresh fish for dinner tonight, a delicious meal to enjoy in a wilderness setting.

CHAPTER SEVENTY

The night sky was clear of cloud cover; the crescent moon shining directly over the couple's cabin as Steward worked on preserving his fish. The smoke from the lake trout drifted into the forest, catching the attention of an unwanted predator. The delectable odor of the fish being smoked, lured the animal towards the cabin. The wolverine stopped in the cover of the forest which bordered Steward's property, watching Steward prepare the lake trout. The animal's stomach ached with hunger as he came up with a plan. He would wait until Steward left the fish he was smoking unattended, then come out of hiding, rush the cabin, grab some fish, and run off into the dark forest with his prize.

Steward threw more wood on the fire before returning to his cabin to talk to Blossom. The wolverine watched as Steward entered the cabin and made its move, dashing out of the forest and raiding Steward's supply of fish. The theft by the wolverine only took seconds, and Steward heard nothing. After talking to Blossom, she joined her husband outside. As Steward returned to the smoker, he noticed a large piece of fish was missing, a section of lake trout had been torn off a larger piece he was smoking. Steward instantly knew who the culprit might be, as there was only one animal in the forest with the courage to raid someone's camp while they were nearby. That animal was a wolverine, the most feared predator for its size in the Canadian north.

Now, Steward would not be able to leave his smoker for fear of another raid by the animal. The wolverine was watching, hoping Steward would make the same mistake and leave the fish alone again. Steward and Blossom manned the smoker all night, preventing the wolverine from returning and stealing more of the couple's fish. Steward finished his work just as the sun was rising above the horizon, signalling another warm summer day in the Yukon. Blossom had retired to bed two hours earlier, promising she would be waiting for Steward to join her.

As Steward was returning to the cabin, he noted a small band of Canadian geese flying over his head, landing in the nearby lake. Joining Blossom in bed, Steward fell asleep in the arms of his wife immediately. The couple slept until after noon, when they were awakened by a loud crashing noise outside the cabin. Steward grabbed his rife and ran to the cabin window. An adult black bear had knocked over the smoker and was destroying it.

The bear had been attracted by the residual odor from the trout while hunting for food. Steward decided against killing the animal, sticking his rife out the open cabin window and discharging two shots above the bear's head. Startled, the animal ran off into the forest, realizing he had barely escaped with his life. To Steward, this incident was a reminder of nature's dominance in this wilderness and isolated land in the far north, a land which God forgot to civilize, left on its own.

CHAPTER SEVENTY-ONE

S teward and Blossom woke after midnight to the sound of a lone wolf howling. Steward recognized the howl as Rudy's, who was calling for a mother he never knew. Unknown to Rudy, his birth mother had been shot dead at the hands of a hunter collecting wolf hides to sell, their fur increasing in value as the interest in wolf fur soared. No matter how hard Rudy tried, he would never find his mother, leaving him to doubt if she ever loved him.

Rudy had been abandoned virtually from birth by a mother who found him too small to worry about, which bothered the wolf greatly. Steward knew Rudy was troubled, caught between two worlds, he found it impossible to decide which he belonged in. At this point, Steward knew he needed to leave Rudy to his own doings. The mistakes the wolf would make in his future could lead to his death at a young age. Steward accepted this as the probable fate of Rudy, his once beloved pet and sled dog.

Steward and Blossom, as well as the couples they knew in the forest would thrive as their futures held promise. Their families would increase in size as some of the women became mothers. With encouragement from Bev, the unofficial head of the family, the couples helped one another in times of need with grace and understanding. Respecting life and helping one's fellow man were two important prerequisites for a successful life in the north.

The sun slowly rose over the horizon. Steward opened his eyes gazing out the cabin window at the beautiful blue waters of the lake. He rolled over in the bed and hugged his wife tightly, wondering what the future held for them. A life in their cabin was certain, in a land the couple loved like their ancestors before them. It was a land known as God's country, where the spirit of their Creator would always protect them from this savage and unforgiving land called Canada's north.

QUEST
FOR GOLD
AND FUR

CHAPTER ONE

It was late spring in the year eighteen hundred ninety-nine. The Yukon gold rush was on, as men and women of all ages flooded into Dawson. Thousands of feet trampling the soft spring earth had turned the city into a vast sea of mud. Dawson was a scene of chaos. Dogs, pack animals, and men hungry for adventure filled the city, waiting their turn to travel to the goldfields of the Klondike. Many gold seekers turned their backs on the Yukon upon experiencing the hardships while working this land for gold.

Supplies from the port cities of Seattle and Vancouver arrived by riverboat up the Yukon River by way of the west coast. Loads of goods arrived daily in Dawson, delivered via large shipping companies filling a need to feed and supply the men and women with goods travelling north to the Klondike. The Canadian government had set rules regarding provisions needed to journey to Dawson and beyond. However, once these were exhausted, gold seekers needed to restock.

With wild abandon, would-be prospectors partied in the streets and saloons which blanketed the city of Dawson. Men lost their money, as well as anything of value they possessed, during poker games and encounters with prostitutes. Petty thieves robbed drunks passed out in the streets, rifling through their pockets for items of worth.

Joe and Mary were a young couple who found their way to Dawson in that fateful year, which ended in tragedy for many of the new arrivals. However, the couple's circumstance was different. Joe was from this area and knew people who lived here well. He had left two years earlier, travelling to Seattle where he met and married Mary, a recent immigrant from Europe. After spending time together in Seattle, Mary agreed to join Joe to travel to Dawson to live in the area where he had grown up. After arriving, Joe and Mary had received permission to camp just outside of Dawson from a respected elder in Joe's tribe, Bev. She had agreed to let the couple set up camp on her spacious property for the summer months. Bev was always happy to accommodate a wayward tribal member's return, helping where she could. Joe and Mary planned to settle in the Dawson area and search for treasure in abandoned or burnt-out cabins in the area. They planned on searching for gold nuggets in the numerous creeks which flowed through this part of the Yukon. An adventure for Joe and Mary, which had not been anticipated, was about to begin.

CHAPTER TWO

Joe and Mary had arrived in Dawson by boat, via the Yukon River. The couple carried few personal belongings but were in possession of a large sum of money. Joe had started a chimney cleaning business in Seattle and had saved a substantial amount of cash. Mary's father had sent her to America from Europe for a better life. He had given her enough money to make her life in Seattle easier than most recent arrivals to this new land. Mary had been staying with her brother, who had immigrated two years earlier to America.

Mary's brother disliked Joe simply because he was a native. Mary's brother was sure his father would feel the same way about the couple's budding romance. When Mary packed a few belongings and told her brother she was leaving to marry Joe and travel to Dawson with him, he raged in anger. He told Mary this was not what their father would want. He then turned to Joe, who was with Mary, calling him a heathen and accusing him of kidnapping his younger sister. He blamed Joe for convincing her to accompany him to this forsaken land called the Yukon. Joe took offence at what this white man said to him. With a closed fist, Joe hit Mary's brother hard in the face. A crack was heard as Joe's punch broke his nose, ending the fight before it started.

Joe grabbed Mary's hand to leave, as blood gushed from her brother's face. This event shattered Mary's relationship with her family, no future contact would ever be made between them. Her well-to-do family in Europe blacklisted her as an outcast, as they disapproved of her marrying outside her social circle. This rich white family did not want the blood of a native to tarnish the family name.

The ship left Seattle on a rainy afternoon. It followed the Pacific coast to the Port of Vancouver, where it was unloaded before returning to Seattle. Joe and Mary bought passage on another vessel in Vancouver, to travel up the inside passage. From there the couple would go over the pass and eventually make their way to Dawson City in the Yukon. The couple found little refuge on the boat loaded with people and goods. Travelers were forced to find their own space to sleep, which proved to be an improbable task on such a crowded platform.

The trip was long and arduous, but the couple finally arrived in the booming gold rush town called Dawson. The city was known as the gateway to Canada's north and a stepping off point to the goldfields of the Klondike. The couple arrived carrying their few meager belongings with them. With Joe leading the way, they walked to Bev's house. The exhausted couple were welcomed by their host and fed a wholesome meal. After dinner and dessert, Joe and Mary bathed and retired to a comfortable bed laden with clean linens. Their sleep was undisturbed till the first rays of sunlight shone through the window early the next morning. The reality of their new life in the Yukon was beginning, the moment upon awakening made this apparent.

CHAPTER THREE

Bev let the couple sleep, not awakening them for breakfast until after 8 a.m.. Joe lay awake before Bev's call for breakfast, the smell of frying pork greeting his sense of smell. He shook Mary lightly, encouraging her to wake up, as Bev's call for breakfast came from the bottom of the stairs. The couple climbed out of bed, dressed, and went downstairs to eat.

While dining, Bev talked about life in Dawson and how the goldrush had brought thousands of would-be prospectors to town. Chaos and unruly behaviour reigned, with over consumption of alcohol contributing to shootings and fights, resulting in many deaths on the streets. Bev warned Joe and Mary to stay away from the saloons, where shootings occurred daily.

Bev had a large tent stored in her house, which she lent to Joe and Mary until they could find more permanent housing, such as a cabin. After breakfast, the couple went outside and scouted a spot to set up their camp. Bev's home sat on fifty acres of forested land. The couple walked into the woods, until they came to a meadow where the first wildflowers of the season were blooming. As spring turned to summer, the field would fill with colour. Joe and Mary decided to set up their camp here, in the middle of the wildflowers. The clearing would give them an open view of their surroundings, serving as a deterrent against predators coming into their camp.

There was an ample supply of dry wood in the surrounding forest, necessary to fuel a fire for cooking and heat. Outdoor supplies, such as axes and saws were nearly impossible to buy in Dawson; the demand for such equipment outweighed the supply. Joe and Mary would use tools owned by Bev until they could purchase their own.

If they paid in advance, Joe could order goods which would arrive in four weeks by boat. Joe soon ordered a quantity of items needed for their search for gold this summer. Gold pans, shovels, saws, and pickaxes for breaking rocks were some of the items he ordered. He also bought two rifles, a handgun, and enough ammunition to get the couple through the summer. Joe would place another order for goods to be shipped on the last boat of the season to come to Dawson.

Joe and Mary gathered up the tent and set up their camp in the meadow. The couple collected large rocks and built a fireplace. This camp would be their home for the summer, but they would eat dinner with Bev nightly, ensuring enough nourishment to sustain their survival in this harsh land. Joe and Mary would pay a generous stipend to Bev every month for the services she was providing for the young couple.

Conversation at dinner that evening turned to the pack animals which lived in her barn. Bev asked Joe and Mary if they would take two adult donkeys, and their young son, to graze in the pasture of green grass and tasty wildflowers. The couple told Bev they would be happy to do this for her tomorrow morning.

After dinner, the couple returned to their camp, where under a starlit night their sleep was peaceful. The tranquility which surrounded them was a silence which could not be ignored, a Yukon evening never to be forgotten in a land of wilderness and inner peace.

CHAPTER FOUR

*J*oe and Mary slept well at their new encampment. A soft wind blew across the meadow, causing the window flap on the couple's tent to flutter in the breeze. The sunshine on the canvas made the interior warm. The Yukon spring was in full bloom, as the short growing season advanced quickly through the warm months of the year. Nature allowed man little time to finish jobs needing to be accomplished before the long, cold months of winter arrived.

Mary told Joe the soil in the meadow was dark and rich in texture. They agreed the area would be a good place to grow root vegetables. Bev had a medley of vegetable seeds saved from her garden from the previous year. She had offered to share them with the couple, if they prepared an area to plant them in.

Joe and Mary walked to Bev's house to pick up the pack animals from the barn. Bev accompanied them to the donkeys' enclosure and introduced Omar, Honey, and Baby Jack to Joe and Mary. The animals would be tethered in the meadow with long ropes, allowing them to roam and eat. Joe and Mary would prepare an area for a garden while babysitting the pack animals. Bev loaned Joe a rifle, in case of a predator attack on the donkeys while they were in his possession. Joe could keep the rifle until his supplies from Vancouver arrived by boat in four weeks. He could also use the gun to hunt small game, which was plentiful in the woods around their campsite.

In the early afternoon, Bev visited the couple's new home to help finish the preparations of their garden. With Bev's expertise, the job was finished before dark. This included planting vegetable seeds and watering the garden. The couple took the animals to the creek which flowed through Bev's property, allowing the donkeys to enjoy one last drink of fresh spring water before being returned to the safety of their barn.

With their work completed, Joe decided to start a campfire and cook some fresh venison which Bev had given them. A member of her tribe had dropped off the meat for her, as she was looked upon as an elder in her tribe and was taken care of by the younger hunters. These men supplied food she was unable to provide for herself. Joe and Mary would cook this meat and provide dinner for Bev tonight.

The smoke from the cooking venison wafted through the forest. A lone wolf watched from the shadows, saliva dripping from its fangs. Bev explained that Rudy, a previously domesticated wolf, was occasionally seen on her property. She hated wolves, but assured the young couple Rudy posed no threat to humans. She explained Rudy had been raised by her nephew, from a pup he had found abandoned in a wolf den. Rudy had returned to the wild after someone released him from his enclosure.

He had been spotted up to fifty miles away from Bev's Dawson home, roaming this large expanse of land and bothering no one. He was a wolf taught by the hand of man, not by nature.

CHAPTER FIVE

An old fur trapper, who was a friend of Bev's, showed up at the door of her house one afternoon. He had been trapping for thirty years in the Yukon wilderness. Leonard arrived with a strong husky named Rusty, who carried a pack of goods on his back. The last time Leonard had seen Bev was earlier in the spring. He had come to town to sell the fur he had harvested over the winter, and after doing so stopped to visit. At that time, Leonard did not tell her of his future plans, only that it had been a hard winter and he was glad the trapping season had ended.

When Leonard settled in at the kitchen table to join Bev for a cup of coffee, he announced his days of living in the bush were over. Leonard had turned seventy and appeared to be the picture of health, but his legs had been giving him problems. Leonard had saved a substantial sum of money over the years, trapping fur and panning for gold. During his life in the bush, Leonard had unearthed a gold nugget he believed to be the biggest found in the Yukon. He had concealed his once in a lifetime discovery in a special hiding place. However, his cognitive abilities had drastically declined over the years, leading to memory loss. Leonard could not recall where he hid the gold nugget but knew it was somewhere in or near his cabin. Leonard had already decided he would not say anything to anyone about this oversized nugget he had lost.

Leonard had family in Seattle and had decided to spend his last days in a more moderate climate with access to goods and modern conveniences. He told Bev he was leaving Dawson in a week and would not be returning. He asked Bev if she knew anyone who would like to take over his cabin. Leonard would donate the cabin and the outbuildings, along with all the contents. A prerequisite for this deal was the new owner would have to be willing to take his dog, Rusty, who would still live on the property he loved. Bev knew the cabin was on a lake full of waterfowl and fish and told Leonard she knew the perfect couple to take him up on his offer. She told him about the newly married couple, encamped in the wildflower meadow a short distance from her home. She said Rusty would be well taken care of by Joe and Mary, and if he returned tomorrow she would introduce them.

Pleased with this news, Leonard left Bev's house. He was staying at a hotel in Dawson until he finished his business here. Shortly after Leonard left, Bev walked out to Joe and Mary's camp to tell them about Leonard's plan. They could not believe their luck, acquiring Rusty would be a bonus. The couple wanted a dog and Rusty was not only trained but knew the property the couple would be moving to well. Bev told Mary and Joe to be at her house at noon tomorrow to meet Leonard and Rusty, the couple's future canine companion.

The couple's sleep was restless, as excitement mounted about their meeting with Leonard tomorrow. The dream of owning a log cabin was now a reality for the couple, a cabin in the wilderness they could call their own.

CHAPTER SIX

T he early morning bird song echoed through the meadow and the surrounding forest. Joe and Mary lay awake in the tent, the cool morning air entering their shelter from the outside. Mary retrieved a covering stored near their bed. The couple snuggled closely together under the warm blanket which was now spread over them. They fell back asleep in each others' arms.

Outside the tent, the day was bright and clear. A fox hunting for mice in the meadow managed to catch a tasty morsel for breakfast. The sound of bees filled the air, as the insects searched for the sweet nectar from the wildflowers to take home to their hives. Joe and Mary exited the bed, getting dressed for the day. The couple would soon need to leave their camp to go to Bev's house. She had told the couple Leonard would be joining them for lunch.

The meeting with Leonard went in the right direction from the start. Over lunch, a deal was agreed upon with Joe and Mary. The man happily signed a piece of paper which stated he was giving ownership of his cabin, the surrounding buildings, and all their contents to the couple. Rusty would continue to live there and be taken care of by Joe and Mary. After drawing a detailed map on how to find his property, Joe and Mary bid farewell to Leonard. He told the couple the cabin was a three hour walk from Dawson.

With their business concluded, Leonard said goodbye to his friends. He hugged Rusty, crying loudly. Rusty and Leonard had shared many adventures together over the years. This man and his dog would always share a special place in their hearts for one another. This was the last time Leonard was seen in Dawson, as a return trip was never in his plans. Memories of his life in the Yukon, and the secret from his past, now lay buried with Leonard, under the cold earth of his grave in Seattle.

Joe and Mary began to plan their move to the new home. They would use Omar, one of the pack animals housed at Bev's, to carry supplies to their cabin. Bev promised to take care of Mary's vegetable garden until harvest, once the couple moved.

Over the next couple of days, the couple gathered what they needed in supplies. They used Omar to transport these goods back to Bev's until they were ready to leave. Omar was glad to get away from his wife and kid, who he sometimes found overbearing. He was willing to give Joe and Mary respect, unless he felt they deserved otherwise. Omar heard the couple talking about the trek to the cabin and hoped there would be a secure structure for him to stay in while there. A donkey's scent to a bear or a wolf was an invitation to a tasty meal. A secure compound in the forest was necessary to keep the donkey safe.

Tomorrow, the group would be ready to leave Bev's property. A new family would soon become members of the forest community. Their survival would be a unique experience in a land which their Creator felt mattered.

CHAPTER SEVEN

oe and Mary were up early, preparing for the journey to their new cabin. Joe retrieved Omar from the barn and loaded the goods they had purchased in Dawson on his back. Mary gathered up their personal belongings and put them in two packs they would carry on their backs. A fond farewell and many thanks of appreciation were expressed to Bev from the departing couple. With Rusty leading the way, the group left Dawson for the wilds of the Yukon.

After walking for an hour, Mary and Joe reached a large open area, lush with green grass and bordered by a small stream. Joe decided to let Omar eat before continuing their journey. The donkey would be able to finish his meal with a drink of cold, refreshing water from the spring-filled creek. While Omar ate, Joe and Mary laid on a large flat rock, looking skyward. Wispy clouds filled the blue northern sky and the bright sun shone down, making the couple drowsy. Rusty lay near the couple, snoring in his sleep. Omar finished eating. His stomach was full, so he laid down in the meadow for a nap. The group slept for an hour, enjoying the sun during this unusually warm, spring day.

Joe woke with a start, having had no intentions of falling asleep on the warm rock. He had the feeling someone, or something, was watching him. He turned his head ninety degrees; what he saw made him feel his eyes were betraying him. Standing one hundred feet away, watching the group, was a lone, adult, male wolf. He stared at Joe before turning and disappearing into the forest.

Rudy had followed the group from Dawson. The wolf was curious. He recognized Omar from previous encounters they had had when he lived at Steward's and wondered where Omar was going. He had been discreetly following behind them. Joe roused everyone from their nap and the group continued their short journey to the cabin.

After a long walk, Rusty started barking excitedly, bounding down a well-worn path they had come upon. Joe sensed their destination was near. As the couple approached the cabin, a fast-flowing creek caught their attention. The creek led them to a pristine northern lake, surrounded by rock cliffs and green forests. On its shore sat Leonard's cabin, a pristine structure built and maintained by a man who had spent most of his adult life here. Leonard would always be in the hearts of Joe and Mary and his spirit would remain with them in this piece of wilderness the couple would now call home.

CHAPTER EIGHT

A squirrel on the roof of the building chattered loudly at the entourage who appeared out of the forest. Joe and Mary approached the cabin and noted the extra lumber Leonard had secured the door with before leaving for Dawson. Bears and wolverines were the two main culprits he did not want to let have access to the inside of his cabin. Their search for food could sometimes leave irreparable damage to the interior of a structure. Racoons and skunks also would call an open cabin home, using it for shelter when needed.

Joe secured Omar to a long rope and let him graze in an area of green grass which surrounded one of the outbuildings. He opened the cabin door and Rusty was the first inside, where a familiar setting and his favorite place to sleep greeted him. The young couple followed Rusty into the cabin. The interior was orderly and clean, attesting to the fact that Leonard was meticulous in his ways, a character trait not shared with most trappers who lived in this harsh land. Except for mice, there was no indication of any other animal using, or ever being inside, the building.

Rusty was already laying in the dog's favorite spot, beside the woodstove. Rusty was hoping Joe would light a fire, as he loved the feel of the warmth which radiated off the hot stove. Joe looked around the interior of the cabin, taking in his surroundings. There was a table and two chairs and a clean, comfortable bed, complete with linens, behind a divider Leonard had built. A fine woodstove with newer stove pipes was also an important asset, something the couple would not have to worry about. Leonard knew the importance of having a safe stove when living in a cabin in the wilderness. The stove and the fire contained in its belly were the only things to keep man alive during the winter months.

Leonard had built an additional structure onto the cabin, with an inside door. This is where he had stored wood used for cooking and heating. An added feature was access to the outhouse through the same doorway. Leonard had also told Joe and Mary he had built a smoker for preserving fish caught from the lake. Joe knew any game not eaten immediately should be smoked as well, as this practice would help preserve their food supply, especially during the summer months when there was no refrigeration.

Mary wanted to light a fire in the stove to get rid of the dampness which had settled into the cabin. Joe told Mary to wait until he checked the chimney. He wanted to make sure an animal had not built a nest, thinking the building was abandoned. Joe accessed the roof of the cabin by climbing a tree which abutted the side of the building. He scaled the branches until he reached the roof, walking across it to the chimney. When Joe looked down the chimney, he understood why the squirrel had verbally attacked the group upon their arrival; it felt it was protecting its property. The rodent had built a nest in the chimney, claiming this lucrative spot for itself. If a fire had been lit in the stove before all the leaves and sticks could be removed, the cabin would have filled with smoke and a fire could have ignited in the chimney.

The squirrel arrived home just as Joe was puling the last of the animal's building materials from inside the chamber. His resuming chatter toward Joe showed his indignation at witnessing the destruction of his home. Joe felt bad about the eviction, and started feeding Charlie when he could. Mary named the squirrel after he decided to stay in the vicinity, building a nest high up in the tree Joe had climbed to get on the roof of the cabin. Charlie made himself at home here, feeling he was entitled to extra attention after observing Joe destroying his home. He would become the couple's pampered pet and neighbour; a privilege Charlie would not be denied.

CHAPTER NINE

Joe started a fire in the woodstove and within a brief time, the wood was crackling and in flames. Wisps of black smoke rose into the clear blue sky from the cabin's chimney. A crow sitting high in a pine tree overlooking the cabin called out, letting his presence be known. Joe and Mary finished the tasks they had been working on inside the cabin. They left Rusty by the stove, going outside to check on the accommodations for Omar.

Leonard had told the couple there was a secure building on his property which was used to house pack animals who stayed overnight or for extended periods of time during the summer months. Joe had unloaded the goods from Omar's back earlier and the couple were now ready to show him his temporary home on the property. They were thankful Leonard had built sturdy buildings. His father had constructed cabins and barns for a living, allowing Leonard to learn the tricks and trades of building by paying attention to his father's teachings about construction.

Omar went willingly with Joe and Mary to his new shelter. The donkey hoped the structure would be strong enough to ward off any attack by a hungry bear or a pack of wolves waiting for an opportunity to make the helpless donkey dinner. This was Omar's biggest fear, getting eaten by a hungry wolf or bear. Omar was surprised when he saw where he would be staying, a well constructed building which would keep him safe from any predator looking for an easy meal.

Next, the couple inspected a storage shed with a spacious enclosed work area attached. Inside the attached room was a work bench, used to clean small game harvested from the forest. This room's primary use had been for harvesting fur from animals caught on Leonard's trapline. Before meeting Leonard, Joe and Mary had planned on doing some trapping this winter but only with a minimal number of traps.

The couple's next stop was the lake. Their new cabin was located two hundred feet back from the shoreline, a short walk from one of the only stretches of sand on the lake. These bodies of water were an important part of man's survival in the Yukon. Fish, waterfowl, and small mammals found here provided a plentiful source of food for the early settlers who lived here. An unlimited supply of fresh water could be harvested from the lake year-round. Along with many freshwater springs close by, the cabin would never run out of water.

Tucked away under the low hanging branches of a pine tree was a canoe. Joe pulled the craft from its shelter and examined its seaworthiness. The paddles for the canoe had been secured under the boat when it had been placed beneath the tree. Like his other possessions, Leonard had taken care of his canoe, knowing how important this small boat was for his survival. The turquoise water of the lake beckoned Joe and Mary to launch the craft into the lake. The canoe slid through the placid waters of the lake, geese and ducks taking off as it approached their fishing and resting places, disturbing the wild birds. Recreation, not hunting, was on the couple's minds as they quietly paddled through the peaceful waters of this beautiful lake. It was a piece of nature Joe and Mary could call their own, in this land of wilderness treasures.

CHAPTER TEN

The wildflower season in the Yukon was in full bloom. The early rains and warm weather in the spring had triggered an explosion of colour to sweep across this usually barren land. The bees, drinking the sweet nectar, and butterflies, attracted to the bright colours of the flowers, filled the meadows of the north with life during the short summer season.

Joe and Mary had decided to travel to an abandoned cabin Joe's father had taken him to when he was a young man. Leonard had confirmed the cabin and property were still somewhat intact in the bush, not far from his own home. He had indicated its general location on the map he had provided to the young couple. Joe and Mary were creative adventurers, who planned on seeking gold and other valuables left behind by deceased trappers and gold seekers who had worked this area in the past. They hoped to uncover dead men's treasures of nuggets, gold dust, and old coins, as well as pieces of heirloom jewellery won in card games or brought from the old country when they immigrated to the area. These men died with their valuables still hidden for safekeeping, never to see the colour of their money again.

The early morning sun promised a warm day, as the couple prepared to leave on their first adventure. Joe went to the barn and retrieved Omar while Mary prepared the supplies they would need for their journey. Rusty waited patiently to leave, following Joe around as he prepared Omar for the trip. Joe secured the cabin door, not knowing for sure when they would return. With their supplies loaded, the group set out.

From a distance, Rudy watched the procession disappear into the forest. After waiting an extended period, he walked toward the cabin. The wolf wanted to investigate this new family's dwelling without interruption. He sniffed around the cabin and outbuildings, paying particular attention to Omar's enclosure. The scent of the donkey sent spasms of hunger to course through Rudy's thinning frame. He was no longer the powerful animal he once was. Living in the bush alone meant he did not eat for days at a time, leaving him weak and hungry. Thoughts of eating Omar fueled the hunger-filled brain of Rudy the wolf. He left the vicinity of the cabin satisfied with what he had found. Rudy would return to Joe and Mary's cabin in a few days, when they returned from their trip.

After travelling along the treeline, Joe's party entered the forest. There were many grouse in the habitat they were walking through, allowing Joe the opportunity to shoot this fine eating bird using the gun he had borrowed from Bev. The trek to the abandoned cabin was not long; the group would find themselves at their destination at lunch time.

Omar and Rusty loved being on the trail together out in the fresh air travelling to unknown destinations.

However, Omar did have reoccurring memories of near-death experiences in the bush, which he could not dispel from his thoughts. But Omar trusted this immediate family to take care of him, overwhelming any illusions of harm that could befall him.

Rusty, who was ahead of the group, started barking. He had found an old trail and alerted Joe to its presence. Following it a short distance, they came to a decrepit cabin, collapsing and decaying with age. A slow-moving brook meandered beside the structure, its waters disappearing into the forest. Not prepared for the winter, the man who once lived here, a returnee from the Klondike, had frozen to death. His body had been dragged off into the bush to be eaten by wolves, another soul lost to the harsh realities of nature and its brutal treatment of man.

CHAPTER ELEVEN

Upon approaching the remains of the cabin, Joe and Mary noticed the vegetation covering the exterior of the building. The logs of the old structure could be seen through the vines that had crept up the outer walls. Joe tethered Omar to a tree which bordered an area of green grass, close to what was once a hospitable dwelling. The couple would set up their camp in this open area, where Omar was already eating.

After Joe and Mary's work was done, they explored the structure they had found in the woods. With only stories to believe about the building's past ownership and the purpose it served, the cabin opened a mystery which needed to be solved. Mary pointed out the chimney of the building to Joe. It lay crumbled and broken on the roof, its remains now serving as a home for nesting birds and wayward rodents.

The couple approached the cabin, ready to start their search for any valuables the man who once lived here may have left behind. Rusty reappeared from his exploratory mission around the cabin, where after finding nothing important he returned to his owner's side. A squirrel, sitting high in a tree, chattered his displeasure at Rusty's sudden appearance.

The door of the cabin lay open, as if with outstretched arms, willing the couple to enter. Over time, its abandonment had led to the decay of the structure. Animals had obviously entered the cabin, destroying anything intact looking for food. An old wood stove lay crumpled under logs which had fallen from the roof of the cabin. A colony of mice now made the belly of the stove their home. The inside of the cabin felt forlorn and desolate. Decay and rot were what the couple found throughout the building.

Joe, Mary, and their nosy canine, Rusty followed each other outside. Upon examination of the exterior of the building, they found evidence of wildlife living under it. Rusty seemed alarmed at the scent coming from one of the entrance holes which had been dug under the cabin. Joe and Mary would keep watch for an unwanted predator strong enough to harm Omar or Rusty. Joe suspected this home belonged to a badger, an uncommon, not so friendly mammal, who can be found in the north.

Having found nothing of interest, the couple returned to their campsite. They gathered wood for their campfire tonight. Joe had shot two grouse on their journey here and needed to clean the birds. The couple would eat this gift from nature for dinner. Mary prepared the fire, while Joe took care of dressing the game birds. With dry wood, the fire was soon burning hot, and the aroma of cooking meat drifted through the forest.

The couple enjoyed their meal sitting around the campfire, as Rusty was fed scraps of the cooked grouse.

Joe had brought dried food for Rusty to eat on this trip, which was not the dog's favorite, but he learned to live with it when there was nothing else. The fire crackled in the quiet night, burning down to its last embers, until only the coals remained glowing in the dark. A shooting star shot across the midnight sky as the couple slept. Their sleep was undisturbed, until the early morning light woke them at the start of another day.

CHAPTER TWELVE

oe and Mary were awakened by Rusty's consistent barking. Omar was calling out loudly, trying to escape his tether. Joe immediately became alert to the situation on hand, retrieving his rifle knowing there was imminent danger. The rising sun cast little light into the forest, creating only shadows which could be perceived as the enemy.

Joe told Mary to quietly stay where she was while he investigated the situation. As he peered into the early morning light, he caught movement in the forest one hundred feet from where he was standing. A dark shape emerged from the shadows. It was a hungry bear coming for the breakfast he felt he deserved.

Omar was in a panic knowing the bear's objective was to kill and eat him. The bear advanced toward Omar, ignoring Joe's yells to retreat into the forest. Two shots rang out from Joe's rifle, as Joe was forced to shoot. The animal fell dead, revealing it to be a young bear recently divorced from his mother, hungry and in need of a meal. The hunter had become the hunted, ending up as food himself for a hungry predator called a human.

Joe butchered the bear, keeping the most desirable meat for himself and Mary. Rusty would be fed his fill once the meat was cooked, an all-you-can-eat smorgasbord of an adversary who shared the forest. After the animal was butchered, Joe, with Rusty's company, dragged the remains of the young bear deep into the forest where the scavengers would strip the carcass of its bounty of food.

The couple prepared some of the meat they had harvested from the animal. After eating their fill, they rewarded Rusty with a large steak for being a brave dog. He had warned the couple of the danger Omar faced from the hungry bear who invaded their camp. Omar considered the whole ordeal as just another escape from death. Almost getting eaten by a deadly predator had become a common occurrence in this savage land in which he was forced to work. Omar knew someday his luck would run out, leaving Honey a widow and Baby Jack without a father.

After eating their fill of tender young bear meat, the couple continued their search for valuables on the property. It had been rumoured the owner had returned from the Klondike with a cache of gold. However, he had been unprepared for the harsh, almost unlivable, conditions of surviving his first winter in the Yukon. It was believed the former gold seeker died of exposure to the cold, taking the location of his valuable cache with him to his death. If Joe and Mary could be lucky enough to solve this unproven mystery, the couple would be well on their way in their quest for gold. Solving this forgotten legend was the couple's dream, a wish they hoped would not be denied.

CHAPTER THIRTEEN

The wild roses, planted a long time ago by a previous owner, were blooming profusely. The man had carefully dug up a specimen from elsewhere and moved it to his cabin. Over the expanse of time, the roses had multiplied, and now took up a large area of the property near the cabin. The pink colour of the flowers created a feeling of order and peace, which graced the abandoned property.

Joe and Mary re-entered the cabin. The couple pulled the fallen beams from the roof off the crumpled woodstove. Disturbed mice ran from the belly of the stove, running for cover against this rude interruption to their sedentary lifestyle. The couple searched the area around the stove, finding nothing unusual. A thorough inspection of the interior of the cabin yielded no clues as to how to solve the mystery which surrounded them.

The couple returned to the outside of the building, looking up at the vine-covered exterior. A bird nesting in a crook of the logs flew out of her nest, leaving her babies calling out for her return. Mary remarked to Joe how beautiful the pink roses were and how large of an area they covered. She reminded Joe this beautiful rose garden was planted many years ago, with just one plant which had flourished. Nature was the rose bed's guardian, not the hand of man.

The couple inspected what they had perceived as a badger hole, believing it was obviously deserted as the animal had not made an appearance since their arrival. Unbeknownst to Joe and Mary, the badger had returned home the previous night after a long absence. He was now sleeping peacefully in his underground den. Looking carefully around the exterior of the cabin, the couple again were left empty handed.

A steady wind blew through the treetops of the forest. The rustling leaves would not be silenced until the grip of winter returned, leaving the tree branches naked and cold, waiting for the return of life in the spring. Omar and Rusty were enjoying the sunshine together, lying in a warm spot dozing through the day.

Joe and Mary returned to their camp. They had erected a temporary canvas shelter they had brought with them on this trip. It served as a refuge from the elements, such as sun and rain. Today the couple needed to get out of the wind, which was from the north and cold. It was a change in the weather which Rusty and Omar did not seem to mind.

The badger awakened, coming out of his underground lair to the surface. He was shocked at what he found, a donkey and a dog sleeping in the sun and a couple of humans looking as if they were lost. The animal retreated to his den, not wanting a confrontation with these adversaries. The badger knew this unwanted company would be leaving shortly. He would wait them out, staying in his den until they left.

Joe and Mary would continue their search in the morning, before packing up and heading toward home in the afternoon. They had to prepare for their trip back to Dawson City, to return Omar to Bev. It was a destination Omar had been longing for.

CHAPTER FOURTEEN

The morning sun shone brightly down on the sleeping couple. The cold north wind had been replaced during the night by a warmer breeze from the southwest. Joe thought it was a perfect day to find the hidden gold, which had so far eluded these treasure hunters. The couple ate the last of the jerky they had carried with them from their cabin, their only readily available food until arriving back home.

Joe and Mary decided to follow the creek which flowed past the abandoned cabin. The stream was spring fed, originating in the higher elevations and ending in a distant lake. Such waters are where gold nuggets could be found. In the spring, the snow melt causes turbulent water to wash away loose soil from the banks and headwaters, allowing this precious mineral to be washed downstream. Gold nuggets could be found by panning in the eddies off the main current of the creek.

The couple had carried their gold pans with them and soon found an eddy to try panning in. Within thirty minutes, the couple's luck proved good. Mary found three small nuggets, while Joe found one large nugget, its weight comparable to Mary's three precious stones. Rusty, who had been scouring the forest for food to fill his hungry stomach, suddenly started barking. The dog was yards in front of the couple, pulling what looked like a leather satchel from a hollow stump.

Rusty had chased a squirrel into the opening of the fallen tree trunk. The small rodent was trying to escape being a meal for the hungry dog. Rusty's frame was too large to go far into the opening, but he had thrust his torso in as far as it would go. He latched on to what he thought was the squirrel with his teeth. When Rusty pulled himself from the tree trunk, it was not with a squirrel in his mouth, but a bag of some sort. Joe and Mary could not believe what they were witnessing. Was this the fabled cache of gold the man in the abandoned cabin had hidden in a hollow tree for safekeeping?

Joe went and retrieved the satchel from where Rusty had dropped it. The bag was waterproof and sewn closed. Returning to where Mary was sitting, he removed his knife from its sheath by his side. With trembling hands, Joe cut the bag open and poured the contents onto a flat rock. Gold nuggets sparkled in the sun, as well as gold and silver coins, both Canadian and American. Two pocket watches and some heirloom gold jewellery from England were also among the valuables Rusty had found.

Joe took the contents of the bag and buried them in their personal belongings for the trip home. The couple broke camp, joyfully loading Omar's back with their goods. The journey home would be happy, knowing the mystery at the abandoned cabin had been solved by a dog named Rusty. His new owners had been made much wealthier with little struggle, not a common occurrence in this land called the Yukon.

CHAPTER FIFTEEN

Much to the badger's delight, the entourage of interlopers packed up their camp and departed from the area. With Joe leading Omar, the group left the abandoned cabin for their journey home. The day was warm and sunny with a clear blue sky, not a cloud in sight. The mood the group was experiencing was cheerful. Even Rusty was enjoying the moment, feeling the happiness flowing outwards from the hearts of his new handlers. Rusty was openly trusting with Joe and Mary, who had fulfilled Leonard's wishes and cared for the dog with acceptance and love. This travelling group made their way through the forest, having no idea they were being followed.

Rudy, who considered this forest part of his territory, had been present in the area where Joe and Mary had camped. The wolf had picked up Omar's scent, his instincts telling this famished wolf Omar was prey. In Rudy's thoughts, Omar was no longer a friend, viewing him as food instead. Rudy followed the group from a distance, hunger causing saliva to drip from his mouth. The wolf envisioned what a good meal the donkey would make filling his hungry stomach.

Rusty ran ahead of the rest of the group, reaching the cabin first and announcing their arrival home with his barking. Minutes later, Joe, Mary, and Omar reached the cabin. The building looked desolate against the backdrop of the much larger forest, which stood behind the small log structure. Upon arriving, Joe tied Omar to a tree close to the cabin. Rusty was waiting for Joe at the door, anxious to enter the building.

Joe opened the cabin door and was met by a rancid smell. Mary had left some raw fish behind by mistake. The meat had rotted in the enclosed cabin, creating an overwhelming stench which would be hard to remove from the structure. Joe entered and opened the windows. The door of the building would also be left open to let fresh air enter the smelly structure. Joe and Mary took Omar, and with Rusty joining them, they went to the lake to watch the waterfowl for two hours.

The lake was an oasis of life in a forgotten land, a serene habitat for all the species of plants and animals calling this wilderness home. The couple watched silently as a beaver swam past their location, unaware of their presence on the shoreline. Rudy was watching from a distance. The direction of the wind was keeping the wolf's scent from reaching the beach, creating a dangerous situation for Omar. In Rudy's mind he could never eat his old friend, Omar, but unfortunately for both animals, Rudy's mind was following its instinctive instructions. Omar was only dinner for a hungry wolf, the donkey was no friend.

CHAPTER SIXTEEN

Joe and Mary, along with Omar and Rusty, returned to the cabin from the lake. Joe placed Omar in the secure location Leonard had built for keeping pack animals safe from predators. Rusty had joined Mary in the cabin. The odour of the rancid fish lingered inside the building. When Joe arrived, he suggested a fire should be lit in the woodstove, thinking the smell of the wood smoke would mask the remaining odour of the rotten meat which permeated the air of the cabin. If Joe was correct, the home would shortly return to its normal welcoming self.

Rusty curled up in what seemed like most dogs' favorite place, beside the woodstove. The warm air generated by the fire relaxed canines and sent them into a comfortable sleep. Joe wanted to retrieve the valuables found in the bush, and with Mary they would take an inventory of what they had. The contents of the leather case had been briefly examined when Joe emptied the waterproof case on the flat rock, close to the site where Rusty had discovered the cache. Joe now retrieved the valuables from under the bed, where he had placed them for safekeeping.

As he carefully dumped the contents of the pouch on the cabin's wooden table, a potpourri of items jumped out at the couple. Joe estimated there was an ounce of gold nuggets of varying sizes and weights, as well as valuable gold and silver coins. One gold and one silver pocket watch, likely won in a card game, along with gold and silver jewellery, completed this valuable collection of the man's personal wealth.

This evening a vegetarian dinner was in order, as no meat was available. Joe went foraging for plants and roots he knew were safe to eat, as this was the best time to harvest these edible gifts nature offered. The tender growths of spring turn into the woody stems of summer, if the wait to harvest such plants is too long. The couple enjoyed the meal, which included no meat, while Rusty was fed dry dogfood. He was happy to eat anything to fill his hungry stomach.

The couple retired to bed around midnight. The forest around the cabin was dark and silent. A low growl emanated from the back of Rusty's throat. Joe stirred in his sleep, unaware of what was going to happen next. Suddenly, the silence of the night was interrupted by a screaming donkey and a barking dog. Joe awakened abruptly and jumped from the bed, grabbing his rifle and bolting out the cabin door without taking time to dress. What he saw surprised him, Rudy terrorizing Omar. It was if the wolf had lost his mind, as he viciously attacked the structure. Omar, in a bid to protect himself from the wolf, had used his back legs to kick at the predator. Unfortunately for the donkey, he had kicked some of the boards loose, exposing himself more to the hungry animal who wanted to devour him.

Joe had a decision to make. He shot and killed Rudy, ending the life of a legend in Dawson City. Steward knew the implications a formerly domesticated wolf being released back into the wild. Rudy had reverted to his ancestral state, living wild in the forest, eating pack animals, and terrorizing men living alone in cabins. Steward would understand the need to end Rudy's life and the rogue ways he had adopted. Steward would always carry fond memories of Rudy, his once prized companion whose friendship he thought would never end.

CHAPTER SEVENTEEN

The morning sunrise brought the promise of another warm day in the Yukon. Joe buried Rudy in a meadow a short distance from his cabin. He erected a wooden cross to mark the wolf's gravesite. Joe hoped when he returned to Dawson, he would meet Steward at Bev's house. He would explain to him the circumstances regarding the wolf's death and extend an invitation to Steward to visit Rudy's gravesite.

Joe and Mary were preparing for their journey to Dawson. The couple planned to return Omar to Bev's house, where he would be reunited with his family. This was a reunion both parties were looking forward to. They packed some personal gear on Omar and Joe secured the cabin. Calling Rusty, who was off hunting in the nearby woods, to join them, the couple left for Dawson.

A lack of rainfall had left the land dry. Creeks, normally fast flowing during this time of year, were almost dry, as their volume of water was but a trickle of what it should be. Two heavy rainfalls would replenish the springs which fed these freshwater creeks, returning their flow to normal.

The group reached Dawson with no mishaps and soon found themselves at Bev's door. Bev was delighted to see their return. She told Joe to place Omar in the barn and then join Mary and herself in the house for coffee and a piece of berry pie. Joe led Omar to the barn. Witnessing his reunion with his wife and son, Baby Jack, was heartwarming. The donkeys were happy being together as a family once again.

Joe returned to Bev's house and sat with her and Mary in the parlour drinking coffee and eating pie. Bev made pies according to what fruit was available at that time of the year. Joe told Bev about Rudy's demise, after the wolf had turned on Omar. In Bev's heart she was glad this demon called Rudy had been put down. Bev's hatred for wolves was deeply entrenched in her heart.

Bev told Joe and Mary their camp in the meadow had been left standing to accommodate the overflow of guests who converged at her place during the summer. She asked the couple to stay for dinner and spend the night, either in their tent or in a warm bed upstairs in her house. The couple chose the latter, which would also include breakfast in the morning. They planned to give Bev a gold nugget upon leaving her house to show their appreciation for her hospitality.

Bev served up a venison roast for dinner. She had been able to secure potatoes from her friend who worked at the docks in Dawson City. It was difficult to find any vegetables in town this time of year. Over dinner, Bev told Joe and Mary Omar's owners were expected to arrive tomorrow to spend a week helping make improvements to the house and barn and then taking Omar home with them. Jason and Wendy needed the donkey to pack in supplies to their cabin for the summer. The couple were stuffed after a dinner accompanied with fresh rolls and a delicious cake Bev baked. Sometimes life in the Yukon was just too easy; visiting Bev's house was always an example of that.

CHAPTER EIGHTEEN

*B*ev yelled a fifteen-minute warning up the stairway to wake Joe and Mary for breakfast. They rolled over in their bed, the smell of fried pork greeting their senses upon awakening. The couple had decided to spend one more night in Dawson before returning to their cabin. Joe and Mary had promised Bev they would do some gardening for her. An explosion of growth in the spring helped the plants mature quickly during the short growing season this far north. This resulted in Bev's flowerbeds becoming full of weeds, hiding the beautiful flowers she had planted. The vegetable gardens also needed to be looked after.

The couple finished eating breakfast and then went to work in the yard. After spending two hours pulling unwanted plants from Bev's flowerbeds and garden, the couple's work was interrupted by the visitors Bev was expecting. Bev's niece, Wendy, her husband, Jason, and their young son, Kuzih, had arrived to pick up Omar. The donkey would not be happy to be going on another work trip so quickly, especially after his horrifying experience in the bush with Joe and Mary.

Bev made lunch and the group joined her inside the house to eat and visit. Wendy's dog, King, who had accompanied them, befriended Rusty immediately. The dogs were left outside to play and enjoy each other's company. Joe told Jason they would move out of the bedroom to their old encampment in the meadow to sleep tonight. This would allow Wendy's family more visiting time with their Aunt Bev. Jason told Joe that would be a nice gesture on his part.

After lunch, Joe and Mary walked into Dawson, a short distance from Bev's house. They wanted to check on the status of Joe's supply order and were disappointed that it wouldn't arrive for at least another week. When the couple returned to Bev's, they moved their belongings from inside the house to their tent. Joe and Mary loved sleeping in their encampment, as the meadow projected a sense of peace and serenity to the couple, allowing them a long undisturbed sleep. They would not wake till the first rays of sunshine announced the beginning of a new day.

Mary lit a campfire. They planned to cook the main course for dinner tonight for Bev and her family. While Joe and Mary were in Dawson, they had picked up fresh lake trout from an Indigenous friend of Bev's, who always had fish for sale. The couple would prepare the trout over the outdoor fire and then return to the house to join the rest of their new friends. Bev had agreed to prepare the side dishes, which along with fresh baked bread and pie for dessert, proved to make the meal delicious.

The group traded stories late into the night, a friendship growing between the newly introduced couples. At times, these new friendships last forever. Joe and Mary were accepted into Bev's extended family that evening, a privilege not shared by many in this unforgiving land.

CHAPTER NINETEEN

A scratching on the side of the tent woke Joe from his peaceful slumber. The early morning light cast a shadow of something walking outside of the tent. The nature of the walk told Joe it was a racoon, most likely on his way home from his nightly hunt for food. The animal was scratching on the side of the tent looking for a way to enter. After investigating the area for a few more minutes, the racoon continued his trip home by way of the forest.

Joe got out of bed and let a waiting Rusty outside for his morning bathroom break. Barking soon followed, waking Mary from her sleep. Rusty had chased an unaware squirrel, who had been hunting for leftovers around the campfire, up a tree. The squirrel's loud chattering showed his annoyance at Rusty for interrupting what had been a peaceful morning for the small rodent.

Joe and Mary packed up their personal gear from the tent. The couple were planning on leaving shortly to return to their cabin. They had said their goodbyes last night to Bev and their new friends, Jason and Wendy. The couple were not sure when they would return to Dawson, as shortly after returning home they planned a trip to an abandoned gold mine.

The mine had been blasted out with dynamite, leaving little to the imagination of the condition it was left in when the men who created it disappeared. It was rumoured that the prospectors had returned to Dawson with a sizable amount of the precious metal in their possession. The men, in a drunken state, had bragged in the saloon about a rich vein of ore in the mine, flaunting their gold for all to see. The prospectors refused to divulge the location of the mine to the curious patrons.

Four hoodlums in the saloon were outlaws, dangerous men from the lower forty-eight, here to make easy money, the criminal way. They followed the two drunken prospectors from the saloon, accosting them with handguns and forcing the men in a dark alley. The men were robbed of their gold and shot. They died in the alley, never revealing the location of their gold mine.

Joe knew where the mine was located. While hunting with his father before leaving for Seattle, the pair had come upon an anomaly in the mountainside. Large boulders were strewn about, blasted out of the rock. Joe's father had told him the landscape had been created by crazy white men blowing things up with dynamite. Later, upon hearing the legend, Joe knew the pile of boulders they had found must have been what the men called their gold mine. Curious about this story, Joe wanted to return to the area he and his father had discovered to investigate.

The couple and their dog, Rusty, left Dawson to return home. The day was cloudy with rain showers. The trio walked in stormy weather all the way to their cabin. Their home looked picturesque in the forest, as it sat lonely, waiting for its family to return. It was an oasis of peace in a hostile land.

CHAPTER TWENTY

After returning to the cabin, Joe and Mary decided to take the canoe and hunt for waterfowl for dinner. Many ducks and geese made this lake their home, and like most northern waters, it contained large numbers of fish in a variety of species. Lake trout was the most desired fish consumed by the early prospectors and fur trappers in the Yukon, whereas whitefish was the most populous species in these northern lakes. This fish was used to feed their dogs, but was also popular for human consumption, saving lives with its availability during the food droughts of winter.

The water on the lake was placid. The reflection of the couple paddling the canoe caught their attention as they quietly plied the waters. Joe was looking for susceptible waterfowl, who he could fall with a shot from his rifle. The warm sunshine and calm breeze made paddling the canoe across this beautiful lake a pleasant experience. The scenery surrounding the couple unmatched anything Mary had ever witnessed before.

Paddling the canoe close to the shoreline, Joe pointed out a large presence to Mary. An adult bull moose was drinking water from the lake. The couple talked of the massive size of the animal as they quietly paddled past the moose, whose uncaring attitude toward them surprised them both. Killing this animal during the summer months was out of the question, as there was no refrigeration to keep the meat from spoiling. During the winter months, a secure outdoor freezer dug into the ground by the cabin owner kept meat frozen and safe to eat all winter.

The honking of Canadian geese caught the couple's attention. The birds flew in from over the treeline, landing in the lake fifty feet from the couple's canoe. A group of fifteen geese soon began feeding in the shallow water, ignorant of the fact a canoe, with a man and a gun, was in their presence. Joe, taking advantage of the situation, fired his rife twice, killing two birds. The rest of the geese, realizing the danger which had been bestowed on them, quickly fled the scene. Their two dead comrades were left floating in the still waters of the lake.

The couple paddled over to where the lifeless geese lay in the water. They retrieved the bodies of the birds, placed them in the canoe, and paddled back to their cabin. Waiting patiently along the shoreline for their return was Rusty. The dog did not like to be left alone at the cabin, always thinking his owners might never come back, leaving him to die a slow painful death at the hands of nature. Rusty met the canoe at the shoreline with tail wagging, glad for the couple's safe arrival.

Summer had arrived in the Yukon. Wild berries were growing throughout the land and becoming a food source only available for a brief time during this season. Mary and Joe had picked a few while on their trek home from Dawson and were looking forward to eating them with the goose. The couple would share nature's bounty with Charlie, the resident squirrel, who also enjoyed this sweet berry treat.

Joe cleaned the geese in preparation for dinner. He lit a fire in the smoker for one bird, while Mary would cook the other inside on the woodstove. This amount of cooked meat would provide nourishment for the couple and Rusty for two days. The couple and Rusty shared dinner around a campfire, enjoying the quiet of the night. Only the mysterious song of a loon coming from the dark recesses of the lake broke the silence of the night. The call of the loon provided comfort to the weary souls living in this land of few rewards.

CHAPTER TWENTY-ONE

A gentle breeze blew through the open cabin windows, causing Joe to stir in his bed, pulling the blankets up over himself and Mary. He snuggled into his wife's back, pulling her close against him. The couple planned on getting up early to travel to the mine which Joe and his father had previously discovered. Joe told Mary it was a four hour walk from their cabin. The couple would camp one night at the location and search for gold the prospectors may have hidden there.

Joe exited the bed, leaving Mary under the blanket. He let his dog outside and prepared coffee for himself and his wife. Rusty's barking caught Joe's attention. He threw on his boots, grabbed his rifle, and went to investigate what the dog was fussing about. Exiting the cabin, Joe noticed a mist hanging over the waters of the lake. Further investigation led to the source of the problem; through the mist he noticed the carcass of a large bird. This is what had drawn Rusty's attention. The bird was a Canada goose, which he had apparently wounded when he shot the two geese yesterday. It had flown off at the time, but died later, falling into the lake. The body of the dead goose had floated close to his landing, attracting the attention of his dog.

Joe removed the bird from the water and would give it a proper burial later. He returned to the cabin and joined his wife for coffee. The couple decided to work around the cabin today. They needed food for their journey, which they hoped the lake would supply. Joe wanted to catch and smoke some fish for their trip to the prospector's gold mine, which they had decided to put off till tomorrow.

Fishing on the lake later in the day, Joe was surprised to see another canoe on the water. Joe knew the lake connected to another body of water, but never expected to see a man paddling a canoe in his lake. The man waved a friendly gesture at Joe and Mary as he approached their canoe. When the stranger moved closer, he introduced himself as Steward, the owner of the wolf Joe had shot. Steward told the couple he had seen his aunt, Bev, in Dawson, who told him where Joe and Mary lived. Steward realized he lived on a lake which connected to theirs, allowing him to easily stop in for a visit.

Joe told Steward to go ahead to his cabin, where they would join him shortly. The couple had caught enough fish for their trip tomorrow, so they turned their canoe around and headed home. Over coffee, Joe told Steward about Rudy attacking Omar's shelter, almost breaching his enclosure. Joe told Steward if he had not taken Rudy's life, Omar would have been the first of the wolf's many victims. Steward agreed Joe had done the right thing, shooting Rudy and ending his life. Steward told Joe he held no grudges or regrets against him, knowing Rudy had reverted to his wild state.

Joe took Steward to Rudy's gravesite. This interaction with Rudy's grave brought back fond memories for Steward of Rudy when he was his obedient sled dog. Memories of a past with his wolf occupied Steward's thoughts at his gravesite. He would never forget the love he shared with Rudy, his once trusted companion.

CHAPTER TWENTY-TWO

Steward was glad he had made the trip to Joe and Mary's cabin to view Rudy's gravesite. Steward's thoughts could now rest in peace, knowing how his ex-wolf's life ended and where Rudy's final resting place was. Steward was glad he met Joe and Mary and upon saying goodbye told the couple he would return for a longer visit, perhaps bringing his wife, Blossom, with him. Steward told Joe it was a short canoe ride across two lakes to reach his cabin. He mentioned to the couple he bred sled dogs at his property and if a need arose this winter where the couple needed dogs, or a dog team, Steward would be more than happy to help them out. Friendly goodbyes left the couple with a good feeling about Steward. Joe and Mary would accept an invitation to visit Steward's cabin and meet his wife and their sled dogs.

Joe lit a fire to smoke the fish he and Mary had caught this morning, which would take most of the day. After the fish was cooked, it would be carried as food for the couple's camping trip to the mine tomorrow. The rest of the day was spent organizing the needed supplies for their adventure.

The following morning was mostly sunny and warm, with a few wispy clouds floating gently across the clear blue sky. Joe and Mary were ready to leave the cabin. They had rigged a small pack for Rusty's back, making him help carry some of the supplies needed for this venture. The group left the cabin, hoping Joe's instincts and memories would take them to this hidden spot in the Yukon wilderness.

After an uneventful four hours of travel, the group reached the general area of the mine. Over the years the vegetation had grown thick, making their target area hard to find. Joe thought Rusty's nose might be of some help, so he removed the pack from Rusty's back and encouraged him to investigate the area. Rusty went to work, pursuing a thorough investigation leaving no stone unturned.

In short order, Rusty found what appeared to be a saddlebag once concealed under a rock, now partially exposed. Joe walked to Rusty's find and pulled the bag from its hiding place. He returned with the bag to where Mary was sitting. Upon opening the bag, a rush of disappointment washed over Joe's face. The bag was empty.

Joe and Mary temporarily gave up their search, choosing to find a site where they could camp comfortably. The couple needed to find flat ground away from the rock face. Their search did not take them far, as after a short descent they found an area sitting on the banks of a fast-moving stream. The couple had a good view of the rock face, which they planned to explore later today. Joe and Mary set up their camp, gathered wood, and built a campfire. After these chores were finished, the couple stopped for lunch, drinking the water from the spring-fed stream.

Studying the rock face, the couple noticed the afternoon sun's rays hitting a section of the rock wall. The couple could see a small opening in the rocks, which looked like it could be an entrance to a mine. This is not what the stories about this place had led them to believe. Joe, Mary, and Rusty were ready to go investigate these new developments to an old story. The couple hoped to not end up with the same result they received earlier, as two disappointments in one day would be unsettling.

CHAPTER TWENTY-THREE

Joe and Mary finished lunch and with Rusty in tow, headed toward the rock wall where they had made out what may be an entrance. Getting to their objective involved climbing around some large boulders to reach it. After scrambling up some loose rock and rounding two large boulders, the couple reached the opening to an underground cavern. Joe pulled some larger rocks away from the entrance. An area large enough to enter beckoned the young couple forward.

While in Dawson, Joe had purchased a torch from an old miner who had a claim in the Klondike which he abandoned. The man wished to leave for Portland on the next boat or barge he could catch out of Dawson, having soured on the idea of finding gold. He was wishing to return home, where he hoped his wife and child were waiting. He had crafted a kerosene torch which gave off added light, used for exploring caves and dark places. The man had carried this prized possession to Dawson when he returned from the Klondike and sold the torch to Joe when he ran out of money.

Joe lit the torch and entered the cave, followed by Mary. Rusty chose to stay outside and guard the entrance. After their eyes adjusted to the darkness, the torch revealed they were in a setting carved by nature, not man. The walls were wet with moisture, the air temperature inside the cave was cold. Joe and Mary moved down a corridor, which led to a spacious room. As the couple entered the room, Joe shone the torch, illuminating the walls and ceiling of the cavern they found themselves in.

What the light from the torch revealed shocked the couple; the walls were covered in rudimentary drawings depicting a primitive culture. In the room were common possessions of these Indigenous people who had resided in this area a long time ago. Among them were tools, such as ancient hand-crafted knives, instruments for cleaning game, and bows and arrows to shoot and kill large animals. This underground setting was not a gold mine but a place where the ancient people would come to find shelter from the elements.

Mary and Joe decided not to disturb the contents of the room. The couple would tell no one of this discovery they made, to save the cave from being looted by unscrupulous thieves. They would keep this exciting discovery to themselves, exiting the cave and concealing the entrance. Rusty, who was waiting outside for their return, led Joe and Mary back to their camp.

The talk around the campfire that evening was about their unusual find. The couple felt they would find no gold in the rocks they had investigated today, believing they had been looking for gold in the wrong place. The prospectors who worked this site probably never mined the gold they found, using that story to cover the real source of the precious mineral they carried to Dawson. Tomorrow, Joe and Mary would search for the real source of those men's wealth and solve this mystery with a cache of gold.

CHAPTER TWENTY-FOUR

The campfire snapped and crackled, the burning wood sending sparks into the night air. Mary lay back in Joe's arms, gazing skyward. What seemed like a million shining stars looked down on her. Mary's thoughts turned to her family. She remembered the anger her brother displayed when Mary told him she was going to Dawson with Joe and the threat from her brother about a permanent split with the family if she did so. The fear of losing Joe, which would leave her a widow, caused Mary to believe she would face almost certain death if left to fend for herself in this land of hardships, where survival was not always a given, even in the best of times.

The couple, with Rusty lying near them, fell asleep by the campfire. Rusty wakened from his sleep when a pack of hungry wolves howled in the distant forest. There was jubilation in their song, the wolves having just killed a deer, their favorite meal. Rusty laid his head back down and fell asleep, knowing the wolves posed no risk to the party he was travelling with.

Pleasant sounds coming from the bush woke the couple at daybreak. The song emanating from the forest was like a symphony, as if an avian band was playing their favorite bird songs. Joe and Mary rose from the hard ground and stretched their stiff muscles. The couple had wanted to rise early, as they planned on following the creek today, searching for gold. Rusty had carried the gold pans on his back from the couple's cabin.

The couple hoped to follow the water to its source, which should be an underground stream flowing out of the mountain. They left their camp, excited as to what adventures the day would bring. Rusty bounded ahead, surprising a squirrel eating a nut which had fallen from a tree. Seeing the dog, the squirrel abandoned his breakfast and scampered up a tree, while voicing his displeasure with Rusty for ruining his day.

After walking for an hour, Joe and Mary could hear rushing water, soon coming upon where the creek began. The water flowed from beneath the mountain, an underground river rising above ground and eventually flowing into a lake far from where the couple were camping. A large backwash had formed where the water escaped from being underground.

Mary was staring at gold, which shone brightly at the bottom of this clear freshwater estuary. The couple had found the horde! Now, it was time to harvest the precious metal. Using their gold pans, they recovered every glitter of gold from the creek bottom before returning to their camp wealthier than when they left earlier in the day.

The couple had no idea of the value of the gold they had found. Joe would take some of this treasure to Dawson, selling it when he went to pick up the supplies he had ordered.

While in Dawson, Joe and Mary also wanted to talk to Bev about wintering over another donkey. The couple would like to acquire their own donkey, instead of having to borrow an animal and be responsible for its survival while it was in their care. Joe and Mary hoped to find an adult donkey to purchase from the livery stable while in town. If successful, they planned to buy building materials to strengthen the animal's enclosure. If attacks by predators became frequent, the donkey would have to be boarded at Bev's, giving the woman a generous reward in gold for doing so.

Joe and Mary would leave for their home in the morning, spending one more night at their camp. The couple were happy with the results of their successful adventure, finding a cache of gold was not what they had expected.

CHAPTER TWENTY-FIVE

Joe and Mary followed the fast-moving creek back to their camp. The couple changed their minds and decided to pack up their belongings and leave on the journey back to their cabin this afternoon. Joe was elated about how lucky they were to have found the gold. He was now ready to plan a trip to Dawson to sell some of this precious metal the couple had found in the bottom of the creek bed.

The trip back to the cabin was not pleasant. The hot sun and high humidity made the walk through the forest difficult. Rusty was hot and thirsty, the fur coat he wore was better suited for a cold climate than a hot day like today. As a trained sled dog, Rusty preferred the cold and snow of the winter season over the warmer months of summer.

Upon arriving home, Joe and Mary opened the windows and doors of the cabin to let the building cool off inside. They decided to take Rusty and go swimming in the lake, where the water stayed cold all summer. This allowed for a refreshing dip to cool off after a hot day in the Yukon, like today. Rusty was in the water first. As soon as the dog realized he was going to the lake, he ran at full speed. With a leap which sent him through the air, Rusty splashed into the water like a kid on a rope swing. Following closely behind were Joe and Mary, with a bar of soap. Having a rare bath with soap was on their agenda while in the lake.

The trio stayed in the water until the sun sat low on the horizon. The couple returned to their cabin to retrieve the only other set of clean clothes they owned. Joe's supply order included clothing for himself and Mary.

The couple decided to sleep outside tonight, as they had a special place by the lake where they slept on warm nights. Having no fresh food, the couple ate what they gathered from the forest. Joe and Mary would resume fishing or hunting tomorrow for fresh meat. Joe lit a small campfire for ambience, looking forward to spending a romantic night with his wife by the water.

The couple watched as the sun disappeared. The loon called for its mate, its mysterious song echoing across the lonely lake. Joe had kept the campfire small, but the occasional breeze caused the almost dormant coals to reignite in flames. Mary lay in Joe's arms, savoring the moment of love she was experiencing with him. A loud splash from a jumping fish broke the silence on the lake. Rusty lifted his tired head up, wondering what the noise was. Hearing nothing more, he laid his head down and fell back asleep. The quiet of the night led everyone to believe there was only peace in the Yukon.

CHAPTER TWENTY-SIX

The loud honking of Canadian geese woke Joe and Mary from their peaceful sleep. A loud splash followed, as the birds landed in the lake only yards from where the couple had been sleeping. Joe grabbed his rifle, which was lying beside him. He took aim at the unsuspecting birds, discharging his rifle twice. Two of the birds lay dead in the water, only yards from shore. Joe retrieved the bodies of the dead geese from the lake. Later in the morning he would clean and prepare the birds to cook for dinner.

Joe and Mary returned to their cabin. The air had cooled during the night, leaving the temperature more seasonal. Joe called for Rusty, who he had not seen since he woke up this morning. The dog appeared out of the nearby trees, carrying a rabbit in his mouth. Breakfast by the cabin would be the end for this mammal Rusty had somehow caught. Joe and Mary had planned on leaving for Dawson tomorrow. Today, they packed the belongings they would need, while Rusty finished his breakfast.

The following morning, Joe secured the cabin with the extra lumber he kept for this purpose. With Rusty leading the way, the trio left on their trip to Dawson. The day was sunny and warm; the calendar had just turned to the month of June. Joe hoped the supplies he ordered had arrived and were waiting to be picked up at the dock. He was concerned about getting the new saws, needed to cut firewood for his woodstove. Joe had ordered these necessary tools and hoped they had arrived, along with the rest of his order, as there were no saws available in Dawson to be purchased.

After an uneventful journey through the bush, the couple arrived at Bev's house. Bev was always glad to see company and gracefully invited the young couple into her home. Joe asked Bev if she had enough room in her barn for another donkey. The couple explained to Bev that ownership of their own pack animal was their goal. Bev told Joe and Mary owning a pack animal and keeping it safe from predators was a challenge when living in the bush, but she had more than enough room in her barn to board another donkey. This was the answer Joe and Mary wanted to hear.

Mary told Bev they planned to stay overnight in the encampment in the meadow, as it was much easier for Rusty, who preferred to be outdoors. The couple left Bev's house and went into town, the gold broker and livery stable being their destinations. Joe had brought a small amount of the gold they had found in the creek to sell. The broker happily exchanged their nuggets for cash, paying them a fair price. The livery owner recognized Joe and greeted him and Mary warmly. The couple inquired if the proprietor happened to have a healthy pack animal for sale. The owner told Joe he was in luck; he had purchased a good donkey from a man who came into his stable just the day before. The gentleman was a discouraged gold seeker. His mining partner had been shot during a drunken dispute with a man with a gun, his life ending in front of the local saloon. This pair's adventure had been destroyed before it ever got off the ground, such was the way of life in the Yukon.

CHAPTER TWENTY-SEVEN

The owner of the stable took Joe and Mary and introduced them to Jake. He was a healthy donkey looking for a good home. Joe purchased the animal and took him from the man's stable back to Bev's house. Jake was placed in the barn, in an enclosure beside Omar and Honey, and their son, Baby Jack. The presence of Jake in the barn made Omar jealous. Jake was younger and better looking than Omar, and Honey had noticed the attractive new male in the barn. She was excited about Jake's presence next to her. Bev came to her barn to meet Jake. To Bev, Jake was another bundle of warm fur to wrap her arms around when she visited the animals in her care. Rusty and Jake bonded well, friendship and trust developing immediately between the two animals.

Joe and Mary left Jake in the barn while they walked to the docks to see if Joe's order was there. The dockmaster, a big burley man, greeted the couple, telling Joe his supplies had arrived the previous day and he had locked them in a room for safekeeping. Joe told the man he would retrieve his pack animal and return this afternoon to pick up his supplies. Joe and Mary left the docks and returned to Bev's house, as she had invited them to join her, Wendy, and Jason for lunch. An invitation for a meal from Bev would not be turned down by the hungry couple.

While eating lunch, Jason and Wendy told Joe and Mary they were getting ready to return home and needed Omar's services to pack in some supplies. Once they returned home with Omar, he would also be used to move wood from the bush to the cabin. When the trees had been downed, they were left to dry where they lay. Now they were ready to be cut into stove size pieces, which could be placed in a cart and pulled by the donkey to the cabin. There, the wood would be unloaded and stacked for use this winter.

After lunch, Joe and Mary retrieved Jake from Bev's barn and walked with him to the docks to pick up their much-needed supplies. It was never too early to prepare for winter when living in the Yukon. The dockmaster opened the locked door where their goods were stored with his key, and Joe checked his order against the manifest, concluding everything was there. Joe gave the dockmaster money for taking care of his order and making sure nothing was stolen.

Joe and Mary loaded their order onto Jake's back. Jake seemed quite happy carrying the load, putting up no fuss at being expected to do this task. Jake knew how it worked, the more cooperative he was regarding the job he was expected to do, the better he would be fed. The couple's first impressions of Jake's attitude towards work were positive. Joe and Mary felt the donkey would be a good fit for their growing family.

Jake liked how calm Joe and Mary were compared to the men who had previously owned him. He loved his new accommodations and Bev's welcoming attitude towards him. The donkey, much to Omar's dismay, adored Honey who was living beside him in the barn. Jake felt like a lucky donkey, an emotion a pack animal rarely experienced in this savage and untamed land called the Canadian north.

CHAPTER TWENTY-EIGHT

Upon returning to the barn, Joe and Mary noticed Omar had already left with Jason and Wendy. Joe unloaded Jake's back and put the animal back into his enclosure beside Honey. Joe would reorganize what they needed to take home and reload Jake's back tomorrow. The couple returned to Bev's house to accept her dinner invitation, which she had offered earlier in the day. They enjoyed coffee together before returning to the barn to pick up Jake and take him to the meadow where their camp was set up. They wanted to give Jake the opportunity to eat his fill of green grass before his trip tomorrow. While Jake was grazing, the couple planned on lying down for a nap. The day was sunny and warm, with a breeze blowing from the south, a perfect day for a nap in an outside setting with a backdrop provided by nature.

Rusty stood watch over his new friend, Jake, making sure the donkey was not accosted by a predator wanting to eat him. If danger became certain for Jake, the dog would alert Joe by barking loudly. The donkey ate his fill of grass from the meadow and laid down to let his stomach digest the food. Joe and Mary were napping peacefully, along with

Rusty who was sleeping with one eye open watching Jake. A feeling of calm and serenity had settled over the meadow.

A sudden honking from two excited donkeys made everyone who was napping stir. Bev was leading Honey and Baby Jack to the meadow to eat. When the donkeys saw Jake and caught the odor of the green grass, they got excited, expressing their approval by braying, waking everyone sleeping in the meadow. Joe and Mary returned Jake to the barn, not wanting to leave this virile donkey alone with Honey. After securing Jake in his pen, the couple returned to their campsite. Bev was still with the donkeys, watching Honey and Baby Jack eating the sweet clover from the meadow. Bev returned to her house to prepare dinner, while Joe and Mary stayed to watch the pair finish eating. The couple then returned the donkeys to the barn to join Jake.

Joe and Mary then returned to their camp to work on weeding the vegetable garden Mary had planted in the spring. The vegetable seeds Mary had planted were growing into healthy plants, guaranteeing a good harvest of vegetables in the fall. The couple worked hard in their garden, until they heard Bev yell that dinner would be served in an hour. Joe and Mary stopped their work, cleaned up, and joined Bev at her house for a visit before dinner. Rusty was also invited to join them for dinner, as Bev was making a special dish for Joe and Mary's dog.

Bev had acquired some venison, which had been shot yesterday, from the tribal member who was assigned to watch over her. As an elder of the tribe, Bev was granted privileges not enjoyed by other members of the tribe. An intermittent supply of fresh meat was left at her door, and whatever meat was left for Bev, she cooked. The meat she did not eat was fed to the poorest members of her tribe who lived in Dawson.

At Bev's insistence, Joe and Mary accepted her invitation to stay in the house with her tonight. She offered to prepare a hearty breakfast for the couple before they left for their cabin in the morning. They consented to spend the night indoors, as the couple occasionally looked forward to sleeping in a comfortable bed away from the insects. After dessert and coffee in the parlour, Joe and Mary retired to bed exhausted. They were looking forward to their return home tomorrow, to their cabin in the woods, a special place they called their own.

CHAPTER TWENTY-NINE

The couple awoke at the same time; a songbird with the sweetest voice was sitting on the sill of the open window singing its morning song to Joe and Mary. The couple could hear the activity downstairs, as Bev prepared breakfast. The aroma of fresh baked bread left their bedroom smelling like a bakery. A short time after the couple woke from their nighttime sleep, Bev yelled up the stairway, announcing breakfast would be served shortly.

Joe and Mary dressed and went downstairs to join her for the morning meal. Bev had cooked venison and eggs for breakfast. She served this delight with fresh baked bread from her oven. Rusty enjoyed a piece of venison for himself, fried by the cook to perfection. Mary stayed and helped Bev clean up the breakfast mess while Joe went to the barn to prepare Jake for the journey home. Thirty minutes later, Joe returned to Bev's house with Jake loaded down with their goods. The couple thanked Bev for her hospitality, passing her a gold nugget before saying goodbye.

The group of travellers left Bev's house for the short trip back to their cabin. Dinner tonight would be the game birds Joe was hoping to shoot while they were on the trail. The trek to the cabin was uneventful and Joe was able to shoot three grouse for dinner. With Joe's help, Mary collected the tastiest plants she could find on their way home. Mary would cook these gifts of food from the forest and serve them as side dishes with dinner tonight.

Upon reaching the cabin, the building looked forlorn and empty. Joe removed the extra boards he had used as added security when they left the cabin overnight or for several days. Mary entered the cabin while Joe unloaded Jake and put the goods he had carried from Dawson in the building the previous owner had used to process furs. The building contained a woodstove and a work bench and had a sturdy door, which protected the building from the outside elements. Joe then took Jake to his new quarters and fed him some grain he had picked up while at the livery stable. Joe would work on strengthening Jake's enclosure tomorrow.

With these chores completed, Joe joined Mary in the cabin where she had a fire burning in the wood stove. She would cook the greens she collected inside, while Joe cooked the grouse outside on a hot fire. They were young grouse, small, which Joe realized as he cleaned the birds for dinner. He had no doubt all the meat from these birds would be eaten tonight. He prepared the outdoor fire for cooking; the hot coals of the wood would slowly cook the birds to a tender state. This would be a meal unmatched in the wilderness, a delicacy enjoyed by few.

CHAPTER THIRTY

The smell of the cooking game bird on the fire was tantalizing the appetites of the young couple and their dog, Rusty. A fox looking for dinner, smelled the odor of cooking meat, following his nose to Joe and Mary's cabin. The fox watched as Joe cooked the last bird, hoping Joe would take the cooked grouse inside the cabin to eat. Then the fox would be able to look for any food left behind undisturbed.

The delicious aroma of the cooked gamebirds filled the cabin with a delectable odor. Rusty sat on his haunches by the table, patiently waiting for his share of the bounty. The fox stealthily walked through the area where Joe had been cooking. After a thorough search for food, the animal found nothing to eat. He returned to the forest to continue the quest to fill his hungry stomach. Shortly after eating dinner, the couple, exhausted from the day's activities, decided to go to bed early. Joe had Rusty stay outside to watch Jake until he could reinforce the donkey's enclosure, which Joe planned on working on tomorrow with Mary.

The forest was dark and foreboding. The sweet smell of donkey in the bush was a tantalizing scent for a hungry bear; a delicious meal for a famished predator waiting in the wings. The bear was not the only animal in the forest who was interested in Jake. A wolverine had also picked up Jake's scent and had arrived at the cabin before the bear. The wolverine had surveyed the area and concluded he could gain access to this prey, taking him to the ground and severing the donkey's throat with his powerful jaws.

When the bear arrived, he believed this prize was his and a smaller animal was not going to take his dinner away from him. The bear was young and had never come across a wolverine before. Rusty was sleeping soundly beside the cabin, his snoring indicated he had let his guard down and was not watching Jake.

The two hungry predators advanced quietly toward Jake's enclosure. Jake was sleeping soundly, unaware of the impending attack against his new home. A low growl came from the back of the wolverine's throat, knowing he had to challenge the bear for the prize. Thinking about the sweet taste of donkey meat caused saliva to drip from the bear's mouth onto the ground. The savage instincts of the wolverine took over. In a screaming attack, he jumped up and locked his powerful jaws into the bear's hindquarter. With howls of pain as the wolverine's teeth sunk in, the bear twisted around trying to get the smaller animal to loosen its grip. In the stillness of the night, chaos had broken out.

Rusty began barking frantically; Jake screamed in terror listening to these two predators fighting outside his enclosure. The bear and wolverine were locked in combat, the smaller animal seeming to have the advantage. Joe stood in the cabin doorway, rifle in hand, surveying the crazy situation. He walked closer, watching this fight between two opponents who were unaware of his presence. Joe raised his rifle over his head, discharging two shots. The startled animals, now in fear for their lives from a new threat, ran off into the darkness of the forest.

Joe was dumbfounded at the startling event he had just witnessed. He calmed his animals down and returned to bed with Mary, hoping tomorrow would be a less stressful day. However, that was a wish rarely fulfilled when living in this wilderness, where only survival matters.

CHAPTER THIRTY-ONE

The morning dawned cloudy and cool. During the night a late season cold front had moved into the area, dropping the temperature well below normal. Joe rose from the bed, shut the cabin windows, and retrieved a blanket. He laid back down with his wife, tucking the blanket tightly around them both. Rusty, who had heard Jake moving about, was now at the front door of the cabin barking, wanting inside. Annoyed, Joe got out of bed again to let Rusty into the cabin. This time Joe decided to stay up. For now, he would let Mary sleep.

Joe fed Rusty some dry dog food. This food was not Rusty's favorite, but he would gladly eat it during times of hunger. Joe dressed, wanting to go see if Jake was still frightened from the episode of terror he had experienced in the night. Upon arriving at Jake's enclosure, Joe found the donkey to be nervous and unsettled, pacing around his small pen. Upon closer examination of Jake's home, Joe found it to be unsafe for the donkey to live in. Not having the proper materials to fortify the structure to guarantee Jake's safety, meant the donkey would have to be taken to Bev's barn to be boarded. Otherwise, he might end up as dinner for some hungry predator living in the forest. Joe and Mary would return Jake to Dawson tomorrow.

As Joe entered the cabin, Mary reminded him they had no food. The couple decided to go fishing, using Joe's net to replenish their supply of fish. They needed to catch enough fish for dinner to feed themselves and Rusty. Any fish leftover would be eaten on the trail to Dawson tomorrow.

The canoe slid effortlessly across the water. The sky had cleared, leaving the sun to warm up what had started as a cool day. The couple paddled their canoe to their most productive fishing area and within a brief time they had six fish, enough to feed the hungry trio tonight and tomorrow. The couple decided to leisurely paddle around the lake before returning to their cabin. The rocky lake was big but not huge, covering two different habitats. Part of the lake was shallow and had a muddy bottom. This wetlands area harbored numerous species of birds and mammals. The rest of the lake, where the lake trout lived, had a rocky bottom and was deep.

Mid-June had arrived in the Yukon. The vegetation had grown thick; the trees bearing their full summer canopy. The atmosphere on the lake was quiet, the occasional quack from a waterfowl was the only sound to break the silence. The couple returned to their cabin elated at being a part of nature in this territory they called home, a small piece of paradise in an otherwise forlorn land.

CHAPTER THIRTY-TWO

After returning to their cabin from the lake, Joe chose to clean the fish immediately, taking the lake trout to the shed to prepare them to be cooked. Mary started the smoker and stacked wood nearby for Joe to use. Joe's plans were to smoke the fish instead of cooking it over an open fire. After the trout were cleaned, the smoker was ready. The constant smoldering of the wood sent columns of smoke drifting aimlessly through the forest. The smell of the cooking fish attracted a hungry fox and two ravens to the area.

While the fish was smoking, Joe took Jake to a meadow a short distance from the cabin. Here the grass was lush and green and would provide the animal with a good meal. After letting Jake eat for an hour, Joe took him to the lake to drink and then returned him to his enclosure. Joe gathered up the salvageable lumber he had stored for strengthening Jake's pen. As he was working on this job, he noticed much of the wood of the structure was rotten. Unfortunately, the shelter was beyond being repaired into a haven for long term use and needed to be replaced. He decided to use the decrepit building to house Jake for short term stays only.

While staying here, Jake would be under the watchful eyes of Rusty, Joe's faithful guard dog.

Joe returned to the cabin to find Mary weeding the garden. The previous owner had planted rhubarb and asparagus, which were both mature enough to eat. Mary was planning on making a rhubarb and wild strawberry pie for dinner, as she had purchased baking supplies on their recent trip to Dawson. After weeding her garden, she cut enough rhubarb to make both a pie and a pudding. With sugar added, the tart rhubarb made a delectable wilderness dessert.

The afternoon soon turned into dusk. Mary had baked her desserts and was waiting for Joe to finish smoking the last of the lake trout. The couple enjoyed dinner together with Rusty, who relished his share of the meal also. The rhubarb desserts were delicious, Mary planning to make more over the course of the summer.

The evening sky was black, as a threatening cloud cover had moved into the area. Crashes of thunder and flashes of lightning sent Rusty running for cover. Soon rain poured down on the cabin, causing a cascade of water to run off the roof. After expending a short burst of energy, the storm exited the area as quickly as it had begun. A sudden peace swept over the forest, only the water dripping from the trees could be heard.

Joe put Rusty outside to stand guard, keeping watch over Jake. Joe and Mary went to bed, hoping to get a good night's sleep before their trip to Dawson in the morning. A pack of wolves, attracted by Jake's scent, were on their way to Joe and Mary's cabin. The wolves had not eaten in days and were famished. The pack arrived at the cabin, surveying the situation. Rusty lay asleep by the cabin, allowing the six wolves to surround Jake's enclosure quietly, not waking the sleeping donkey. On the alpha wolf's command, the pack members simultaneously attacked Jake's structure. The terrified donkey, realizing he was under attack again, cried out in terror. Rusty's barking and Jake's bellowing sent Joe into an adrenaline-fueled rage. With no remorse, he shot to kill, unloading six rounds into the center of the wolf pack. Joe closed the cabin door. He would pick up the bodies in the morning.

CHAPTER THIRTY-THREE

Joe awoke with a sense of panic, as he realized he had fired aimlessly into the pack of wolves in a fit of anger. He was concerned Jake might have been hit in the barrage of gunfire. He woke Mary and told her he was getting dressed to see what carnage he had created last night with his rifle. He opened the cabin door, allowing Rusty access to the inside of the building. When Joe looked at Jake's pen, he understood why Rusty was in such a hurry to get inside, as three dead wolves lay beside Jake's enclosure. Joe walked closer calling out for Jake. An eerie silence answered. Joe realized at that time what he had done; he had shot Jake.

Upon entering the building, Jake lay dead on the ground of his enclosure. Jake had been standing in the wrong place at the wrong time. A bullet from Joe's rifle had blown apart the rotten wood and entered Jake's heart, killing him instantly. Joe lowered his head in shame, blaming himself for Jake's death. He realized he could never take back what happened to Jake and the vision of him laying dead on the ground would haunt Joe forever.

Joe returned to the cabin, telling Mary what happened to Jake. Mary consoled her husband the best she knew how.

She tried to convince her husband that sometimes in life mistakes were made and lives were lost. It was just a part of the larger picture called life. Unfortunately for Jake, the only means of disposing of a body this large in the wilderness was letting the corpse be devoured by scavengers. Mary told Joe she would help him move Jake's body to a desolate location far from the cabin.

On the other hand, the fur from the dead wolves was valuable. Joe would tan the wolf hides and sell them this winter in Dawson. He had been considering running a trapline this winter. If Steward had an extra husky, he would borrow the dog from Steward and pay him a rental fee. Rusty would need help pulling the small dogsled which was stored in the fur processing shed.

The couple's entire day was spent taking care of the disposal of the remains of the dead animals. It was a day steeped in stress, reminding the couple nature was not always on their side, delivering a blow when it was least expected. These were the ways of the Yukon.

CHAPTER THIRTY-FOUR

Joe rolled over in bed and opened his eyes. The sun was just rising over the horizon, marking the beginning of another day. The sound of honking geese flying over the cabin caught Joe's attention. He had noticed many baby geese on the lake with their parents and had decided he would refrain from shooting the adult waterfowl until the young birds were grown and no longer in need of care.

A feeling of loss filled the cabin with grief. Rusty, now aware Jake was gone, also harbored a sadness in his heart. The dog moped by the fireplace, his head on his paws and his straightforward gaze unbroken. Joe called to Mary, waking her from her sleep. He told her under no circumstances would he allow any pack animals to stay in Jake's old enclosure in the future. He told her he would prefer to tear down the structure because most of the wood was rotten and he feared it would fall down this winter during a blizzard. If left standing, this old building would always remind Joe of the horrible mistake he made on that tragic night, when Jake lost his life. He wanted the old building gone as soon as possible.

When Mary was up and dressed, the couple decided to go out on the lake with the canoe to harvest something to eat. They also needed to secure food for Rusty, who was hungry and grumpy. They went to the shallow end of the lake where Joe had seen an abundance of muskrat, their homes like straw houses sitting on top of the water surrounded by the beaver dam. This small mammal was Joe and Mary's prey, as muskrats can be eaten as food and their undamaged fur can be sold in Dawson. Joe would try to shoot these animals in the head, so as not to damage their hides.

The beavers who lived in this part of the lake had built a large dam and did not like sharing their territory with the muskrats. They viewed these smaller animals as freeloaders and would prefer to rid their pond of all of them. Joe and Mary paddled the canoe to the beaver area, the over population of muskrats evident upon their arrival. One hour later, Joe had shot six muskrats, four of them dead from bullet wounds to the head. The couple returned to the cabin with the meat and fur. Joe gutted the muskrats and harvested their meat, with any parts deemed inedible for humans saved for Rusty. The choice meat would be fried on the cookstove by Mary. Joe would work on tanning the muskrat pelts later in the day.

Joe and Mary spent the afternoon tearing down Jake's old living quarters. They separated the good wood from the bad, with the latter set aside for use in the campfire and smoker. The structure came down easily and by early afternoon the job was almost completed. Only the four original corner posts were left standing. Joe pulled on the first post, which was rotten and broke off at the ground. The second post, being more solid and with little rot, had to be dug out. After digging around the post and pulling the rocks away which surrounded the wood, Joe and Mary were able to free the post and pull it from its confines. Joe happened to look down into the hole the post had come out of, shocked to see the top of a metal box.

His heart pounding with excitement, Joe called Mary to come see what he had discovered. A half-hour later, after digging to make the hole larger, Joe pulled a small metal box out of the ground. He sat down and handed it to Mary to open. She did so with no hesitation, like a child opening a gift at Christmas. Inside the box were five, twenty-dollar gold pieces, the old trapper's take for the fur he had caught during a past winter season. It had been buried long ago in a place forgotten by a man who had succumbed to senility, a trapper's curse in this northern wilderness.

CHAPTER THIRTY-FIVE

Joe and Mary returned to their cabin, with Mary carrying the gold coins clutched tightly in her hands. There was more gold to be found on the property. The extra-large gold nugget Leonard had hidden was still lost, waiting to be found. However, the story about a nugget said to be the largest ever discovered in the Yukon could just be a tale thought up by the mind of a senile man who spent too much time living alone in the bush.

Mary went inside the cabin to start cooking the muskrat meat, while Joe cut up some of the lumber from Jake's old enclosure. He planned on having a campfire tonight, as it had been a beautiful afternoon and Joe expected the evening to be the same. Joe and Mary, with Rusty's help, ate all the meat Mary had prepared on the stove. The muskrat had a potent smell and a strong flavor, unlike any other meat found in the forest.

After dinner was finished, Mary brought out rhubarb pudding for dessert. Joe suggested he start the campfire and they could eat the pudding later, outside under the stars, and Mary agreed. Rusty was lying by the cold campfire waiting for Joe to light it. He loved the feel of the warm air on his fur coat, regardless of the temperature outside.

The night was dark, only the moonlight shone down casting shadows into the forest. The couple sat in silence enjoying a moment of peace which nature provided them. The campfire crackled, sending sparks high into the night sky. Mary retrieved the rhubarb pudding from the house and the couple ate their dessert, enjoying it immensely. Jake's demise still saddened Joe greatly. He could have used Jake for several jobs this summer, the most important of which was hauling wood from the bush to the cabin. Joe would have to find other means to solve the problems he had created for himself.

Around midnight, the call of a loon echoed across the silent lake. Seconds later, the call was answered by a second loon. It was the bird's mate, lost in the darkness on the opposite shore of the lake. This exchange by the loons was a cue for the couple to retire to bed; they took Rusty inside the cabin with them. A peaceful sleep was expected by the couple after such a relaxing evening. At times, living here seemed so carefree and easy. However, one should not be fooled by this way of thinking, as the Yukon can take one's life and show no empathy at any time.

CHAPTER THIRTY-SIX

One day in mid-July, heavy rain falling on the roof of the cabin woke the couple from their peaceful sleep. Intense thunder and lightning accompanied this unexpected storm. Joe and Mary lay in each other's arms, listening to the thunder moving off into the distance. The rain gradually dissipated, as the clouds moved out of the area. Mary was thankful for the rain, her garden would love this gift of nourishment nature provided to her thirsty plants.

The sun shone down on the cabin, drying the roof and the surrounding forest with its warm brightness. The couple rose from their bed. Joe let Rusty outside, while Mary lit a fire in the woodstove, hoping to take the dampness out of the cabin which had been caused by the thunderstorm. Shortly before noon, the couple were surprised to hear a shout of greeting.

Looking out the door, Joe was happy to see Steward, who had stopped by for a visit on his way to Dawson to return Omar to Bev's house. Steward had been using the donkey to help with some work around his property. Joe invited his friend in for coffee, which Steward readily accepted. Steward brought a gift of smoked venison for Joe and Mary.

He had shot the animal two days earlier and had smoked all the meat to preserve it. Mary asked about Steward's wife, Blossom, who had stayed home to look after the sled dogs.

Joe told Steward about the tragedy involving Jake. Steward told Joe it was difficult to keep pack animals alive in the bush and he had lost two donkeys to wolves in the last ten years. He shared he no longer liked to keep any pack animals overnight at his cabin, fearing attacks by predators in the middle of the night. Joe told Steward he needed the services of a pack animal to help him haul wood which the previous owner had cut, but left in the forest. Leonard had told Joe and Mary about the wood he had felled and left in the bush when the couple agreed to take his cabin and make it their home.

After thinking about it for a moment, Steward offered to assist Joe move the timber with the help of Omar. The two of them could work on this project this afternoon, and Steward could spend the night and finish the job in the morning. Omar would be safe locked in the fur shed overnight with a bucket of Jake's leftover oats and Rusty to keep him company. Agreeing to this plan, Joe and Steward got to work.

Leonard had marked the locations of the fallen timber he had readied to be pulled out of the bush. Omar would pull these small and medium size logs back to the cabin, where they would be cut up into smaller pieces for use in the woodstove this winter. The men and Omar worked on this job with Rusty accompanying them, while Mary went fishing for dinner. After Mary's late afternoon return from the lake with fish, Steward and Joe quit their work for the day. Three hours of labor in the morning would finish the job.

Joe took the fish from Mary, and with Steward's help, cleaned and prepared the fish for dinner. Steward offered to cook the lake trout over the campfire. His expertise in this type of cooking could not be denied. The fish was cooked with some young vegetables harvested from Mary's garden, making for a delicious meal. The evening was peaceful, with the full moon shining down on this wilderness land, a light from God symbolizing peace to all who live here.

CHAPTER THIRTY-SEVEN

Over the course of the evening, Joe and Steward talked about the dog Joe wanted to use this winter. Steward told Joe one of his younger huskies, who he had raised and trained, was ready to be used as a sled dog. Steward said he was a strong dog with a good temperament and would be a good match to work with Rusty this winter. Joe said he would come to Steward's cabin and pick up the dog in the late fall.

Neither Joe nor Mary had ever met Steward's wife, Blossom, or seen their cabin and property. Steward felt it was time for them to come to visit and spend the night, knowing Blossom would love meeting new friends. Joe offered to return Omar to Bev's house, feeling it would only be fair as Steward had helped him gather the felled logs. Steward thanked Joe, happy to take him up on that offer.

In the morning, shortly after their work was done, Steward left for home. Blossom would be surprised when he returned to home early, believing his trip to Dawson would take much longer. Blossom was happy to learn Mary and Joe were taking Omar to Bev's house. She was also pleased to hear Joe and Mary were coming to visit, looking forward to finally meeting the man who had shot Rudy.

The sound of birds singing early in the morning filled the forest with sound. Mary rose from the bed first, followed a short time later by Joe. The couple were planning to leave the cabin early today to return Omar to Dawson City. After eating a quick breakfast, Joe retrieved Omar from the fur shed where he had spent another quiet night. With Rusty in tow, Joe and Omar returned to the cabin. Within a brief time, Mary was ready to leave. She had packed food and a change of clothes for each of them.

Joe had taken the wolf hides and muskrat pelts he had in the fur shed and secured them to the back of a not so happy donkey. Omar would have to live with the smell of wolf accompanying him until the hides were removed from his back when they reached Bev's house. Joe secured the cabin door and with Rusty leading the way, the travellers hit the trail to Dawson.

After travelling a short distance, Rusty, who was further down the trail, started barking loudly. Joe detected from his bark he was in some type of distress. He found Rusty at the bottom of a tree, barking loudly at a porcupine in the higher branches. Rusty had received a gift from this mammal, three quills protruding from Rusty's lip. Joe pulled Rusty back from the tree and inspected his face. The quills in the dog's mouth would have to wait to be removed at Bev's house, where there were tools he could use to remove them safely.

The remainder of the couple's journey was uneventful; the group reaching Bev's house shortly after lunch. They returned Omar to the barn, where Joe unloaded the furs from the donkey's back and hung them over the railing of an empty enclosure. Later, he would show Bev the gift the couple were giving her. The hides of the wolves were of high value, as the rage sweeping Europe created great demand for such fur.

Joe and Mary went to the house, where a surprised Bev greeted the couple warmly, telling them she expected to see Steward accompanying Omar. Mary explained to Bev how they happened to be returning him. Bev thought Joe had made a fair deal with Steward regarding the donkey. She told Joe she was sure Omar was glad to be home, where the donkey felt safe and loved. Omar was back in the company of his wife and son, his family together once more.

CHAPTER THIRTY-EIGHT

Joe took Rusty to Bev's outside workshop, which her husband had built. After her husband died, Bev kept all his tools and his workshop in good order. Joe knelt close to Rusty and within minutes he had removed the porcupine quills from the dog's lip. Rusty ran off, no longer annoyed by the pain which had emanated from his mouth.

Joe and Mary joined Bev in her house. They told Bev about Joe's unfortunate incident regarding Jake, their deceased pack animal. Bev told Joe not to blame himself for Jake's death, explaining accidents happen when decisions are made during the chaos of the moment. She fed Joe and Mary a late lunch, which was appreciated by the hungry couple who had not eaten since early morning. Bev also invited the two of them to stay for dinner and the night, sleeping in a nice warm bed upstairs. The couple graciously accepted her kind offer.

Joe told Bev he had brought some animal pelts with him from his cabin. She followed the couple to the barn, where she was shown the wolf and muskrat pelts. Mary told Bev all the pelts were hers. Bev told the couple the furs would be donated to the leaders of the Indigenous tribe she belonged to. The hides would be sold, and the money used to help the poorest members of her tribe who lived in this area.

While in the barn, the group went to visit the donkeys. The animals were glad to see the people who kept them fed and safe from harm. Joe and Mary headed into Dawson to buy two commodities they were running short of, coffee and sugar. While in town, they stopped at the livery stable and picked up oats for the three donkeys living in Bev's barn. This was a treat the animals would not be expecting.

Dawson was crowded with people, largely gold seekers ready to risk their lives for that precious yellow metal. Most of these men were homeless and had nowhere to go. They slept on the streets of Dawson, a dangerous and dirty place. Joe and Mary walked back to Bev's house, a sanctuary outside the hell's pit of humanity living in Dawson City.

Bev was cooking dinner; moose steak and fresh, early vegetables from her garden were on the menu. Rusty would be sharing this meal with his human companions tonight. Berry pie was in the oven for dessert, along with Bev's baked bread to be eaten with dinner. Bev's dinners were like an all-you-can-eat buffet, no one ever left her kitchen table hungry.

After a delicious meal, which left the participants feeling full with no room in their stomachs for any more food, sleep would come easily. This is how Joe and Mary went upstairs feeling. The comfortable bed they were sleeping in tonight helped them drift off almost as soon as their heads hit the pillows. The couple enjoyed a night of quiet peace, which would not be disturbed till sunrise of the following morning.

CHAPTER THIRTY-NINE

Joe awoke to a light rain falling outside, hoping the skies would soon clear and become sunny. The couple, with Rusty in tow, were planning on leaving Bev's this morning and returning to their cabin. The smell of food cooking downstairs drew Joe's attention. He woke Mary, knowing soon Bev would be calling them to eat breakfast. Five minutes later, Bev yelled at the couple to wake up and come downstairs.

Joe and Mary dressed and followed Bev's command, joining her at the kitchen table. The rain had stopped falling and the sun was peeking through a break in the clouds, drying up the water dripping from the eaves of the house. After finishing breakfast, the couple embraced Bev, saying they would see her on their next visit to town and telling her they were going to stop in the barn to say goodbye to the donkeys. The couple had taken a liking to these animals, who they found friendly and loving. Omar greeted the company with a welcoming bray. Mary fed the donkey family some oats and the couple hugged all three animals before leaving the barn and heading out on the trail home.

Bev had told the couple to be on the alert for a bear, who had recently attacked and killed a hunter in the woods outside Dawson. The bear had consumed the man he had ambushed in the forest, leaving only his remains for the scavengers to fight over. The bear had also killed the hunter's dog, who had tried to protect his owner. An errant wolverine had made a meal of the dog's body, after the bear had left the kill site. Ravens and a fox had fought over the few remaining pieces of flesh scattered about where the bear had fed. The Mounties in Dawson had issued a warning over this dangerous predator, and currently a contingent of Mounties and volunteers from Dawson were out looking for this killer with the taste of human flesh on its mind.

Joe and Mary entered a wooded area after walking through a meadow awash in colourful wildflowers. A silent atmosphere greeted the couple as they entered the forest. No birds were singing or insects spreading their mating calls among each other. The hair on Rusty's back was on end, as he sensed and smelled danger. Soon, a low growl came from the dog's throat. Joe gripped his rifle tightly, his increased adrenaline keeping him on high alert. A crow cawing in the distance was the only sound to break the tense silence which surrounded the couple.

The large bear attacked with stealth. Rusty ran to head the bear off, jumping into its path, giving Joe seconds of extra preparation to face this menace. The charging bear, with one swipe of his paw, knocked Rusty to the side into the brush, where he landed unharmed. Two loud gunshots rang out from Joe's rifle, hitting the animal in the head. Both bullets entered the bear's brain, killing him instantly.

A triumphant Joe and Mary stood over the dead animal, with Rusty sniffing at the carcass.

A sudden yell from two men caught the couple's attention, the voices wanting to know their location. Joe answered back, telling them where to find them. Within minutes, two Mounties appeared out of the trees. They had been searching for the bear which Joe had shot. The men told Joe to take any meat they wanted from the bear. The officers would then take care of harvesting the remainder of the meat before returning to Dawson with the good news. A serious threat to the people living in the area had been removed, the man-eating bear was dead. His flesh would now be consumed by the most dangerous of predators, man.

CHAPTER FORTY

Joe and Mary said goodbye, wishing the Mounties luck. The couple, with their dog Rusty and carrying a small amount of fresh meat, continued their journey toward home. The rest of the trip was without mishap. Sighting their cabin, Joe noticed the extra wood he had used for securing the door had been removed. Upon further inspection, the signs pointed to someone breaking into their cabin while they were gone. The intruder had ransacked the cabin, apparently looking for valuables.

Whoever it was had been unlucky in his search. Perhaps he had been in a rush, fearful of getting caught and being shot in the back. Maybe it was a refugee from the Klondike fields, with little to lose except his life. Whoever it was, the search had not been thorough. Luckily, none of the valuables Joe and Mary had hidden in a secure location were missing. The couple wondered where this stranger had come from and where he was going. Joe and Mary were hopeful he had continued his journey, probably to Dawson. They did not want to encounter this man again, in the bush or at their cabin.

The couple, deciding a thorough cleaning of their cabin was overdue, went to work. When the couple finished, Joe pulled out a business card he had found on the floor. He had picked it up and put it into his pocket, planning to look at it when their cleaning was done. Joe and Mary studied the card. They were shocked and alarmed when they realized where the card came from, an unscrupulous gold dealer with an office in Dawson. It was said he had been affiliated with a known thief and liar named One-Eyed Jack, who died tragically when his own dog ripped out his throat. The couple surmised their unknown visitor was either the gold dealer himself, or one of his associates. Either way, they had no idea why anyone would want to search their home. They were unaware of Leonard's tale of finding a huge gold nugget and had no way of knowing who he may have shared this story with. Joe doubted if the thief would return, as he had found nothing of value and knew he would be shot if he was caught around Joe and Mary's cabin.

Joe and Mary decided to take the canoe out on the lake, wanting to take their minds off of the mess which had greeted them when they arrived home. A relaxing paddle, sightseeing and fishing was their plan. The afternoon sun shone down on the couple as they launched the canoe into the placid waters of the crystal-clear lake. Joe and Mary paddled quietly, watching the ducks and geese who were enjoying eating their fill of their favorite foods. Joe put out his fishing net, while Mary maneuvered the canoe. In a short time, their teamwork produced many whitefish and lake trout.

As it was getting late in the day, the couple decided to return to their cabin. Joe wanted to smoke some of their catch along with the bear meat, while Mary would fry the rest of the delicious fish caught from the cold northern lake which fronted their cabin. The lake had provided a bounty of food to this hungry couple living in the wilderness; a privilege afforded to few.

CHAPTER FORTY-ONE

oe and Mary paddled the canoe toward the shoreline. A small, sandy beach in front of the cabin provided a good spot to land the vessel and pull it onto the shore. Rusty met the couple at the shoreline with tail wagging, happy to see his owners return safely from the lake. Mary disembarked from the canoe first to go light fires in the woodstove and smoker. Joe gathered up the lake trout and whitefish from the bottom of the canoe and carried them to the fur shed. The work bench would provide Joe with a large area to clean and prepare the fish for cooking.

Mary had fires started both in the woodstove and the smoker outside. The burning wood from the smoker left the area enshrouded in a cloud of gray. A calm day with no breeze, exasperated this situation further. However, Joe thought it would be a good day for smoking fish, as the smoke would not be blown away. This would allow the fish and meat to cook faster, turning out more succulent and tender to the taste buds of the consumer.

As the late afternoon turned into evening, Joe started a campfire. The couple planned on eating the fish outside. The night promised to be warm, with a cloudless sky. A hungry fox waited in the wings for a handout. Joe had spotted the small animal while smoking fish earlier, trying to hide out of sight. The fox was hoping something to eat would be left after the couple retired with their dog to the cabin for the night. Joe had an idea. With the remains from the fish in the fur shed, and Rusty having eaten his fill, Joe would feed the fox, who would be happy to eat the leftovers. It was a meal this hungry animal was sure to accept.

When Joe finished smoking the fish, the couple and Rusty gathered around the campfire and ate their catch from the lake. The fire crackled as the dry wood burned in the campfire, sending smoke straight up into the sky till its presence became lost in the blackness of the night. The fish Mary had cooked on the woodstove would be saved for tomorrow night, served with produce from Mary's garden. Such vegetables would soon be unavailable, as the summer months turned into fall, which in turn quickly changed into the winter.

Joe let the campfire burn down to coals, extinguishing the rest of the heat with water from the lake. The trio returned to the cabin to sleep. The tired couple removed their clothing and lay in their bed. The sky had darkened, with cloud cover obscuring any light from the sky; thunder could be heard in the distance. As the storm approached, the thunder grew louder, and flashes of lightning lit up the interior of the cabin. Rusty cowered under Joe and Mary's blanket, afraid of the storm, which passed quickly. Serenity soon returned to the forest. The couple fell asleep in each other's arms, happy to share a love, necessary for their survival.

CHAPTER FORTY-TWO

The summer months passed quickly in the Yukon; September brought signs of autumn everywhere. The wildflowers which had covered the meadows in bright colors all summer had completed their cycle of life. The plants were now dying, their flowers turning into seeds. These seeds will soon fall to the ground, helping to bring life back to the meadow next year.

The couple had worked on cutting more dry wood from the forest to keep the woodstove burning all winter. They had left the wood in the bush to be picked up this winter. The dogsled pulled by Rusty and Joe's new dog he was acquiring from Steward would be utilized for this task. Joe and Mary needed to make one more trip to Dawson for supplies before the cruelties of winter set in. On their last trip to town, Bev had told Joe and Mary she knew and trusted a man who would pack in supplies to their cabin for a fee. This would solve the couple's problem of not owning a pack animal.

The nights in the cabin were getting colder, which required the couple to keep the woodstove burning longer to keep the cabin warm. One night in the middle of

September, the first flakes of snow fell while the couple were sleeping. Upon wakening that morning, Joe found a dusting of snow on the ground and on the branches of the trees. Joe thought they should not wait much longer to take care of the business which needed to be completed in Dawson. The freezing and thawing cycle later in the fall, would make the trail to Dawson City muddy and more difficult to navigate.

After talking it over, Joe and Mary decided it would be best to leave tomorrow. The couple would go to Bev's house upon their arrival in town. They hoped Bev could introduce them to her friend who would help them pick up the supplies they needed and deliver them to their cabin. If the man accepted this job, Joe would pay him handsomely when he was finished.

The trip to Dawson was uneventful, the couple and their dog arriving at Bev's home before lunch. Joe mentioned to Bev they required the help of her friend to deliver their supplies for the winter into the bush. She told Joe she had mentioned the job to Jacob, her friend who owned a mule. He had told Bev to have Joe and Mary come see him when they arrived in town. Jacob was interested in helping Joe and Mary, especially after Bev spoke so highly of them.

Getting directions from Bev, Joe and Mary left to go meet Jacob. He lived in a small house in Dawson. The home was a stinking mess from the dog feces and urine waste left by his team of huskies, which he kept in his back yard. He had a well-constructed enclosure for the two mules adjacent to his house. In the past, Jacob had lost a couple of these valuable animals to hungry predators who had ventured into

Dawson looking for food. He had built a solid structure to ensure the safety of his current pack animals.

After introductions and a brief discussion, Jacob agreed to pick up Joe and Mary's needed supplies. The couple spent the rest of the afternoon shopping and purchasing the necessary goods, which Jacob would pick up two days later. This would allow Joe and Mary enough time to complete their visit with Bev and return home before Jacob and their supplies arrived in the bush.

With their shopping completed, Joe and Mary returned to Bev's house for dinner. They were pleased Bev's only living sibling, also named Mary, joined them. Around the dinner table, Bev's sister told stories from her youth. She was the eldest sibling in Bev's family and had recently turned ninety-years-old. After dinner, Mary's son was coming to accompany her back to her small home in Dawson.

After yet another delicious meal, Joe and Mary retired to bed early, leaving the two sisters to talk alone. Within minutes of their heads hitting the pillow, the couple were fast asleep, their dreams full of hope for their future.

CHAPTER FORTY-THREE

An unusually loud chorus of songbirds filled the early morning air with sound. Joe and Mary lay awake in their bed listening to nature's harmony, the melody flowing in through the open windows of their bedroom. The couple exited the bed and got dressed, knowing Bev would be calling them for breakfast anytime. The couple wanted to surprise Bev and be downstairs before she called out.

Joe and Mary quietly went down to the kitchen and seated themselves at the table. Bev's back was turned as she stood over the stove, paying no attention to what was happening behind her. She was happily cooking, humming her favorite song as she worked. When she turned to retrieve something from the table, she threw up her hands in surprise and let out a burst of laughter, enjoying the joke Joe and Mary had played on her.

While the trio sat and ate breakfast, Bev asked Joe and Mary if they could feed and water the donkeys in the barn immediately after eating. The couple readily agreed, as they were so thankful for everything Bev had done for them since their arrival in Dawson last spring and they loved her donkeys.

Omar and his family were always happy to see humans, as it usually meant two things, affection and food would be lavished upon them. As soon as the barn door opened, the welcoming committee sent out a greeting. All three donkeys stuck their heads through the railings of their pens, ready and waiting to be scratched upon the couple's arrival. Mary retrieved the bucket of oats and some wild apples from a pile in the corner. The apples had been collected earlier in the fall as treats for the donkeys. The animals were fed and loved before the couple left the barn.

Joe and Mary headed to Jacob's house to ensure he would be picking up their supplies tomorrow. They provided a list of which merchants they had purchased items from and the receipts for their goods. They also told Jacob exactly where their cabin was located. Jacob assured the couple that he and his mule, Molly, would pick up their supplies first thing in the morning and then head for their cabin. He was certain they would arrive in the early afternoon.

Joe and Mary returned to Bev's house to pick up their belongings and their dog Rusty and leave for home. They said their goodbyes to Bev, telling her they would see her at Christmas for dinner. The day was cloudy and unusually cold, hinting of snow for their walk home. After walking for one hour, snow flurries filled the grey sky. Joe and Mary picked up their pace, hoping to make it to their cabin sooner. However, the air turned colder and the snowstorm intensified in strength. Joe knew they had to find shelter and wait to see if the snow subsided.

The couple climbed to a higher altitude, knowing there were many caves in the rocks high above. Rusty, who was ahead of Joe and Mary, started barking loudly. Reaching Rusty's location, the couple noticed a large overhang of granite rock which would provide shelter from the storm. The travellers waited under this outcropping until the snow blew through the area, leaving sunny skies to prevail.

CHAPTER FORTY-FOUR

After waiting under the outcropping for forty-five minutes, the snow stopped. The sun peeked through a break in the clouds causing a glare to reflect off the snow on the ground. Joe, Mary, and Rusty continued their way home. The clouds which had earlier spread snow across the trail had dissipated, the sun now dominating the blue sky. Within an hour, the snow on the ground had melted. The rest of the journey home held no further delays or trouble on the trail.

Joe and Mary were glad to get home to familiar surroundings. A fire was soon burning in the woodstove to remove the dampness and chill from the cabin. Rusty lay by the stove, warming up his cold extremities and preparing himself for a nap. Clouds had moved back into the area, bringing more snow flurries. The nights had been getting longer, as the daylight hours became less.

The couple had to stick close to home tomorrow to wait for Jacob to deliver their goods from Dawson; they were expecting him sometime after lunch. Jacob arrived when he said he would, with a cooperative mule named Molly carrying the supplies on her back. The men unloaded the mule, putting the contents in the fur shed to be sorted later and put in their proper places. Jacob left with a five-dollar gold piece in hand for his services, a healthy sum of money at the time.

Something Joe and Mary had borrowed from Bev, which they would thoroughly enjoy, were a couple of books. Her deceased husband had been an avid reader and had left a large book collection when he died. Bev treasured these books her husband once owned. To her they were invaluable, and she cared for them as such. Joe had selected a book about Indigenous life in the Yukon while Mary had chosen an action adventure. Mary's book was about a young couple and their life of survival in the wilderness.

As the late fall progressed into early winter, the sky was full of migrating geese looking for open water and warmer temperatures. Joe and Mary needed to travel to Steward's to pick up the dog they were going to use for a sled dog this winter. Joe told Mary they should go to Steward's cabin tomorrow before the weather turned colder and they were confronted with their first blizzard of the season.

The following morning found the couple on their way to Steward and Blossom's home. The walk was an all day journey from their own cabin. The day was sunny, but cold, with no accumulation of snow on the ground. However, that can change quickly, and without warning, in the Yukon. It was a land of harsh realities, leading to the deaths of men who defied nature, unnecessary ends to those who ignored nature's warnings with their ignorance.

The walk to Steward's was easy, as most of the terrain consisted of level ground. Steward's dogs sounded the warning someone was approaching the cabin, causing Blossom and Steward to come outside and greet the couple warmly. Joe and Mary finally met Blossom, whom they had heard much about. Steward said Rusty was fine to come into the cabin with them, as their dogs were kept outdoors.

Steward and Blossom's home was spacious, with a bedroom separated from the living area. The large woodstove warmed the entire cabin to a comfortable temperature. Steward told Joe and Mary he had some bad news. Star, the husky he was planning on loaning to Joe and Mary this winter, was dead. A young female wolf had come around, luring this young stud to take her as his wife. Overcome with passion, the husky had broken free from his restraints and run off with his new girlfriend. Unfortunately for Star, the male wolves in his newfound love's pack disagreed with the young wolf's decision. The alpha male had killed Star and banished the young female from the pack, forcing her to live in the forest on her own.

This was bad news for Joe and Mary, which would make them alter their plans of how many traps they could set this winter. However, Rusty would be able to handle the sled alone. Blossom and Mary took an instant like to each other and socialized like two lonely women. It was obvious they both enjoyed having female companionship. Steward extended an invitation for Joe and Mary to spend the night, which they graciously accepted. Rusty was welcome to sleep by the woodstove in the cabin, a spot Joe knew the dog would enjoy. A social evening was in store for the two couples, with a game of euchre planned for later.

CHAPTER FORTY-FIVE

The two couples sat around the table playing cards. Euchre was played for recreation, being the most popular, non-gambling card game in the Yukon. The coal oil lanterns shone dimly in the cabin, allowing just enough light to see the cards the couples were holding. A cold north wind was blowing through the bare branches of the trees in the forest, their colourful leaves lying in piles on the damp forest floor.

Soon the blizzards would come to the Yukon, covering this Canadian wilderness with a blanket of white snow. The huskies, who had been lying idle all summer, were anxious to resume their jobs pulling dogsleds this winter. These canines will revel in the snow once it arrives, knowing they will be leaving the captivity of their chains shortly.

Around midnight, Joe let Rusty out for a bathroom break before bed. He called the rest of the group to the door to see the spectacular light show nature was putting on; the aurora borealis lit up the dark Yukon sky. A potpourri of coloured lights danced across the night sky; a miracle of colors created by a power humans did not understand. After being mesmerized by the beauty of the night for a short time, Joe called his dog and the two couples retired back inside Steward's cabin for the night. The full moon was visible through the cabin window when sleep came for Joe and Mary. They enjoyed spending time with Steward and Blossom and would return in the future for another visit.

Over the course of the evening, Steward had informed Joe some of the men in his family hunted together in the early winter for moose and deer, hoping to fill their outdoor freezers. Steward extended his hand to Joe, inviting him to join them on this year's hunt. He told Joe the men were meeting at his cabin in two weeks, and they would love Joe to join them. A successful hunt meant meat for at least part of the winter in each of the participants' outdoor freezers. In two weeks, time, there would be enough snow on the ground to run the dogsleds. Joe was looking forward to going on the hunt and securing meat for himself and Mary.

The following morning Joe and Mary said goodbye to their friends. Blossom gave them a gift of smoked trout, which they had harvested from the lake the cabin sat on. New snow had fallen overnight, meaning Mary and Joe could look for moose or deer sign on their way home. They did find plenty of animal tracks on their journey, but none belonging to the prey they were looking for.

Arriving home, Joe and Mary's cabin looked forlorn, sitting with six inches of snow surrounding it. Joe unbarricaded the cabin door and entered the cold structure. Mary started a fire in the woodstove to warm the cabin to a comfortable temperature. Rusty took his position by the stove, waiting for the heat to radiate from its belly to warm his stiff and aching joints. After warming up and eating a dinner of smoked trout, which Blossom had given them, the couple retired to bed. They relaxed in the peace and serenity their life sometimes offered, living in this land of enchantment known as the Canadian north.

CHAPTER FORTY-SIX

The following morning, Joe and Mary worked on sorting their traps. Joe had purchased seven new leg traps to replace the twenty-five-year-old rusty ones the previous owner had left in the shed. Some of these old traps were salvageable, but most needed to be thrown out. If a trap did not work properly, the animal would not usually give the trapper a second chance to catch it. With the traps ready for use, the couple returned to the cabin for lunch.

Joe had retrieved some venison from the freezer which Mary fried on the woodstove. While eating, the couple heard noises coming from overhead. Rusty's ears perked up and a low growl came from the back of the dog's throat. Joe pulled on his coat and grabbed his rifle. By the time he opened the cabin door and went outside, the noise coming from the roof had stopped. He saw nothing that piqued his interest. Walking around to the back of the cabin, he could see prints in the snow leading to the tree whose branches hung low over the cabin roof. He moved closer to inspect the animal prints which were clearly identifiable in the snow. They were from a wolverine, probably hunting for food who happened to pass by the cabin. His curiosity had taken him to the roof, where he could get a better look at his surroundings. After not finding anything of interest, the wolverine moved on, looking for bigger and better things to explore. Returning to the cabin, Joe let Rusty outside and told Mary what he had found.

After lunch, Joe wanted to enlarge the outdoor freezer. Digging would not be a problem, as only the first six inches of ground were frozen. Joe told Mary he was going to retrieve a shovel from the shed and begin to work. Mary said she would be joining him shortly.

Joe retrieved a shovel and started scraping dirt from the sides of the walls of the underground freezer. As he worked, his shovel hit a leather bag which seemed embedded in the wall. He dug around the bag, freeing it from its tomb. Joe reached up and pulled the satchel from the wall. Opening the drawstrings which kept the bag tightly closed, Joe was shocked to find a gigantic gold nugget. Joe estimated it to weigh two ounces, never envisioning a gold nugget this large. It was rumoured Leonard had found something special, but no one ever paid attention to his ramblings, his senility and his incoherent conversations had been unbelievable.

Forgetting about his digging for a moment, Joe went to the cabin to share his good fortune with his wife. Not believing her eyes, Mary asked if the nugget was real or just a piece of fool's gold. Joe told Mary he was certain it was real. After putting the nugget in a secure location, Mary and Joe returned to the freezer to finish the job Joe had started earlier. This cellar would hold large amounts of moose and deer meat, keeping it frozen over the winter.

Their work completed; the couple walked to the lake. A frosting of ice was forming around the perimeter, close to the shore. Depending on weather conditions, in six weeks the ice would be thick enough to run a dogsled on. Joe would be able to cut a large hole in the ice for fishing with the net. He would also cut a hole in the ice close to the cabin, so they would have a ready supply of water if the spring froze up during a frigid spell this winter. Returning to the cabin, Rusty followed the couple into the building, going to his favorite spot by the woodstove. Joe looked at Rusty thinking he wished he had it so easy. Joe's thoughts were that being a dog might not be such a bad life after all.

CHAPTER FORTY-SEVEN

The time for the moose hunt came quickly. Mary accompanied Joe to Steward's cabin. While the men were out hunting, Mary was looking forward to visiting with Blossom. Jason was coming on the hunt, along with Joanathan, another member of Bev's family whom Joe and Mary had not yet met.

The entire hunting party had arrived at Steward's cabin just before noon. After eating lunch, the men decided to go into the bush and search for moose and deer sign. The hunting party planned to use two dog teams for transportation, with Steward and Johnathan's being used today. The men headed out on the dogsleds, with Steward leading the way. Steward guided the group to a wetland area with tall grass. During the day, moose often fed on the lower branches of the evergreen trees found here, with grasses pulled from the swamp rounding out these animals' diets. Moose also tended to lay down in the tall grass to sleep, concealing themselves from their enemies.

Rusty, who had joined the men on the hunt, would be sent into the swamp to flush out any moose hidden in the tall grass. The two sleds arrived near the grassy area which bordered the wetlands. Immediately, the sound of gunshots shattered the silence. A deer had run out of the trees not fifty feet from the first sled. Jason had shot the deer on impulse, killing the animal only yards from where they sat.

The men let Rusty go. Barking loudly, he bounded into the tall grass. After fifteen minutes of searching for a moose, the dog gave up and returned to Joe. The men were happy to have shot the deer, which they would take back to Steward's cabin to butcher. The deer was small, fitting on the sled easily. Joe and Jason walked behind the sled, or ran beside it, until they got back to the cabin. When the sleds neared the cabin, the women heard the dogs barking and came out to greet the men. Spotting the deer on the sled, meant they would be eating well tonight.

Steward started the smoker while Johnathan lit a roaring campfire to keep the men warm while they harvested the meat from the deer. The entire hunting party would stay the night and resume their hunt for the moose tomorrow. The men planned to cook the venison over the open fire and enjoy each other's company. Mary and Blossom would prepare their own dinner inside the cabin, glad to get away from the men's hunting stories.

Sitting around the campfire once the butchering was complete, Johnathan shared a secret he had been keeping for just such a moment. He had purchased a small bottle of Canadian whiskey while in Dawson, which the men would share before dinner. It was a special treat for the wilderness diners sitting in the forest.

Steward cooked enough meat for everyone, including Rusty, to eat their fill. Tomorrow, if the hunt was successful, the men would be eating moose meat instead of venison. The night was dark as the last coals from the campfire burned low. Everyone, including Rusty, was sleeping inside the cabin tonight; Steward and Blossom's floor serving as everyone's bedroom. It was a much warmer place to sleep than out in the snow, if they could put up with Rusty's snoring.

CHAPTER FORTY-EIGHT

The hunters were awake and up from Steward's floor before sunrise. Within a short time, the dogsleds were ready, the huskies pulling on their harnesses waiting to go. Steward led the way, mushing his dogs into a steady run. He had decided to check at the other end of the swamp, where an expanse of tall grass bordered a stand of evergreen trees. This was an area where Steward had seen moose before, in the tall grass with only their shoulders and heads visible while they were eating.

After thirty minutes of driving the sleds forward, Steward gave the signal to stop. Johnathan would stay with the dog teams while the rest of the men, with Rusty, would go on the hunt. After a thirty-minute walk, the men reached their target area. Moose tracks were plentiful, raising the hopes of these men for a successful hunt. The large number of fresh imprints in the snow led Steward to believe a moose was bedded down in the grass close by.

The men had spread out, fifty feet apart, bordering the grass beds. Joe sent his dog into the swamp to find the hiding moose. Rusty bounded through the tall grass barking loudly. The hunters waited patiently; their rifles ready to fire with little notice. Minutes passed with no movement, only Rusty's loud barking broke the stillness of the morning air. Soon, louder and more rapid barking indicated the dog had found something. The men watched as a large bull moose, with a full rack of antlers, lumbered through the tall swamp grass toward them.

Three shots rang out as soon as the moose exited the swamp. The giant animal staggered forward, falling on its knees. More shots followed, two of the bullets hitting the moose in the head, ending the majestic animal's life. The moose lay dead in the blood-soaked snow. Rusty ran over and climbed on the body of the moose, looking like he had defeated his foe. The hunting party was jubilant at their success. When butchered, this moose would provide meat for four families for half of the winter season.

The two hindquarters were removed from the moose first, using a saw made for butchering large game. These were taken back to Steward's cabin by Johnathan and stored in the fur shed. He informed Mary and Blossom of the successful kill, asking them to help move the meat back to the cabin. They quickly agreed, taking the other dogsled and following Johnathan back to the kill site. When the women arrived, their sled was loaded with meat and they were sent home to add their cargo to the stash in the fur shed.

The other two sleds would soon follow, ladened with the remains of the moose. The head of the animal, minus his rack of antlers, was left where he died, with other unsalvageable parts piled beside it. This would provide a feast for carnivores and scavengers alike. As the men were preparing to leave the area, a snow squall hit. The squall was so intense the dogs and sleds could only be seen as shadows in the blinding snow. After a short period, the winds subsided, and the snow stopped, allowing the men an easy path forward to Steward's cabin, and a well-earned rest upon arrival.

CHAPTER FORTY-NINE

*J*ason and Steward pulled their loaded dogsleds over to the fur shed. Mary had built a fire in the building's woodstove to warm the interior, keeping the moose from freezing until the men had finished butchering it. Steward and Jason unloaded their sleds, piling the unprocessed moose meat onto the worktable. The smell of venison cooking drifted to where the men were, reminding them of what was on the lunch menu. Slabs of venison steak greeted the men when they returned to the cabin. After not eating breakfast, the men were famished. The plate of venison Blossom and Mary had cooked was soon picked clean, with the men looking for more.

After lunch, the hunters took a half hour break, before returning to work in the fur shed to butcher the moose. While they were in Steward's cabin, a wolverine had picked up the scent of the moose and followed his nose to the homestead. The men had not secured the door to the fur shed, never expecting an intruder in the short time they would be gone. The wolverine slipped through the unsecured door, jumping up on the work bench to help himself to the finest cuts of moose meat. In his moment of bliss, this predator did not hear the group of men returning. Rusty's barking brought the wolverine back to reality, and with a long jump off the work bench, the animal dashed out the open door right between Jason's legs. The men laughed at the site of a vicious wolverine running into the forest, until they saw what the biggest glutton in the forest had done to their kill.

Steward and his friends worked diligently on processing the remaining moose. Dusk was just forming on the horizon when they finished. This time, they secured the door against any more theft and returned to the cabin. The women had cooked up some of the fresh moose and a platter of meat, larger than the one served earlier, sat on the table. The men, taking advantage of the bounty, ate their fill, not worrying about food for tomorrow.

The group planned to spend one more night together, before returning to their prospective cabins with their sleds loaded down with meat. Rusty, with a full stomach, was already sleeping peacefully by the woodstove. The men soon joined Rusty on the floor, letting Mary and Blossom share the bed. In the early morning, the men were awakened when Rusty started walking across their bodies to get to the front door. Once there, he hoped someone would let him outside.

The occupants of the cabin all got out of bed, the hunters looking forward to returning home. Soon they had divided the meat, readied their dogsleds, and were saying goodbye to Steward and Blossom, thanking them for a successful hunt. Steward would deliver Joe and Mary's moose meat to them later. This morning they rode home on their small dogsled pulled by their reliable work dog, Rusty.

CHAPTER FIFTY

Joe and Mary returned home with Rusty, who was a one-dog-team, pulling their sled back to the cabin. Joe and Mary were happy with Rusty's lone performance, believing he would suffice as the only dog they needed for working their small trapline this winter. Upon reaching their cabin, Joe first removed the extra security he had placed across the cabin door. Mary entered the cold cabin ready to work her magic, bringing a feeling of warmth and belonging to this wilderness structure.

Joe unloaded the couple's few personal belongings from the sled and placed them in the cabin. He then motioned Rusty to pull the sled over to the fur shed. During the winter months, the sled was kept outside, sitting beside the building. During the months when there was no snow on the ground, the sled was kept inside the structure.

Joe unhooked Rusty from the confines of his harness and praised him for the fine job he had done working with the group of men to help make the moose hunt successful. Joe and Rusty walked to the lake. The water was covered in ice, which was not yet strong enough to sustain the weight of a dogsled. Two more weeks of cold temperatures and all the lakes in the Yukon would become the highways of the north.

Rusty and Joe returned to the cabin, joining Mary in a warming environment. Rusty took up his favorite spot by the woodstove. The dog often had sad thoughts about Leonard, his previous owner, wondering why the old man had suddenly disappeared from his life. Rusty was happy living with Joe and Mary, feeling he was treated well, and his primary needs were taken care of. A sense of mutual respect had developed between the couple and their dog, a valuable partnership when residing in the north.

The following morning while discussing their trapline, Joe and Mary were interrupted by the barking of sled dogs approaching the cabin. Within minutes, Steward arrived with his sled piled high with moose and deer meat from the hunt. A warm greeting was given to Steward and a gracious thank you was said for delivering the meat to their cabin. The men unloaded the precious food from the dogsled and placed it into the outdoor freezer. After finishing, Joe invited Steward inside the cabin to warm up and enjoy a cup of coffee before starting his trek home.

Steward was more than happy to accept the offer, joining the couple in their cozy cabin. Steward shared some bad news with Joe and Mary. Blossom had suffered a second miscarriage. It was an unforeseen and tragic event for the couple, something they had shared only with each other. Joe and Mary were saddened by the news and asked how Blossom was doing. Steward said she was fine and was fully recovered, but thoughts of a new baby were out of the question for the time being.

Steward left Joe and Mary's cabin, hugging the couple warmly while saying goodbye. They watched as Steward with his dog team disappeared into the forest. Joe and Mary's worries about securing enough food for the winter were over. They had acquired enough meat, which along with fish and small game added, appeared to be sufficient to keep themselves and Rusty eating well this winter. This positive ending was not always a given in this savage and untamed land.

CHAPTER FIFTY-ONE

C hristmas was drawing near, and Joe and Mary had been invited to celebrate the holiday with Bev's family at her house in Dawson City. The couple would leave for Dawson the day before Christmas, spending Christmas Eve and Christmas Day there. They were looking forward to a delicious dinner and participating in Bev's family's gift exchange. Names had been picked out of a hat to decide who each person would get a gift for. This created a fair exchange, considering the large number of people invited for the Christmas celebration.

Of course, everyone enjoying Bev's hospitality would also bring a gift for her. This was a way for each family member to show their appreciation to her, as she spent so much time trying to make Christmas happy for everyone. These gifts were usually hand-made crafts, often created by the givers themselves. Bev loved all the presents she received at Christmas time.

Joe and Mary decided to celebrate a small Christmas at home before leaving for Dawson. The couple took Rusty and went into the forest to select a small tree, taking it back to their cabin. Mary had made some decorations from her collection of forest finds she kept on hand for such projects. She had used these finds to also create a beautiful ornament for Bev's Christmas tree and a decorative piece to be displayed above Bev's fireplace as her Christmas gift. The ornate object was decorated with gold flake Mary had collected from the bottom of her gold pan. Joe told Mary Bev would love this beautifully crafted work of art when she sees it at Christmas.

Mary and Joe celebrated their Christmas by exchanging their reflections of love toward one another, followed by a warm embrace and a loving kiss. These were the only gifts given during the couple's private celebration. The following day, they gathered up the belongings they would need for their stay at Bev's house, hooked Rusty's harness up to the sled, and left their cabin for Dawson City. Rusty pulled the sled well. Joe expected to arrive at Bev's in two hours, providing they did not encounter any disruptions on the trail.

Unfortunately, shortly after reaching the halfway point to Dawson, the couple stumbled upon an unsavoury sight. At first look, Joe thought it was a dead animal. But as they drew closer, he realized it was a half-eaten human body. Upon closer examination of the remains, Joe concluded the victim had probably died from exposure and then been eaten by an animal. Whatever had been feeding on the body had most likely been scared off by the approaching sled and did not get to finish their meal.

Joe left the remains where they lay and continued their journey. He told Mary they would report this find to the Mounties in Dawson. The day was sunny but cold, with a north wind slicing across the faces of the travellers as they came to the outskirts of town. The smoke from the many chimneys being used filled the sky over Dawson.

The couple's arrival at Bev's house was met by a chorus of barking, the dogs from the sled teams parked in the front of her house announcing new visitors. Bev's company had already started to arrive, Joe and Mary were the latest to join them to celebrate the holiday.

CHAPTER FIFTY-TWO

With news of Joe and Mary's arrival, a welcoming committee met the couple at the door. Jason and Wendy with their son, Kuzih, and Johnathan and Shining Star, along with their son, Grey Eagle, were present. Bev was busy working in the kitchen, warmly greeting the couple once they entered the house.

Steward and Blossom would be joining the celebration tomorrow, and after eating Christmas dinner at noon, they would return to their home. Steward worried about leaving some of his huskies at his cabin. They were an asset he did not want to lose through neglect on his part. His biggest concern were wolves coming during the night and attacking the chained huskies while they slept. If this scenario were to happen, Steward would come home to find all his dogs dead, killed by a marauding wolf pack. He simply could not leave any of his huskies alone overnight, and there were just too many to travel with at one time.

Before unhooking Rusty from the sled, Joe needed to go to the Mountie headquarters and inform the officers of the body they had found in the forest. Upon arrival, he filed a report, providing the location and condition of the body when it was found. Joe told the Mountie he was afraid there would be little left of the remains, as upon leaving the scene there were scavengers waiting in the woods to pick the bones of this victim of circumstance clean. The body was already half-eaten when Joe and Mary encountered it and may be unidentifiable by the time the constables from Dawson arrived on the scene.

The officer thanked Joe for coming in and reporting this tragic event. His description of the body made the Mountie believe it was that of a man who had been reported missing by his friend in Dawson. The man, whose name was Jim, had been seen acting strangely two days before his disappearance. The Mountie believed he was suffering from cabin fever, nature's way of taking out the weak and unprepared for winter in the Yukon, creating a mysterious force which draws people to the forest to die.

Joe left the station, telling the Mountie where he could be located if they needed to question him further about this matter. He returned to Bev's and joined her other guests. Everyone in attendance lived in isolated cabins in the forest and were happy to be gathering for an annual tradition at Bev's house, one she looked forward to every year. No other guests would be attending Bev's dinner. Her two friends, who usually joined in the festivities, would not be joining them this year because of a decline in their health.

The crowd sat around the large kitchen table to eat the delicious dinner their host had prepared. The smell of fresh baked bread stimulated the guests' appetites even more. A smorgasbord of food sat on the table, moose and venison roasts from the bounty of the men's kill when hunting with

Steward. Her guest's had happily supplied this protein for Bev's Christmas Eve party. Mounds of root vegetables were piled high; potatoes, turnips and carrots all harvested from Bev's garden in late fall. Some of these vegetables would be saved to eat with the Christmas Day meal tomorrow. The food was delicious as always. Memorable stories were exchanged among the couples, as Christmas brings back memories from the past.

Bev assigned bedrooms to the three couples who were spending the night, and they moved their personal belongings into their respective rooms. Bev's home was a special retreat for these people, a time for them to leave their problems at their cabins in the bush. Bev would be sorely missed when she joined her husband in the afterlife God had blessed them with, but for now everyone was thankful she was here.

CHAPTER FIFTY-THREE

Christmas morning at Bev's home arrived early; she expected everyone to be up for breakfast when she called. With only three hours of sleep the night before, Bev had been working in the kitchen preparing breakfast and Christmas dinner. Shortly after Bev's call to her guests, they were all sitting around her kitchen table. Rarely did those living in the bush get to eat a home-cooked breakfast which included farm fresh eggs.

Bev joined her family and friends for breakfast, participating in the conversation which flowed freely around the table. After finishing, Shining Star and Wendy cleared the table and set about doing the dishes and assisting in the kitchen. Everyone helped in completing the chores this morning. Johnathan and Jason fed their sled dogs and their personal pets, ensuring each had fresh water and straw to bed down on. Joe and Mary headed outside to feed and water the donkeys, whose winter diet consisted of grain purchased from the livery stable and dry grass harvested during the summer months and stored in a corner of the barn. The donkeys were always happy to see people coming into the barn, braying loudly in greeting when they saw Joe and Mary. The couple rubbed the necks of the donkeys, who were more than willing to return the love which was given to them. With Rusty watching, Joe and Mary also cleaned the animal's pens before returning to the house.

By the time the work was almost finished, Steward and Blossom arrived with their dog team. Jason and Johnathan helped Steward unhitch the dogs and provide them with food and water, while Blossom retreated to the kitchen to assist in any way she could. Soon everyone was in the house, ready to exchange gifts around the Christmas tree.

The Yukon winter was cold and today was no exception. The north wind had brought arctic air into the region, giving Dawson its coldest temperatures this winter. The group in Bev's house sat around the fireplace in the living room, the fragrant odour of evergreen filling the room with the Christmas spirit. Once everyone was settled, the gift exchange began. Each person in attendance received a present from the member who had previously selected their name. The gifts were typically mementos crafted by the settlers who called this land home, given as tokens of friendship and love. As usual, Bev received more than one gift. Some of the decorative, hand-made objects were placed on her Christmas tree, making it even more festive.

After this exchange of gifts around the Christmas tree, Bev went into the kitchen to put the finishing touches on dinner. Bev insisted she needed no help with the preparation, only assistance cleaning up the kitchen afterwards. The young couples spent time catching up with Steward and Blossom, enjoying being together.

Shortly after noon, Bev announced dinner was ready. The traditional Christmas bird, a large goose, sat on the sideboard, accompanied by a platter of vegetables, the last Bev had harvested from her garden. Freshly baked loaves of bread and creamy butter were on the table, and as a surprise for her company, hot apple pie for dessert. Bev had made the pie earlier and froze it in her outside freezer, leaving it there until it was ready to bake in her oven. Dinner was enjoyed by all who participated, a meal this good they would not enjoy again until next Christmas.

Shortly after dinner, Steward and Blossom had to leave for home. They were unable to stay the night, but were happy they could attend the festivities today, making it a memorable event for the couple. The rest of Bev's company would be leaving in the morning to return to their own cabins and lives in the wilderness. A journey of survival throughout the winter awaited these fearless souls, as the Yukon beckoned them home.

CHAPTER FIFTY-FOUR

Bev's company was leaving today. The men and their wives were up at daybreak, packing their personal belongings. The sun was rising over the horizon, its bright rays reflecting off the white powdery snow. Bev's kitchen table was loaded with leftovers from Christmas dinner, which was breakfast for her departing company. After a half hour of eating, the group of friends and family were ready to leave.

The happy outdoorsmen and women, who had chosen this secluded life in the Yukon, left Bev's home with memories they would carry with them forever. Jason and Johnathan left together with the two larger dog teams. Joe and Mary were the last to depart, with just Rusty pulling their sled. The trail was in good condition, fresh powdery snow which fell the night before made their dogsled glide through the snow like it was riding on air. The trees were covered in a new layer of snow, creating an almost pure white landscape. Rusty pulled the sled forward, passing other travellers on the trail heading to and from Dawson.

After an hour's travel from Bev's house, the couple took a seldom used trail which led to their cabin deep in the forest. Travelling through this section of forest, Joe spotted many rabbit tracks heading in and out of the fir trees He stopped the dogsled and picked up his rifle. Telling Mary to stay with Rusty, he said he would be back shortly. Fifteen minutes later, Mary heard the gun discharge three times. Shortly afterwards, Joe walked out with two large rabbits in hand, providing a different taste for tonight's dinner. It would be a welcome change from their diet of moose and deer meat of the past two weeks.

The remainder of Joe and Mary's trip home was uneventful and soon their little cabin came into view. Returning home from a trip to their own cabin was always a rewarding experience, no matter how humble their dwelling was. Joe opened the cabin door for Mary and unloaded the few belongings they carried with them from the sled. Joe then directed Rusty to the shed, where he disconnected his harness and let him run free.

Rusty and Joe returned to the cabin, where Mary was trying to get a fire burning in the woodstove. However, the smoke kept returning into the cabin, not going out the chimney. Joe told Mary something must be blocking the chimney, and he would get on the roof and have a look. Joe went outside and climbed the tree which gave him access to the roof of the cabin. Looking down into the chimney, he reached in and pulled out handfuls of leaves and sticks. The resident squirrel, Charlie, had again thought the chimney would make a better home than where he had been living. Joe made sure the chimney was free of debris before telling Mary she could start her fire in the woodstove, the risk of accidently burning the cabin down was over.

Warm air from the hot stove soon dominated the small structure. Rusty was curled up in his favorite spot by the stove snoring loudly. Life was good for this young couple now, but this was not a given in their future. The harsh environment can take its toll on even the strong and healthy, a situation Joe and Mary hoped they would never experience.

CHAPTER FIFTY-FIVE

The calendar changed to the new year; January arrived in the Dawson area with a blizzard. Joe and Mary had just set their trapline before the storm hit. All the traps they had set would now be buried under deep snow, meaning the couple would have to dig them out from under the new snow and reset them after the blizzard passed.

The wind was fierce, shaking the cabin to the core. The windows rattled; the cold outside air entered the cabin around the unsealed window frames. Joe had failed to chink the cracks in his cabin walls and windows, allowing cold draughts to enter the structure. This caused the wood stove to work harder to maintain a constant temperature.

Rusty could have cared less about the blizzard outside, as long as Joe and Mary kept adding wood to the fire. The storm ended after twenty hours of wind and snow. Joe and Mary woke from a deep sleep with the sun shining in through the cabin windows. They rose from their bed and looked out the front door, where a winter wonderland greeted their senses. Joe dressed and went outside to retrieve meat and fish from the outdoor freezer, as their supply of food for Rusty had run low during the storm.

Joe called Mary to come outside and look at the lake. A wolf pack, running with stealth, was crossing the lake on their way home from a successful kill they had made last night. After eating breakfast, the couple decided they should head to the lake and open the hole that had frozen over. After clearing the snow, Joe used his axe to break through the ice. The couple utilized this access to place their fish net in the water to catch whitefish for Rusty. During the winter months, their dog lived on fish caught under the ice.

After completing this chore, the couple cleaned the new snow off the dogsled, which Joe would be using to dig out his buried traps tomorrow. He would reset his traps, along with some rabbit snares. Mary would have to stay home, as the snow was too deep to pull that much weight on the sled at once.

The day passed by quickly; the couple busy doing many chores. Mary began to prepare a dinner of venison, hunger gnawing at the stomachs of the trio. The smell of the cooking meat made things worse, with Rusty sitting up whining in anticipation of his dinner. The food was finally served, venison being all that they had. Joe and Mary looked at their meager meal, already missing Bev's cooking.

CHAPTER FIFTY-SIX

The following morning dawned sunny with a clear blue sky. Joe was up at daybreak, leaving Mary in bed to sleep. Rusty was watching Joe with one eye open. He suspected he was going to be pulling the sled this morning and helping Joe work his trapline. This was not one of Rusty's favorite jobs he performed for Joe and Mary.

Joe finished his preparations for this venture and called Rusty to join him as he walked out the cabin door. He hooked the harness to Rusty and pulled the sled away from the side of the building. Joe loaded the few things he needed for today on the sled and commanded Rusty to go. With a mighty pull on his harness, the dogsled shot forward through the deep snow. Joe and Mary were only working twelve traps this season, with one of those traps designed to catch a beaver.

Joe meticulously worked digging out his traps, a long and laborious procedure while dealing with the deep snow. Rusty patiently waited for Joe to finish his work so he could go home to a warm cabin. After finishing the job of retrieving and resetting the traps, Joe motioned Rusty toward the beaver dam. Joe had set a beaver trap under the ice before the blizzard and was hoping this valuable fur was in his trap. Rusty pulled the sled forward until Joe told him to stop. Joe had reached the area where he had set the beaver trap. Looking at the hole, he saw an air bubble. Breaking through the ice, he pulled an adult male beaver up through the hole, making his whole day worth getting out of bed.

Snowshoe hares were plentiful in this area, as a lack of foxes due to a contagious disease had caused the population of these rabbits to explode. Joe loaded the beaver on the sled and motioned Rusty toward home. He would stop in a stand of evergreen trees on their way back to the cabin. On his way out this morning, he had noticed rabbit sign along the treeline. Evergreen trees were a favorite for rabbits, with their branches sometimes reaching the ground, providing excellent shelter from bad weather and protection against predators. The rabbits' white winter coats make them difficult to see from both the ground and the air, deceiving even raptors, with their ability to spot prey from long distances away.

Joe mushed Rusty to the location and found a maze of rabbit runways running through the evergreens. The runways were trodden down in deep snow, making for an easier capture of the rabbits. Joe set his snares and then motioned Rusty to go home. Upon arriving at his cabin, Joe proudly showed off the beaver to Mary. Mary laughed, telling Joe she did not think beaver grew that large and the pelt should be worth extra money because of its size.

Joe took the beaver to the fur shed, removing its hide and butchering the salvageable meat off the carcass. Beaver meat was a favorite food provided by nature to the people living in the bush. Rich in protein, the animal made good stew when vegetables were available. The fried meat also had a good taste when cooked on the woodstove. Dinner tonight would be the fine cuts of the beaver meat fried to perfection, a meal often enjoyed by hungry fur trappers and their faithful dogs alike.

CHAPTER FIFTY-SEVEN

Fur trapping in the Yukon is a hard life, as traplines need to be checked daily. Any dead animals in the traps need to be removed and the traps reset with fresh bait. Failing to do so, lets the wolverines and raptors help themselves to animals caught in the traps, ruining the fur for the trapper.

Joe ran into some issues during the month of January, losing several mammals in his traps to an elusive wolverine always looking for a free meal. The vicious predator was treating Joe's trapline like his private diner. After a visit by Steward and his wife, Steward suggested an old Indigenous trick for catching wolverines. This trick involved moulding bait around a trap and hanging it from a tree branch, out of the reach of the wolverine. The wolverine would climb the tree, trying to reach the bait from the top. The extra effort the wolverine must put forth to get his prize, makes him careless, allowing him to be caught in the trap. Steward told Joe this method of execution does not work all the time. But when it does work, there's a feeling of glory upon seeing an archenemy hanging from the tree, dead.

Joe found the perfect tree to test Steward's method of ending the wolverine's rampage. To his surprise, the trap worked the first night. He found the animal hanging dead the next morning when he checked to see what the results of his wolverine trap would be. He froze the wolverine's body whole, having promised Steward the animal would be his if the trap worked as Steward had described. Steward had told Joe while visiting, he had caught six wolverines so far this season, saying he had never seen so many wolverines since moving into his cabin.

One day in late January, Joe heard dogs barking while inside the cabin. Going outside to investigate, he saw two men travelling on a large dogsled in the direction of the cabin. As the men drew closer, Joe realized it was two of the Mounties who were stationed in Dawson. He recognized one as the man he had filed the police report with regarding the body found on the trail to Dawson at Christmas. Greetings were exchanged and the men were invited into Joe's cabin. The constables gave Joe and Mary a goodwill gift of coffee and sugar, which the couple had run out of a week ago.

The constables told Joe and Mary they had found Old Joe, an old-time trapper, dead in his cabin while on patrol last week. His body lay on the floor, frozen as solid as a block of ice. It was rumoured Old Joe had trapped in the Yukon for forty-five years, outliving three of his dogs he had kept as pets. The constables shared Old Joe had no family or friends that they knew of. After a brief search, they could find no papers as to who owned the cabin or the property it sat on. They told Joe and Mary his possessions were there for the taking, but the cabin was in major disrepair and not worth rebuilding.

Joe and Mary were curious and wanted to look at Old Joe's cabin and possessions. Believing valuables were found in the least expected places, Joe and Mary figured this man may have hidden something of value somewhere, after selling fur for so many years and not spending much money. The constables left, telling Joe and Mary to be careful of hungry bears, as two people so far this winter had been attacked and eaten in the Dawson area. The constable laughed, saying he did not want to answer a call about a hungry bear eating them in the forest, instead of them eating the hungry bear.

CHAPTER FIFTY-EIGHT

Joe and Mary escorted the Mounties outside and waved goodbye to their company as they watched the two men mush their sled dogs across the frozen lake. Smoke churned from their chimney, floating off into the almost still air of the forest. When the couple returned to the cabin, a quiet swept over them, making them realize how alone they were in the wilderness.

Joe and Mary longed for the return of summer. The Yukon winter can break even the strongest spirits, sending many to their deaths and some back to where they began their broken dreams of finding vast riches. The relentless cold and isolation were starting to work on the couple's mental health. Rusty was a big help in fighting off the loneliness Joe and Mary were experiencing. Rusty was always quick with a slobbery kiss and consoling whines when they felt down.

Nearing the end of February, Joe had accumulated numerous furs in just two months of trapping. He had trapped a few beavers, a lynx, and a bobcat, as well as two wolverines, numerous ermines, and a plethora of pine martens, which were the most plentiful animal on his trapline. Joe and Mary planned on finishing their trapping season by the beginning of April and had planned for Steward to pick up the fur they had accumulated. Using his large dogsled, Steward could take all the fruits of Joe and Mary's labor in one load. The couple would follow Steward to the broker in Dawson on their sled with Rusty when that time arrived.

The couple lay together on the bed. The north wind howled through the tops of the barren trees in the forest. The blowing snow outside the cabin could be clearly seen through the cabin windows. The fire crackled in the woodstove, heating the cabin to a comfortable temperature. Rusty slept soundly, enjoying the radiating heat from the belly of the stove. Joe's thoughts turned to the many men and women who died in their cabins. These hapless souls perished during long-lived blizzards when they ran out of firewood to feed their woodstoves. Their sentence was death by freezing in an unheated cabin if caught in this predicament.

One evening in mid-February, during the darkest part of the night, Rusty was awakened by an unfamiliar odour. Rusty was disturbed sufficiently about the scent to bark loud enough to wake Joe and Mary. Joe realized Rusty's unusual behaviour was obviously a warning of some kind of danger outside. Joe exited his bed and gazed out the cabin windows. A full moon illuminated the landscape outside, bathing everything in white. The beauty and expanse of the lake were breathtaking when seen in the moonlight.

Joe could not discover what had prompted Rusty's behaviour. He thought Rusty may have smelled a predator outside, but not being able to see anything, he headed back to bed. Joe would check for tracks in the snow in the morning. Laying down, Joe joined Mary in a peaceful slumber until the first rays of sunshine arrived the following morning.

CHAPTER FIFTY-NINE

U pon awakening in the morning, Joe let Rusty outside. Within minutes, the dog's barking caught Joe's attention. He dressed quickly, grabbing his rifle and exiting the cabin. He walked to where Rusty was barking. What he saw he had only heard about in tales and legends of the Yukon. Bigfoot, the legendary man-ape who roamed the wilds of the northern forests, had visited his cabin overnight.

Joe placed his foot inside a footprint imprinted in the snow. He knew now where this legendary creature's name came from. Joe called Mary to see the giant footprints in the snow. Mary was mystified as to how a man's feet could have grown so large. Joe thought better of telling her the truth, afraid of scaring his wife half to death.

Later that evening, Joe told Mary the story of Bigfoot. He explained there was no need to fear Bigfoot, as there was no record of the creature ever being aggressive toward humans. Mary accepted Joe's explanation, but still did not like the idea of this being lurking around their cabin at night. Joe promised he would protect her from this man-ape if they should ever encounter him. He told Mary he would shoot the creature to save her life if need be. He would not hesitate to follow through on this promise if forced to.

After breakfast the next morning, the couple planned to check their trapline. In addition to their fur, Joe and Mary had caught twenty rabbits using snare wire over the course of the winter so far. This meat added variety to the couple's diet, along with any grouse Joe shot while hunting in the forest which surrounded their cabin. Within a short time, Joe and Mary were ready to leave. Joe called Rusty, who came willingly to be hooked up to the sled. When he was finished, Joe directed his dog back to the cabin to pick up his wife. Mary joined Joe on the sled and Rusty was given the signal to go, heading toward the start of their trapline.

Checking the first trap, the pair were greeted by a snarling bobcat with his leg caught in the trap. Joe took out his rifle and shot this animal, one of many who provided him with a method of making money. Joe felt bad about taking any animal's life, but it was a way of living neither Mary nor he would be denied. After checking all their traps, the couple came up with only two more animals, both weasels whose fur was white as snow. Joe ended their trip by changing the location of his beaver trap. The current placement had not caught a beaver in two weeks. He was hoping to catch two more of these mammals, whose fur coats were valuable, before the trapping season ended.

Finished with the trapline for the day, the couple and Rusty headed home. After arriving at the cabin, Joe would skin the fur-bearing mammals he had harvested today and then join his wife in the nice, warm cabin for an afternoon nap. Joe was happy he had met Mary and fallen in love with her. Their meeting had led to a happy life in the Yukon, a rare privilege where one's existence is usually about survival, not love.

CHAPTER SIXTY

Joe and Mary woke from their nap during the late afternoon. Rusty was still sleeping comfortably by the woodstove. Mary got out of bed to start dinner, which would consist of rabbit and grouse. The rabbit would be fried on top of the stove, while the grouse would be cooked in the oven. Mary fed Rusty his dinner outside. He ate whitefish and would indulge in any scraps of food Joe and Mary would give him when they ate dinner. Rusty was your typical dog, always hungry, never filled.

The following morning, the sun was shining, and the weather had warmed. The couple decided to skip a day checking on their traps and go visit Steward and Blossom. Since they had caught the destructive wolverine, the couple had experienced no more loss of fur on their trapline. Even the raptors were not bothering anything caught in Joe's traps.

Joe hooked up Rusty to the sled and with his wife Mary, they traversed their lake by dogsled. Before travelling the passage which led to Steward's lake, Joe came across numerous wolf tracks. He decided to follow the tracks to see where the pack went. Joe did not have to go far. Off the lake in a clearing, it was obvious the wolves' had accosted a moose. A battle had ensued, with the wolf pack being unsuccessful in their attempt to take down the large animal. The moose had escaped the hungry jaws of these predators, probably because of its size. The tracks left in the snow indicated the moose was an adult, who had successfully defended itself, running off and gaining its freedom from the mob of hungry animals wanting to eat him.

Joe turned the sled around, continuing the journey to Steward's cabin. After travelling a distance across the connected lake, Mary spotted smoke rising into the air. Joe turned Rusty to move toward the source of the smoke. As the sled moved closer, the couple could make out the cabin. A short time later, they arrived to the sound of barking huskies; there was always a welcoming party when visiting Steward.

Steward and Blossom opened the door to greet Joe and Mary, always happy to see their friends visit. Steward invited the couple into the cabin and Blossom made coffee. Joe told Steward about the encounter between a moose and a wolf pack. Steward told Joe he had been having a problem with that same pack, who were coming around at night bothering his huskies. He had yet to get a clear shot at one of the wolves, as they ran off into the forest whenever they heard Steward open the cabin door.

Steward suggested he and Joe take their rifles and see if they could find the pack of wolves who were staying in this area. Steward figured if he could take two wolves from the pack, they would probably stop harassing his huskies. Using Steward's dogsled, Joe directed Steward to where he had seen the recent activity involving the moose. The men followed the wolf tracks and after a short distance they could not believe their luck. The tracks had led them straight to the wolves' den. The pack was inside, sleeping after hunting all night.

Excitement mounted at the thought of catching the wolves unprepared, increasing Steward and Joe's chances of a successful kill. The two men hatched a plan. Joe would fire two shots into the air in quick succession, hoping the startled wolves would wake from their sleep and run from the den. Steward would be waiting, ready to shoot to kill as many of these animals as he could, before they escaped into the forest. The men got ready to execute their plan.

CHAPTER SIXTY-ONE

S teward gave Joe the signal indicating he was ready to implement their plan. Joe raised his rifle in the air, firing two shots in quick succession. A moment of dead silence followed the gunfire, as six startled wolves, who had been sleeping, woke up sensing they were in danger. In a panic, the wolves fled from what they had perceived as the safety of their den. Steward was ready, his rifle aimed at the opening of the wolf den.

The frightened wolves ran, as Steward emptied his gun. His bullets hit and killed three of the six wolves, their blood-stained carcasses laying in the snow. Steward was very happy with the outcome of the plan he and Joe had come up with. The wolf pack would no longer bother his dogs and he would be able sell their hides in Dawson for a handsome sum.

Joe and Steward loaded the bodies of the dead wolves onto the sled. The men would follow behind the dogs, walking the short distance back to the cabin. Upon their return to Steward and Blossom's dwelling, Blossom was happy to hear the nighttime forays by the wolves were over. This was something which had bothered Steward greatly and she felt he would be much happier with that problem solved.

Steward and Joe unloaded the wolves' bodies into Steward's fur shed, where he would skin them later in the day. The men unhooked the dog team from the sled and fed and watered the animals before joining their wives back at the cabin. The women had steaming hot coffee ready when the men finished their work. After visiting for two hours, Joe and Mary told their hosts they needed to be on their way home. With well wishes from both sides the couple left, reminding Steward and Blossom the next visit should be at their cabin.

Steward watched as the dogsled, pulled by just one dog, became merely a speck on the expanse of the frozen lake. After a sixty-minute ride, Joe and Mary could see their cabin in the distance. Rusty pulled harder on his reins, knowing he would soon be home. Upon arrival, Mary went into the cabin to start the stove and cook dinner. Joe took Rusty with him to finish some work he had started, but not completed, in the fur shed. When he was finished, he joined Mary in the cabin for some beaver stew, which Blossom had given to her. Mary had thawed the stew on the top of the woodstove to serve it for dinner.

The calendar had just turned to the month of March, but spring in the Yukon was still a long way off. After dinner, Joe was reminded of how long the winter was lasting when he noticed an abrupt change in the weather. Ominous looking clouds were settling over the area, accompanied by a change in the direction of the wind, which was coming from the north. This usually meant a storm was in the making.

Joe carried more firewood into the cabin and brought meat in from the outdoor freezer. The snow started in the early evening but ended quickly. In a stroke of good luck, the blizzard quickly moved away from the cabin, saving the couple from having to dig out their traps from deep snow and reset them in the morning.

Joe and Mary retired to bed early, after their busy day. Tomorrow, Joe would check his trapline in the morning and when he returned, he would talk to Mary about visiting to Old Joe's cabin. Joe hoped their trip there would be an adventure in the making.

CHAPTER SIXTY-TWO

Joe and Mary had decided over dinner the previous night, they needed to go to Old Joe's cabin before the snow melted. It was nearing the end of March, and the sun was getting warmer as the days grew longer. Using the dogsled for transportation now would be easier than walking to the cabin later. Joe studied the map of the cabin's location, which the Mountie had given him. He told Mary it was a one-hour dogsled ride from their home, so the couple decided to leave in the morning. They would pack the supplies they would need just before heading out.

The night was unseasonably warm. The temperatures had stayed near freezing for two days. The melting snow on the roof caused a dripping sound as it drained off the eaves of the cabin onto the frozen ground. The night was quiet, not a sound coming from the forest. Joe and Mary lay in bed together, making small talk amongst themselves until they drifted off into a peaceful sleep to match the serene evening they had enjoyed together.

Brilliant sunshine shone through the cabin windows. Joe got out of bed and let Rusty outside. Mary got up, dressed, and prepared the supplies and food they were taking with them. Joe went outside and called Rusty, harnessing him and hooking him up to the sled. Joe directed Rusty to pull the sled in front of the cabin door, where he helped Mary load the few belongings they would need for the day. Joe secured the cabin and they left for Old Joe's homestead.

The temperature had dropped, freezing the snow, allowing the dogsled to glide easily over the surface of the frozen ground. About halfway to their destination, Rusty started acting nervous. Sensing something was wrong, Joe stopped the dogsled and took the safety off his rifle. He caught movement in the nearby trees. Unbeknown to Joe and Mary, the three surviving wolves from the pack Joe and Steward had previously ambushed had picked up Rusty's scent and begun to follow them.

The wolves had recognized Rusty's smell as part of the group which had killed the other members of their pack. As the wolves had fled, they remembered the scent of a husky, which was Rusty who happened to be nearby when the wolves exited their den. The wolves were stalking the unsuspecting group as they traveled through the forest. Joe had caught sight of one of the wolves, making him think they were being followed because Rusty was with them. A wolf has one reason to greet a husky, and that is to kill him. The pack will eat any huskies they kill, viewing them as prey.

Joe did not want Rusty to end up on the dinner table of some vengeful wolves looking to even a score. He lost sight of the wolf but was aware the predator was nearby.

Joe and Mary continued their journey to the cabin, conscious of the ever-present danger which surrounded them. One wolf, or a whole pack, the couple did not know exactly what the threat was. But Joe thought they were sure to find out.

CHAPTER SIXTY-THREE

Old Joe's cabin came into view. The couple's first impressions of the structure were not as bad as they had envisioned. The Mounties had portrayed Old Joe's cabin as a decrepit building which was uninhabitable. The front door of the cabin had been boarded up by the Mounties after they removed Old Joe's body. Joe removed the extra boards securing the cabin door, allowing them to enter. The interior of the cabin was just the way it had been left before Old Joe died. This cabin had been Joe's home for forty-five years. The isolation and lack of human contact was what this man desired, and in all those years he had lived in seclusion, with nature as his only friend.

After a thorough inspection of the property, the couple deemed the cabin suitable to live in. Joe got up on the roof checking for rotten areas of wood but could find nothing worrisome there. He examined the chimney, which seemed structurally sound and in good working order. The woodstove was in good shape, along with the furnishings inside the cabin. Joe thought about what the Mounties had told them about Old Joe's cabin. He realized the men knew the cabin was in fine shape but wanted to surprise Joe and

Mary went they visited the structure. The couple were now the owners of two fully equipped cabins in the wilderness of the Yukon.

Rusty loved his new stomping grounds; he explored the forest around the cabin taking special notice of a porcupine he encountered. Rusty, previously having quills in his lip from this prickly creature, knew enough to keep his distance. The dog was intrigued by a hole an animal had dug under the cabin. The hole in the snow went under the building, indicating this animal had dug out a den a while ago, when the ground was not frozen.

After a brief discussion, Joe and Mary decided to spend the night in their newly acquired cabin. Joe started a fire with the wood left beside the stove. He had previously noted a large supply of firewood was stacked outside, against the cabin wall. A fire was soon burning, warming the interior of the home to a comfortable temperature. Rusty took up his favorite spot by the woodstove, immediately falling asleep with his back toward the heat radiating from the metal. Rusty would not be let outside the cabin without an escort, as there was an ever-present danger of wolves lurking in the woods waiting for their opportunity to kill him, if given the chance.

Joe and Mary decided to inspect the grounds of the old cabin. Old Joe's cabin was sitting on the shores of a pristine, freshwater lake, its waters now encased under a thick coat of ice. A canoe lay sheltered in some trees close to the shoreline. The couple returned to the cabin, stopping to examine the hole an animal had made under the structure before going back inside. Joe had retrieved some fish out of Old Joe's outdoor freezer, which was also stocked with rabbit, waterfowl, and venison, ready to thaw and eat. Joe, Mary, and Rusty enjoyed a meal of fish for dinner, which Mary fried on the top of the woodstove.

The couple's evening was quiet, a solitude of silence surrounding them. Their night's sleep was peaceful, even if in an unfamiliar bed. Being rudely awakened by wolves sniffing around the cabin at sunrise was not what Joe and Mary were expecting. This event woke them to the unexpected reality of whose territory they were really in.

CHAPTER SIXTY-FOUR

Rusty's barking woke Joe and Mary from what had been a peaceful sleep. The couple could hear animal activity outside the cabin, causing Joe to exit the bed and quietly walk over to the window. Looking outside in the dim light of the morning dawn, he could make out the silhouettes of three wolves hanging out around the front door of the cabin. Rusty had caught the scent of these predators first and then heard them prowling outside. He had barked to make Joe and Mary aware of the wolves' presence.

While Joe pondered what to do next, the animals abruptly retreated into the forest. Joe realized they were the remaining wolves, who had escaped during the shooting at their den. Joe dressed and accompanied Rusty outside for a bathroom break. He saw no sign of the three wolves.

Joe returned to the cabin, adding wood to the embers glowing in the bottom of the stove. He talked with Mary about a plan to rid themselves of the wolf menace which was disrupting their lives. Joe told Mary he would go into Old Joe's freezer and remove a sizable amount of moose meat. They would allow the meat to thaw and then partially cook it, before putting it out to lure the wolves into an ambush. Under the light of the full moon, Joe would position himself on the roof of the cabin, lying in wait for the hungry wolves to come for the meat. At that time, Joe hoped to shoot and kill all three animals. Mary told Joe she thought his plan would work.

After breakfast, the couple went outside, leaving Rusty inside the cabin. Joe went to the freezer and removed the meat, taking it in the cabin to thaw. He then went with Mary to Old Joe's fur shed, an outbuilding which was intact but in poor condition. In Old Joe's last years, he had given up trapping, as it was a hard life, and he was an old man with health problems. He had closed the door of his fur shed five years ago and never re-entered the building.

Upon entering the fur shed, the couple were met by a musty odour, the smell of forty years of trapping had never left the building. The shed contained a dogsled in good condition, and twenty-five rusty leg traps, which were no longer usable. Various items which Old Joe thought he might be able to use were scattered about the shed. Under the work bench, the couple found a treasure trove of history. Old Joe had kept a journal for many years, writing down some of the more important things that happened in his life while living in his cabin. He had kept this record of events until arthritis in his fingers dictated he could no longer write.

Joe and Mary were surprised to learn Old Joe was literate. They decided take the book back to their cabin and study it, looking for any entry regarding the money he had earned from trapping and what he had done with these riches. Joe and Mary were sure there were valuables hidden nearby, which they believed to be a mystery which needed to be solved.

CHAPTER SIXTY-FIVE

*J*oe and Mary took Old Joe's journal back to the cabin from the fur shed. They put the manuscript away for the time being, planning on studying it more thoroughly when they returned home. The couple lay back down in the bed. Their sleep had been disturbed by the wolves who had been lurking outside the cabin before daybreak. Hugging each other closely, they quickly fell asleep in each other's arms. The couple did not stir until Rusty stuck his cold nose in Joe's face, waking him from his comfortable slumber.

Joe looked at the sun when he opened the cabin door to let Rusty outside. He surmised it was early afternoon, as the sun's position in the sky suggested it had started its downward trend towards dusk. Keeping an eye on the dog, Joe called out to Mary, who was still sleeping. Mary got out of bed and fixed coffee for herself and Joe. She began to prepare the meat for the trap Joe planned to execute tonight to rid themselves of the wolf problem.

Joe waited until well into the night before putting his plan in action. He laid the meat in the snow; certain its odor would attract the wolves back to the cabin. He climbed up and lay down on the roof, which was free of snow due to the recent warm weather. The forest was silent; only the occasional call of a night owl could be heard. Joe lay in silence, his sights set on the bait which he had placed in the small clearing below him.

Joe heard the wolves' presence first. Cautiously the animals approached the meat Joe had laid out for his ambush. Joe's finger trembled on the trigger of his rifle. The three wolves gathered around the meat, no longer paying attention to their surroundings. Joe shot four rounds from his rifle; Mary heard the gunshots from the roof. Three wolves lay dead in front of the cabin, Joe and Mary's wolf problem solved. Joe would drag the bodies of these animals into the forest tomorrow for the scavengers to feed on. Then they would leave for home, counting this journey as a successful venture.

Joe climbed down from the roof and checked the bodies of the dead wolves. Three of the wolves had been killed instantly by head shots, while one had suffered an extra gunshot wound in his side. Joe joined a happy Mary and Rusty to celebrate this successful wolf hunt. The couple went to bed knowing they would not be bothered by the wolves again, which lay dead in the front yard.

The morning sun rose with the promise of a warm day. The snow was melting, as the predawn temperatures were just above freezing. The couple left Old Joe's cabin in the early morning, before the snow became slush from the warm temperatures. Such conditions would make it difficult for Rusty to pull the sled through the snow.

The trip back to Joe and Mary's cabin was uneventful. Joe realized he would miss being able to use the dogsled as winter gave way to warmer weather. A rebirth would soon happen in the Yukon, bringing life back to this land in a season called spring. The beauty of the north would soon return for another year.

CHAPTER SIXTY-SIX

The month of April brought the first signs of spring. As the Earth moved closer to the sun, the Yukon began to warm up. Joe ended his trapping season at the end of March, as the warmer weather had arrived early this year causing the snowpack to melt. When Joe and Mary had visited Steward at his cabin, they had decided for Steward to pick up their furs before it became too warm to utilize the dogsleds. Steward would deliver the furs to Dawson City to be sold, while Joe would follow him to Dawson and collect his money from the fur broker.

Joe planned to stay one night with Bev and pick up supplies while he was in town to bring back to his cabin. Mary would stay home, her space on the sled was needed to carry some fur to Dawson and transport the supplies on the return trip home. Steward arrived at Joe's cabin on the first of April. Joe had been expecting him any day and was ready to travel to Dawson. The men decided to have coffee with Mary before loading their dogsleds with Joe's furs.

The day was sunny but not warm. Cold air had returned to the Yukon keeping the snow frozen. Today would be a good day to travel by dogsled to Dawson City. The men hugged Mary goodbye, went outside to load their sleds, and were soon on their way. Steward led the way, his dog team highly spirited and wanting to run. Steward told Joe he would go ahead and drop the load of fur he was carrying off at the brokers. He had stated he was also going to visit Bev while he was in town, and he would see Joe there later in the day. With a wave goodbye, Steward left Joe and Rusty on the trail. Steward would reach Dawson thirty minutes before Joe's one-dog sled team.

When Joe arrived at the fur brokerage house in Dawson, the business was chaotic. The local trappers were cashing in their fur after a hard winter of trapping. An employee of the business showed Joe where Steward had unloaded his furs. Joe removed the remaining furs from Rusty's dogsled, placing them with Steward's delivery. The owner of the brokerage house told Joe he would sort his furs later today and would be ready tomorrow to offer him a price for his hard work last winter. Joe thanked the man and left.

Before going to Bev's house, Joe decided to shop for his supplies today. He went to the mercantile to pick up nails and a few commodities, such as coffee and sugar, which they had run out of. Flour, which Mary also no longer had on hand, was not available this early in the spring. While at the mercantile, Joe also ordered a bag of dog food for Rusty. This dried food helped to keep his dog fed when facing food shortages at their cabin. The Yukon served up a hard life to the early settlers who came here, men and women looking for a solitary life and would have it no other way.

CHAPTER SIXTY-SEVEN

Joe and Rusty arrived at Bev's house in the early afternoon. Steward had arrived hours earlier and had already left for home. Bev welcomed Joe, offering him some fresh baked bread and butter. Joe never turned down anything Bev baked or cooked, so he graciously accepted her offer. Bev gave Joe some vegetable seeds she had harvested from her garden in the fall. Bev kept a large supply of seeds on hand for herself and her family and friends who lived in the forest. The seeds would be planted in late spring, giving the beneficiary fresh vegetables during the late summer months.

Joe told Bev he had to wait until tomorrow to get paid for the furs he and Steward had brought to town. She immediately offered to let him spend the night. Joe had planned on doing so, and volunteered to clean the donkey pens in the barn, which was a job he knew Bev needed done and would probably have asked him to do while he was here. Joe loved seeing Omar, Honey, and Baby Jack, who had grown to be half as big as his father.

As soon as Joe opened the barn door, he was met by an excited chorus of voices, including Baby Jack's, who sounded out a welcome to whomever was entering the barn. Joe reached out to the excited donkeys, petting and hugging each one affectionately. Joe spent two hours cleaning the animals' pens, putting down fresh bedding, and feeding and watering the donkeys. After finishing this task, he returned to the house, taking Rusty with him. His dog had been out investigating the property surrounding Bev's home while Joe was busy in the barn.

Bev was in the kitchen preparing dinner when Joe arrived back to the house. Bev's niece and her husband, Grey Wolf and Rose, who had just married, were coming from the winter camp their people had in the forest. They were planning to spend a few days with Bev, a well-known and respected elder of their tribe. Bev told Joe she would introduce the couple to him tonight when they arrived. Joe went upstairs to freshen up, using the pitcher of water Bev had left in his room for him. Bev knew Joe would need to wash up after working in the barn.

Joe lay down on the comfortable bed in his room and fell asleep. Bev let Joe sleep until dinner was ready. When he went downstairs, Bev's company had arrived. He was introduced to Grey Wolf and Rose, the recently married couple Bev had told him about. Bev served a wonderful dinner of venison and home baked bread. There were no side dishes to go with the meat, as that would have to wait until produce arrived from down south by boat or locally grown vegetables were available.

Over dinner, Grey Wolf mentioned to Bev that he and Rose would like to leave the tribal life and acquire their own cabin in the bush. Joe had not told Bev about

Old Joe's cabin, as he had been planning to tell her over dinner tonight. But it got Joe thinking that he would like to do something nice for Bev's niece and her new husband. Knowing Mary would give her blessing, they would give Old Joe's cabin to the young couple to start their new life together as man and wife. This was a gift that even Bev could not imagine.

CHAPTER SIXTY-EIGHT

oe told Bev and the young couple the story of the Mounties coming to their home for a wellness check. The men had told Joe about a cabin which lay empty in the forest after the old trapper who had lived there had been found frozen to death inside. The Mounties told Joe and Mary the cabin was theirs for the taking, as no family could be found for Old Joe, the previous owner. Joe wanted to turn this cabin over to Grey Wolf and Rose, allowing them to start their new life together.

The young couple could not believe their luck or the generosity of this man they had just met for the first time. Bev was shocked at the news and couldn't be happier for her niece and her husband. Joe drew Grey Wolf a detailed map on how to get to Mary's and his cabin. He told Grey Wolf if he and Rose came in two weeks, they would take them to their new home in the forest.

The rest of the evening was spent with Bev's company getting to know one another better and making small talk. When the midnight hour approached, it was time for bed. The tired occupants of the house climbed the stairs, going to their respective bedrooms for a night's sleep.

Before the sun came up, loud barking from Rusty downstairs woke Joe. Knowing something was wrong, he dressed quickly and grabbed his rifle. Opening the kitchen door, he let himself outside with Rusty right behind. Loud calls of distress from the donkeys could be heard coming from the barn. Joe ran toward the sound, where he found the door was ajar. Joe was afraid this had allowed a predator access to the building.

Joe entered the dark barn with caution. The building had become silent. Joe listened in the darkness and thought he heard an animal eating. Finding this odd and fearing for the worst, he retrieved a lantern kept in the barn for emergencies. He took it outside to strike a match to light it, just to be safe. The donkeys remained quiet and the atmosphere in the barn seemed calmer.

Joe re-entered the building, using the light to find the source of the noise he heard. He walked toward the chewing sound. There, in the corner of the hay pile, was a hungry porcupine chomping away on sweet-smelling hay. A wave of relief swept over Joe, as he guided the animal back outside the same door, he had come in. After cleaning the donkeys' pens earlier in the day, he must not have secured the door when he left the barn. Joe was happy the intruder was a porcupine and not a bear waking up from his long winter nap looking for breakfast. He knew he would listen to Bev's wrath for making such a big mistake. The donkeys were lucky it turned out to be a benign threat.

Later, Joe talked to Bev privately, apologizing for not securing the barn door after cleaning the donkeys' pens. As no harm had been done, Bev quickly forgave him and they hugged one another, the matter being dropped. Joe loaded his sled and he and Rusty left Bev's house early, returning to the fur brokerage business to pick up the money for the fur he had brought to town.

The proprietor's price to purchase Joe's fur was more than he had expected. Joe readily accepted the money, planning to take it back to his cabin for safe keeping. At this time, banks were not trusted institutions for keeping one's money safe. If the institution was robbed, the funds were simply gone; the bank was not held responsible for the loss.

After leaving the brokerage house, Joe steered Rusty in the direction of home. He was anticipating seeing Mary and snuggling with her in their warm bed. This was something Mary was also looking forward to upon Joe's return. Companionship and love helped the couple get through the good times and bad, a prerequisite for life in the north.

CHAPTER SIXTY-NINE

After ninety minutes of travel, Joe's cabin came into view. Upon seeing he was almost home, Rusty ran faster, pulling harder on his harness. He was looking forward to getting home so he could lay by the woodstove to warm up his aching body. Mary had been watching for Joe, knowing he was coming home today. She ran out to greet him when she heard Rusty barking as he got closer to the cabin.

Joe and Mary unloaded the sled, carrying the items Joe had purchased in Dawson into the cabin. Joe then had the dog pull the sled over to the fur shed, where he unhooked Rusty, who immediately went into the cabin to warm up by the fire. Joe soon followed his dog inside, embracing and kissing his wife passionately. Joe told Mary to sit down at the table, as he had something important to tell her.

Joe told Mary about meeting Bev's niece, Rose, and her husband, Grey Wolf. They were a young Indigenous couple who had just married and were starting a life of their own. Mary agreed with Joe about giving them Old Joe's cabin, both happy to be able to help Bev's niece and her husband tackle this obstacle they faced in life. They remembered how thrilled they were when Leonard had gifted them his home and were happy to do the same for another young couple.

Joe told Mary about Rose and Grey Wolf coming in two weeks. They agreed that before they took the couple to their new home, they should study Old Joe's journal for any clues to hidden wealth he may have left on or near his premises. But before doing so, Joe and Mary laid down and took a nap together. This was something Joe had been looking forward to when he got home from Dawson. The couple slept for two hours and then awoke to eat lunch and study the journal they carried home from Old Joe's.

Old Joe's handwriting was barely legible, but the couple could read what the man had written. The journal was a snapshot of Old Joe's forty years of living and trapping at his cabin. There was mention of him selling his furs in Dawson and buying liquor to bring back home with him. He talked of finding gold nuggets in the nearby creeks during the summer, while panning for gold. Old Joe never mentioned hiding anything valuable, but he also never said what he had spent his money on, leaving a mystery regarding a hidden stash of money or gold.

Joe planned on taking Rusty and Mary to Old Joe's cabin one more time before handing the building over to Grey Wolf and Rose. They would spend one night there, to allow for a thorough search of the premises and fur shed. The couple would also search the grounds surrounding the cabin, looking for any abnormalities which might point them to an unusual find. Old Joe's life savings may be ready to give up its secret location, which hopefully would be the result of this venture. Joe and Mary decided to leave for Old Joe's cabin tomorrow, in the hopes of finding something hidden on the property. If found, this stash of valuables would be theirs.

CHAPTER SEVENTY

The month of April is a month of contrasts in the Yukon. The first half of the month is usually filled with days of cold weather, followed by days of melting snow. The last half of the month, the temperature during the day is usually above freezing causing the snowpack to melt. This is the time of year in the north dogsleds are stored away, not be used again until the following winter. Because the current temperatures were in a freezing cycle, Joe and Mary could safely use their dogsled for transportation.

The day was sunny and cold, the frozen snow making the trip by dogsled to Old Joe's cabin an easy ride. Rusty was in an ambitious mood, pulling the sled with a fast gait down the open trail. After a fifty-minute ride, Joe, Mary, and Rusty arrived at their destination. Upon arrival, Mary lit a fire in the woodstove, as the inside of the cabin was cold and smelled musty. Soon a hot fire was burning in the stove, causing warm air to spread throughout the cabin.

Joe and Mary sat at the table drinking coffee which they had carried with them. The couple were talking about where in the cabin they should begin their search. They decided to move the bed and bedframe to look for any hiding areas beneath the bed. They thought Old Joe might have prepared a space for his money and gold under the floorboards of the cabin. When the couple moved the furniture from its spot on the floor, Joe and Mary's hearts skipped a beat as they noticed a piece of wood had been cut from the floor and then placed back in its original spot. Joe reached down and easily removed the cut piece of wood from the cabin floor.

Under the floor, Old Joe had dug a hole. Joe reached into the crevice and pulled out a leather bag with a drawstring. Joe's hands shook with excitement as he pulled the bag open. He dumped the contents of the bag on the table. Out of the bag tumbled a large assortment of gold coins, some of them being twenty-dollar gold pieces. Joe estimated the gold nuggets in the cache had a combined weight of two ounces. Joe and Mary had found Old Joe's life savings, which they could now call their own.

The couple replaced the wood back in the hole and returned the bed to its original position. Joe placed the bag of valuables with their own belongings and would take this treasure back to their cabin tomorrow. They decided when Grey Wolf and Rose took over Old Joe's cabin, they would give the newlyweds one of the twenty-dollar gold pieces they had found to help buy supplies for their new adventure.

Joe and Mary relaxed in the cabin for rest of the day, while Rusty spent most of his time hunting small mammals which lived in the forest surrounding the cabin. Tomorrow the trio would return home, their quest for finding the old man's gold a success.

CHAPTER SEVENTY-ONE

Joe and Mary were awake with the sun the following morning. Joe was up first, letting Rusty outside the cabin. Mary pulled her still tired soul out of bed. She added wood to the stove and prepared water for coffee. The temperature outside was hovering a little below freezing. Joe thought it would be best to leave for home as soon as possible. The snow would soon melt, which would make the sled almost inoperable. The wetter the snow became, the harder it would be for Rusty to pull the sled.

Within thirty minutes the group was ready to leave. Joe secured the front door of the cabin, then directed Rusty to go. Old Joe's cabin soon disappeared behind the travellers. The first half of the trip home was uneventful, but that would change. Rounding a bend in the trail, the trio almost ran head long into a mother bear and her cub, who were sitting in the middle of the trail. Upon seeing these animals, Rusty came to an abrupt stop.

Fifty feet from the dogsled, the mother bear stared at the unwanted company contemplating her next move. Joe picked up his rifle, but sensing no menacing behaviour coming from the bear, just held it at the ready. The mother bear decided against confronting this group who had intruded on her space. She picked herself up from the ground, gathered up her cub, and ambled off into the forest. Joe and Mary continued their way, reaching home with no further distractions.

Joe realized the dogsled would soon need to be retired until next winter. The snow would soon be gone and the way of life in the Yukon would change. As the warm weather returned, the ice in the lake began melting, beckoning the return of the waterfowl who called this lake home during the summer. The call of the loon would soon echo across the dark lake during the short months of summer.

Joe and Mary welcomed their new neighbors, Grey Wolf and Rose, to their cabin. With the twenty-dollar gold piece Joe and Mary gave the couple, they were able to buy enough supplies to start their new life together. Grey Wolf's father promised his son a dog team as a wedding gift, something every fur trapper needs when working in the bush.

Mary and Joe's life in the Yukon was a rewarding experience, teaching them about a world few people would know. Theirs was a life of happiness, but they also experienced times of sadness and loneliness. A life which offered them a clear understanding of the power of nature which surrounded them. The spirit of the north guided Joe and Mary to a life they desired in this land called the Yukon, in Canada's great white north.

Grey Wolf and Rose were welcomed into Bev's family, joining her other nieces and nephews who lived in the forest. Like a small village, this group of people, including

Steward, Jason, Johnathan, Joe, and their wives and children watched out for one another while living in the wilderness. Grey Wolf and Rose became part of this small, tight-knit group, continuing their unending adventure, shared with a community of new friends.

Printed in the USA
CPSIA information can be obtained
at www.ICGtesting.com
JSHW012159261223
54228JS00011B/42